Out
to
Lunch

David Bullard

Out to Lunch

JONATHAN BALL PUBLISHERS
JOHANNESBURG & CAPE TOWN
and
Sunday Times

All rights reserved.
No part of this publication may be reproduced or transmitted
in any form or by any means, without prior permisson from
the publisher or copyright holder.

© *Sunday Times*, 2002

Published in 2002 by
JONATHAN BALL PUBLISHERS (PTY) LTD and *SUNDAY TIMES*
PO Box 33977
Jeppestown
2043

ISBN 1 86842 137 6

Front cover cartoon by Richard Smith
Design by Michael Barnett, Johannesburg
Typesetting and reproduction of cover by
TripleM Advertising & Design, Johannesburg
Typesetting and reproduction of text by Alinea Studio, Cape Town
Printed and bound by CTP Book Printers, Caxton Street, Parow, Cape

Contents

Introduction 17

29 September 1996
Let's not forget the rights of thugs disempowered by apartheid 19

27 October 1996
Garbage bag gold for Johannesburg's dedicated team of sewer rats 21

17 November 1996
Catch a tourist if you can – and then tax him the Mokaba way 23

19 January 1997
No room for melanistically disadvantaged musicians 25

26 January 1997
With God and Mandela on his side, the good minister need not fear 27

9 February 1997
Chameleon entrepreneurs make the most of 'black empowerment' 29

2 March 1997
Hold on to your homburgs – Bullard is voting for the ANC 31

16 March 1997
'Sellout' cat has confused pigeons all aflutter with conspiracy theory 33

30 March 1997
Rich and powerful cosy up over lavish dinner while voters wait
for bread 35

4 May 1997
Winnie and the dastardly plot to import 30-million anti-ANC voters   37

8 June 1997
Master of the photo opportunity sees the writing on the wall   39

13 July 1997
'Let them eat cake' is the message from the empty benches of parliament   41

24 August 1997
A railway station with a history of open windows and slippery floors   43

14 September 1997
Never mind the Olympics, Cape Town is playing   45

21 September 1997
Losing parliament could have a silver lining for Western Cape   47

26 October 1997
Stals and his devious deputies pull the wool over miffed traders' eyes   49

2 November 1997
Winnie still savours the sweet scent of survival   51

16 November 1997
Hypocrisy and greed lurk behind labels of 'empowerment' and
   'affirmative action'   53

28 December 1997
Being a counter-revolutionary has its attractions   55

4 January 1998
Viva global domination and afternoon naps   57

11 January 1998
No room for an orgy but your R1m Clifton box says you've made it   59

1 February 1998
Clinton should have stuck to vacuum cleaners in the Oral Office   61

8 February 1998
Accountability takes a back seat in the BMW as leaders take
   wrong turning   63

15 February 1998
Oh for an honestly naughty politician with a decent housing policy   65

22 February 1998
Do-it-yourself cloning kits could cause a rift in the nuclear family   67

1 March 1998
No such thing as a free wooden lizard in the business forest   69

15 March 1998
Not even an apple for teacher puts diligent Trevor at the top of the class   71

29 March 1998
Checking for interns in the wardrobes and assassins in the palm trees   73

12 April 1998
Ladies and Gents, at last the full spectacle of military 'intelligence'   75

26 April 1998
Sorry Jani, I don't fall off horses and my underpants ain't got no holes   77

3 May 1998
Warning: too much time on the phone with psychopaths causes
   racial hatred   79

17 May 1998
Creating desirable winter homes for rats and an undesirable city
   for humans   81

7 June 1998
Will that be economy, business class or the hanky panky section, sir?   83

14 June 1998
Serious training needed to get into shape to not run the Comrades   85

5 July 1998
It's time to stop beating our breasts and start working for the future   87

12 July 1998
Wanted: bright lad for top bank job. No experience necessary　　　89

19 July 1998
British Airways decides it is simply too British for its own good　　　91

16 August 1998
Looking for short, fat white men to make up quota in basketball team　　　93

23 August 1998
Roll up, roll up, comrades – borrow from me and make me rich　　　95

6 September 1998
Queuing up for bar code democracy is a taxing business　　　97

13 September 1998
The mystery of South Africa's invisible white stinkwoods　　　99

20 September 1998
Intelligent leaders should wipe the egg off their faces and apologise　　　101

11 October 1998
Watch out smokers, the Drag Squad will put you behind bars in a puff　　　103

1 November 1998
Get involved – or stop whinging about the decline of our cities　　　105

22 November 1998
Please don't mention Julius Caesar – I could be traumatised for days　　　107

29 November 1998
If you don't know Led Zeppelin, you're too young to handle my money　　　109

6 December 1998
A panic button for Joe Modise could save us all a lot of money　　　111

24 January 1999
Life's a blast in Cape Town in the aftermath of New Year bomb　　　113

7 February 1999
Now that SA has democracy, the people couldn't care less　　　115

14 February 1999
If we're scraping the bottom of the diplomatic barrel, send me to Cannes 117

28 February 1999
Who's going to take a black man trapped in white skin seriously? 119

7 March 1999
Let's not end up with only stale ANC portions on the menu 121

21 March 1999
Bigger than Tom Wolfe, bolder than all the kugels in Sandton 123

18 April 1999
Workers no-balled but illegal Zaïrean basketball players get the red carpet 125

25 April 1999
Bringing some plummy eccentricity to our desolate political landscape 127

2 May 1999
Bring out the cigars for Shilowa as the invisible man says goodbye 129

9 May 1999
Thanks to nice Mandela and dozy Nzo for saving us from being bombed 131

16 May 1999
Liberals should not hang their holier-than-thou washing out to dry 133

20 June 1999
Mute cashiers at Pick 'n Pay can talk – they just don't want to 135

11 July 1999
You can't fish and look at a computer screen at the same time 137

18 July 1999
Hats off to the clever people who sell water to the vain and silly 139

25 July 1999
Just one hour of Mozart and you'll be able to set your video recorder 141

22 August 1999
Three cheers to all my unsuitable drinking companions 143

12 September 1999
All that jazz and open air must really disturb the human brain 145

10 October 1999
Parliamentary pin-up calendar could reveal all about ministers 147

14 November 1999
Bringing home the desperate elegance of real-estate speak 149

5 December 1999
Thanks, Claudia, you've done the free press in SA a huge favour 151

23 January 2000
Call me a chimp or a gorilla, just not a human please 153

27 February 2000
The rule of law is dead – we are living in a taxiocracy 155

26 March 2000
Winning a better class of flying duck above the fireplace 157

23 April 2000
How Seffrica's crigget boss got a call at three in the morning ... 159

7 May 2000
It's unutterable. It's unintelligible. You guessed: it's SA's new motto 161

14 May 2000
Those jolly good days when the colonies knew their place 163

28 May 2000
No, I'm not just gazing at your breasts, I'm working out 165

4 June 2000
Need advice? Statingthebloodyobvious.com will set you straight 167

11 June 2000
Exclusive: Satan says he was less than honoured by Hansie's slur 169

2 July 2000
Sharp marketing needed to make kugels want to chat about DNA 171

9 July 2000
Clear up the cockpit clutter and we can all become Biggles   173

6 August 2000
In-between Hansie duty, Satan finds time to corrupt Harry Potter fans   175

13 August 2000
New evidence that talk is cheap in the President's office   177

27 August 2000
What's the point of all this law when enforcing it is such a chore?   179

10 September 2000
What drives the racism talkshop industry is the colour of money   183

1 October 2000
Cosatu's comic opera delivers superb display of utter brillance   185

15 October 2000
Introducing *Sloth*, the game show where everyone wins, every time   187

22 October 2000
Keep your prize – I have naked women dying to honour me   189

19 November 2000
SABC move to show dog video inspired more by money than ire   191

26 November 2000
The day they found giraffe skeletons on the ocean floor   193

10 December 2000
To shore up your status in Plett, increase your building noise   195

14 January 2001
My Annual Report shows a deficit in fixed social assets   197

4 February 2001
If a low rand is SA's share price, it's an attractive investment   199

11 February 2001
Knowing what voters want hardly a turn-on for SA politicians   201

25 February 2001
I can't stomach the gutless trash dished up in local TV shows   203

1 April 2001
Racially intolerant Martians impress President Mbeki with their insight   205

22 April 2001
Gauteng school text evaluators, lend me your ass's ears   207

6 May 2001
Come now, Nedcor – do you really think we're *that* gullible?   209

13 May 2001
They paid R160 000 to undermine the right to free speech   211

27 May 2001
That's the way, Chris, blame the media – it works for politicians   213

24 June 2001
Stupidity is no excuse for the SAA debacle – off with their heads!   215

1 July 2001
ANC curiously silent on despotic abuses by Swaziland king   217

22 July 2001
What 'Special Price' Yengeni had to say about his Mercedes   219

12 August 2001
Nothing like a bodice ripper to give a bad dog a good name   221

26 August 2001
At last, a use for all those balls and coathangers: traffic-light croquet   223

2 September 2001
Dishonesty in public life ought to be punished as treason   225

28 October 2001
Don't despair: you can still go pretty far on a shrivelled rand   227

4 November 2001
My new mission: to put the fun back into fundamentalism   229

2 December 2001
Bring on the Havanas and pass the port: There's work to be done! 231

20 January 2002
Outing culprits will do little to solve the rand murder mystery 233

10 February 2002
Someone didn't get the joke but, frankly speaking, the laugh's on them 235

17 February 2002
It's a bit rich of the WEF to debate poverty amid five-star luxury 237

24 February 2002
Why we need a sports minister – to keep the race issue in play 239

17 March 2002
The price of fame and the strange, disconnected world of PR 241

24 March 2002
Take a tip from me: SA tourism is about to enter a bull market 243

31 March 2002
State's Aids stance means it wants a lean and mean workforce 245

5 May 2002
Should Mark have spent so much to send himself up? 247

Acknowledgements

Thanks to:

Jonathan Ball and Francine Blum for having the guts to turn *Out to Lunch* into a book.

Richard Smith for the cover picture.

Michelle Leon at Johnnic for finding the columns on the *Sunday Times* computer and transferring them to disc, thereby saving everyone an awful lot of typing.

Northcliff Auto for providing a promotional Mini Cooper.

Mike Robertson, publisher of the *Sunday Times* and previously editor, for his support for the project.

Sue Russell of the *Sunday Times* who had the difficult job of telling the other two interested publishers that their advance fee simply wasn't high enough.

Finally, to my wife and best friend Jacquie who tolerates my eccentric behaviour and sometimes allows me to smoke cigars in the house.

Introduction

I toyed with the idea of asking someone important to write a foreword for this book. I thought it might increase sales if the cover carried the words 'With an introduction by Ken Owen'. Then my publisher pointed out that so many eminent and important people had begged to write the *Out to Lunch* foreword that I risked offending all those who were not chosen ... (sorry Ken). So I decided to go it alone and write my own introduction. I mention this just in case you think I'm being cheap.

The Out to Lunch column sprung to life in March 1994 and is therefore older than democracy itself in South Africa. In the past eight years it has angered, amused, irritated, educated and hopefully provided a kick start to many a reader's Sunday mornings. Described once as 'All Bran for the Brain', I like to think of *Out to Lunch* as the roughage that helps you digest the rest of the newspaper. What it lacks in intellect it often makes up in bad taste.

Over the years I have received hate mail as well as fan mail and I derive great pleasure from the fact that some readers hate the column enough to carefully cut it from the newspaper, scrawl obscene comments all over it, put it in an envelope and take the trouble to post it to me. It is humbling to realise that I wield that sort of power. I wish I'd kept all the hate mail I have received because it would make a hilarious companion volume to this one.

I frequently have to remind people that a columnist is not the same thing at all as a journalist. A journalist is expected to check facts, quote sources to support the story and not allow personal prejudice or judgement to interfere with the truth. A columnist, on the other hand, relies on the facts already collected by the hard-working journalist, doesn't need to quote any sources and can be as prejudiced and judgemental as he or she wishes. Of course, there's always the risk of a lawsuit should you libel somebody. However, the wonderful thing about the English language is that you can get the message across without actually having to risk a court appearance. For example, to refer to Winnie Madikizela-Mandela as 'the nation's favourite babysitter' is far more effective than dredging up all that dreadful stuff about football teams and unexplained deaths.

We live in a politically correct age. Some people think this empowers the weak and encourages us all to respect our fellow citizens. Some people are wrong. Political correctness is nothing more than a sinister plot by world governments to deprive us of a bit of harmless fun and enrich lawyers. When you consider that many politicians started life as lawyers, this makes sense.

The one-legged, whale-loving, single-parent lesbians and their muesli-munching friends don't much like me ... which is great, because I don't much like them either. They think I'm arrogant and opinionated and shouldn't be appearing weekly on the pages of a family newspaper. Fortunately, they are hugely outnumbered by intelligent readers who share my view that life is much too ridiculous to be taken seriously.

And those are the people who inspire me to sit down at a blank computer screen every week and knock off another column when, at my age, I ought to be looking for a well-remunerated corporate job with a pension scheme.

David Bullard
October 2002

29 September 1996

Let's not forget the rights of thugs disempowered by apartheid

I finally realised that the lunatics had taken over the asylum when I watched the news and saw a march of gangsters in Cape Town. They were demanding a general amnesty because, had it not been for apartheid, they would all have had proper jobs and not been forced to become gangsters.

Those of my readers who know their Gilbert and Sullivan will immediately recognise the resemblance to *The Pirates of Penzance*, where the pirates have a similar excuse: 'They are no members of the common throng, they are all noblemen who have gone wrong.'

As I watched the marchers chat into their cellphones and laugh and joke with each other, suddenly everything fell into place.

Quite obviously the need to distribute Mandrax tablets among young children is nothing more than a frustrated desire to become a pharmacist and the occasional removal of a rival's limbs without the benefit of anaesthetic is proof that inside every gangland hit-man there is a surgeon struggling to get out.

The gangsters have given the government an ultimatum; either recognise their demands or in four weeks (just in time for the tourist season) they will embark on a programme of rolling mass action.

They haven't yet been specific about precisely what form this will take, but I think we should understand that even gangsters have standards of excellence.

Pelting foreign tourists with rotten fruit, squirting them with water pistols or calling them rude names would seriously diminish their standing in the international gangster community, so I imagine they are planning something more in the Quentin Tarantino line.

No doubt the government will respond to this threat with their usual sense of urgency.

*

Of course, one of the reasons that our politicians spend so much time overseas (apart from the fact that we pay their expenses) is that it is a damn sight safer than staying in South Africa. A gentle stroll through Harlem at dusk or a saunter through downtown Beirut are infinitely safer than a walk down Commissioner Street in Johannesburg.

This accusation cannot be levelled at the financial world's 'odd couple', Reserve Bank governor Chris Stals and Finance Minister Trevor Manuel, who are trotting around some of the major financial capitals hoping to persuade foreigners to invest before we offend them further by inviting their political enemies over for tea. It has been stressed on TV news that this is NOT a begging mission. They didn't add the word 'yet', so I will.

There seems to be some confusion as to what constitutes foreign investment and what we should get excited about. When we are told that foreigners have bought R1-billion of SA bonds the news is generally presented as proof that there is confidence in South Africa and investment is pouring in.

Sorry to spoil the party, but nothing could be further from the truth. A bond bought on Monday can be sold on Tuesday and practically the only criteria for foreign investment in bonds or equities is capital gain and currency risk; altruism doesn't feature in the investment world. We are one of the many global financial markets competing to improve the performance of emerging market fund managers.

The inflow of funds into the bond market means that the government can fund its growing budget deficit. The flows benefit financial instrument traders and very few others.

Quite why taxpayers are expected to be so agog about the government's ability to borrow money at ruinously high interest rates I cannot imagine. Maybe we have spent so long in the financial wilderness that the fact that anyone wants to lend us money is supposed to be cause for a celebration, but that's another story.

Foreign investment has less to do with speculating on financial markets than with attracting foreign businesses with a combination of tax incentives, a low crime rate, good living conditions and a reliable workforce.

We are patently not doing that, and one of the main reasons is that SA businessmen are apparently sending out 'negative' signals with all their whimpering about crime and violence.

The message from the government is simple; pull yourself together, and next time somebody asks about that ugly gash on your throat, don't mention the hijacking – just tell them you cut yourself shaving.

27 October 1996

Garbage bag gold for Johannesburg's dedicated team of sewer rats

In a recently published survey of 1 500 American globetrotters, Johannesburg was labelled as one of the most undesirable cities to visit along with other Third World garbage tips like Manila, Lagos and San Juan. The survey describes Johannesburg as a 'hellish nest' and ranks it even lower on the list than Nairobi.

In fact, Johannesburg didn't receive a single vote of approval in the poll. Just in case you think this is anti-South Africanism rearing its ugly head I should point out that Cape Town features among the same travellers' five favourite destinations.

The apparent ease with which Johannesburg occupies its position as one of the world's most revolting places to visit belies the tremendous effort that has gone into attaining this accolade.

After all, you don't end up at the bottom of the heap without trying hard and Johannesburgers have pulled together magnificently to ensure that the country's largest city maintains its total lack of appeal for residents and visitors alike. It is all too easy to let standards slip and to find yourself only half way down the list; neither desirable nor undesirable.

I think the reason we have managed to pip other cities to the post is the surprise factor. Visitors arrive expecting First World standards and find Third World standards. First impressions are tremendously important in a contest of this kind and an airport in which it is impossible to take luggage onto an escalator or to find a lift that will transport you to the lower parking level gives us an instant advantage. Those passengers who decide to wheel their luggage out of the airport building on a trolley will find the camber on the pavement just sufficient to ensure that their luggage falls off every few steps.

Low standards are all about teamwork and there is no point in everybody slouching around trying to make life miserable for visitors unless there is total commitment. It takes only one renegade to jeopardise our world ranking. Fortunately, our black taxi drivers are united in their attempts to make the roads around Johannesburg among the most dangerous in the world.

Where else can you dice with a taxi driver who is drunk, uninsured, unlicensed and packing an automatic weapon? In New York the best you can hope for is a surly Puerto Rican who can't speak English and doesn't know his way around Manhattan.

The South African Kamikaze Taxi Association has a rigid code of misconduct which is observed by all members. These include not indicating, deliberately driving too close to somebody who has had the cheek to pull in front and firing off a few rounds at motorists who dare to hoot or make rude gestures with their fingers.

Fortunately the association has an understanding with the traffic authorities which ensures its reputation as a major tourist deterrent. Quite simply it is this; if any traffic officer has the temerity to ask for a taxi driver's licence or to question why 27 people are crammed into one minibus then seven other taxi drivers shall be entitled to pull up and settle the dispute.

The serious business of creating an environment which ensures that we remain an undesirable destination is not something that can be left to entrepreneurs like beggars, unofficial parking consultants and muggers.

Local government has to take an initiative and we are particularly fortunate in Johannesburg to have people who seem dedicated to making the city and its environs look as repulsive as possible.

There is a new policy to allow piles of garbage to be left on main thoroughfares and to refuse to sweep suburban streets, particularly in 'elitist' suburbs. This means that all the storm drains will be blocked with the accumulated garbage of several months and the rains, when they arrive, will be free to damage the roads and pavements giving that pot-hole effect so favoured by Third World nations.

However, the *pièce de résistance* has been the decision to adorn every available lamppost and tree with at least a dozen posters. When they are up they look disgusting and when they fall down and litter the streets they also look disgusting; a win-win situation for local eco-vandals.

Despite the dedication of so many people, Johannesburg's position as one of the world's hell holes wouldn't have been possible without the untiring support of Gauteng premier Tokyo Sexwale who has managed to skilfully avert his gaze from the decline. When the 'Golden Garbage Bag' awards ceremony takes place, it is he who should be making the acceptance speech.

17 November 1996

Catch a tourist if you can – and then tax him the Mokaba way

Peter Mokaba, the Deputy Minister of Environmental Affairs and Tourism, made a speech at the Food and Hotel Africa 1996 trade exhibition last week.

Mr Mokaba is, of course, better known for his rather unorthodox views on agriculture (kill the farmer, kill the boer) and so it was interesting to read what he had to say about the relatively simple matter of attracting tourists to a country with considerably more natural tourist resources than most.

It is possible that the article I read deliberately failed to report some of Mr Mokaba's more brilliant and visionary suggestions, and if that is the case I apologise in advance.

What Mr Mokaba did say though was that tourism is still a remote 'foreign concept' for the majority of black South Africans, many of whom have never been tourists, and that it catered predominantly for the white upper and middle classes.

Mr Mokaba went on to say that 95% of this country's tourism industry was still owned by the white private sector and that a lack of meaningful participation by black entrepreneurs and all South African communities in the tourism industry was just one of several impediments causing the industry to 'remain in the doldrums'.

Other constraints apparently include inadequate resources, a 'myopic' private sector, a lack of infrastructure, high air tariffs, lack of appropriate ground transportation, a bureaucratic marketing arm and ... oh yes, our crime-ridden image.

About the only people who escape any blame it seems is his own department, who have no doubt been battling valiantly against almost impossible odds.

After all, didn't Mr Mokaba come up with the dazzling suggestion of levying a tax on all departing tourists? What a pity nobody told him that in order to depart you first have to arrive.

It seems that Mr Mokaba missed a superb opportunity to promote South

Africa to exhibitors from the US, Canada, India, Singapore and Europe, preferring instead to concentrate on the social inequalities of tourism.

For example, to say that tourism is a foreign concept to the majority of black South Africans is a pointless statement. If tourism caters for what Mokaba refers to as the white middle and upper class it is because they are the people who have money to spend.

A simple business principle is that you aim goods or services at a target market and to offer Mediterranean cruises or Tyrolean skiing holidays to shack dwellers would obviously be ridiculous; just as ridiculous as blaming the poor performance of our tourism industry on social imbalances.

Similarly, the accusatory comment that 95% of SA's tourism industry is still owned by the white private sector is fatuous.

So what? I am unaware of any laws, other than pure commercial ones, that preclude any person of any colour setting up in the tourism business. Mokaba complains that even the magazines and newspapers aimed at black readers still do not carry advertisements for leisure and holiday facilities.

Again, I fail to understand his point. Surely he isn't suggesting that advertisers are deliberately not using the black media in order the keep the beaches white?

While Mr Mokaba is probably quite correct in his accusation that the marketing arm for SA tourism is bureaucratic and unwieldy, he cannot be serious when he accuses the private sector of being 'myopic'.

If anything, the tourism industry could be charged with over-enthusiasm. Spurred on by predictions of a tourist boom, many investors must now be wondering whether they haven't over-committed themselves as they twiddle their thumbs waiting for the promised foreign invasion.

Like any aimless department of government which has no real idea of what it is supposed to be achieving, Mr Mokaba's ministry has 'launched' a White Paper on tourism which identifies the fundamentals for a government-led, private sector-driven, community-based industry.

If you think that sounds like political gobbledegook, you would be quite correct. A rough translation of that statement means that government will tell you what to do, the private sector will be expected to pay for it and the public will have to put up with the consequences.

Mr Mokaba's speech appears to contribute little towards the tourism debate, strewn as it is with 'struggle clichés' about white ownership and similar populist platitudes. It is the speech of a man who evidently has neither enthusiasm nor empathy for his portfolio. Still, I suppose it could have been worse. He could have become Deputy Minister of Agriculture.

19 January 1997

No room for melanistically disadvantaged musicians

'The man that hath not music in himself, nor is moved with concord of sweet sounds, is fit for treasons, stratagems and spoils; The motions of his spirit are dull as night, And his affections dark as Erebus: Let no such man be trusted' – *The Merchant of Venice*. The SABC's decision to withdraw its subsidy for the National Symphony Orchestra moves us a little closer to the uncivilised and barbaric society that the class warriors would wish on us; a world dominated by Big Macs and mindless TV soap operas.

For some reason they have it in their heads that orchestras exist to play music by DWEMs (Dead White European Males) which is only ever listened to by audiences who are similarly melanistically disadvantaged.

One would have thought that a national orchestra is an asset that we should cherish and support, but apparently this is not the case.

Quite the contrary in fact. A national orchestra is a throwback to the dark ages of white privilege and therefore must be purged.

Have you ever heard of the Burundi Symphony Orchestra or the Baghdad Philharmonic? Of course not, and for a very good reason.

Some nations have far more important things to do, like killing each other, to have time to listen to a load of penguins scraping away at cat gut.

It is only in decadent places like London, Paris, New York and Vienna that people have the time and the leisure to sit down and listen to classical music. Govan Reddy's excuse for the cut in subsidy is that as long as he is unable to provide more than a 40% radio service to the Ndebele and Swazi people he cannot justify funding an orchestra.

While it is just about possible (if you try very hard) to empathise with Mr Reddy's point of view, it is difficult to see what the one has to do with the other.

The orchestra has been around for 72 years and, as music director Richard Cock correctly says, plays a valuable role in cross-cultural ties.

A live concert by a symphony orchestra at Zoo Lake or in Soweto is far more likely to contribute towards a black child's spiritual growth than a radio station broadcasting 24-hour rap music with lyrics urging its listeners to go out and kill a cop.

The orchestra is clearly being sacrificed by the SABC in the interests of short-term objectives and political correctness.

I suspect the real cost to the SABC is well below the figures quoted and the saving, once the orchestra has been ditched, would barely pay the entertainment expenses of one of those consultants that government organisations take such delight in employing.

The possible demise of the NSO should rekindle the debate about a national lottery.

The critics claim that lottery tickets are bought by those who can least afford them and that a society which encourages people to believe that they can sort out all life's problems by winning a stupendous jackpot against terrible odds is an unhealthy society.

On the other hand, the idea that contributions from avaricious philistines would go towards supporting an orchestra that they probably wouldn't bother to listen to has a certain charm.

Besides, as we have seen with the British lottery, the masses need some excitement injected into their drab, mindless existences and if the weekly prospect of winning enough money to stay drunk for the rest of their lives makes them happy, why not?

The only reason South Africa does not have a national lottery yet is that the government has yet to decide who should run it.

As the Brits have discovered, the wonderful thing about a national lottery is that the people who eventually get to run it don't need to buy tickets; they win every week.

For this reason, the job would almost certainly be given to a retiring politician and private enterprise wouldn't get a look in.

*

The news that tax collectors are to make house calls in an attempt to recoup some R2,4-billion of unpaid taxes is one of the more intelligent decisions to come from the department of finance.

I never much liked Chris Liebenberg's tax amnesty, which was little more than a 'cheat's charter' designed to make those of us who have been paying our taxes all along feel like suckers.

After all, if we had known there would be an amnesty we would never have bothered to register as taxpayers in the first place.

26 January 1997

With God and Mandela on his side, the good minister need not fear

Towards the end of last year the newspapers reported that the investigations against Dr Allan Boesak had finally been completed, almost two years after the original accusations were made, and that Boesak would have to answer charges that charitable donations from Danchurch, intended for the upliftment of the local community, were apt to flow in unusual directions; namely Boesak's personal account.

The hearing was set for January 17 and Boesak duly appeared on local TV, assuring us in his peculiar falsetto voice that he couldn't wait to get back to South Africa to establish his innocence.

Of course, January 17 has come and gone but still no sign of the errant cleric, who is living and working in the United States with his wife.

I combed the papers last weekend and did notice a small reference that says (surprise) the case has been postponed until March.

Bearing in mind that it has taken the investigators so long to piece together the evidence and build its case against Boesak (all at the taxpayer's expense) it is difficult to understand why it needs to be postponed for another two months. Let us be charitable and imagine that, try as he may, the Rev Boesak simply couldn't get a flight out of the United States, not even in first class where he was used to travelling before this whole unfortunate business.

Of course, the uncharitable view is that our Allan didn't try particularly hard to come back, and with good reason; his reappearance in this country would simply add to the ANC's woes.

You may remember that when Boesak was first accused of financial skulduggery he was being considered for a diplomatic posting to Geneva.

Having lost the Western Cape fairly and squarely in the 1994 election to the National Party, this was thought to be the ideal way to remove him from the local political scene while at the same time rewarding him for his past loyalties to the struggle.

Even as the accusations of fraud flew thick and fast, Boesak steadfastly protested his innocence. People wondered how a simple man of God could afford such as swanky lifestyle with a house in Constantia, luxury cars and a penchant for visiting some of the more refined Cape eateries.

Those of us who publicly criticised Boesak were accused of racism and the matter might have been dragged on interminably had a rescue plan not been hatched.

Suddenly there was flash in the sky ... Is it a bird? Is it a plane? ... No, it's Supermandela! The State President, in the interests of the transparency for which the ruling party is so well known, declared that Boesak was a good egg and a highly talented young man to boot.

There was no reason to end a promising career just because a load of Vikings from the frozen north couldn't make sense of a few simple bank statements. In an attempt to close the matter once and for all and to give it a spurious legality, an unknown lawyer (both before and since) was found by Thabo Mbeki who would conduct an independent investigation into the matter and find, predictably, that there was insufficient evidence against the Rev Boesak.

That done, Allan would be free to represent South Africa in Geneva and, as they say in other good fairy stories, everybody would live happily ever after.

Unfortunately, all didn't go quite according to plan because the predominantly white-owned press didn't believe a word of it and called for a proper investigation by fraud squad detectives.

Neither were the Danes too impressed because they still had large amounts of money unaccounted for.

Another problem was that Boesak's alleged accomplice, Freddie Steenkamp, had already confessed to financial mismanagement and it looked as though he was about to blow the whistle on Boesak.

Unfortunately for Freddie, he was simply not important enough to be looked after by the establishment so he was left to fend for himself.

Dr and Mrs Boesak were luckier, however. They were spirited away to the United States. I don't know if you have ever tried to emigrate to the US. Apart from needing skills that the country requires, you also have to convince them of your unblemished political past; they don't much like commies for example.

I also recall that they are less than enthusiastic about applicants who have pending criminal cases. None of this seems to have worried them in the case of Allan Boesak, though. God does indeed move in mysterious ways.

9 February 1997

Chameleon entrepreneurs make the most of 'black empowerment'

I was relieved to learn at a lunch last week that I am not the only person puzzling over where the 'black empowerment' groups have suddenly found the enormous amounts of money necessary to buy large stakes in some of South Africa's leading companies.

After all, life as we know it began only in April 1994. Before that, most aspirant black entrepreneurs were in political exile or breaking up chunks of limestone on Robben Island. Hardly an ideal environment in which to build up a war chest of a few hundred million rand just in case democracy happened to be around the corner and you felt like buying a mining house.

Yet every day we hear of companies who have risen without trace and have neither a trading history nor any tangible product to sell. However, somehow, by doing absolutely nothing, they have amassed enough cash to take meaningful stakes in other people's businesses. Surely this is one of the greatest miracles of capitalism! The answer is it may very well be for the fortunate few.

In the early days of our bright new democracy we had something called the Reconstruction and Development Programme (RDP), which was the government's attempt to co-ordinate, for the benefit of the poor, all the things that needed urgent attention like housing, water supplies, education and health services. Suddenly, anybody hoping to make a fast buck got into the upliftment racket and claimed a link to the RDP. This had the double advantage of allowing you to brown-nose the new government while at the same time playing on the post-colonial guilt of your potential clients.

Those who managed to exploit the RDP connection in its early days made handsome fortunes out of government contacts although, it has to be said, the poor remained stubbornly un-uplifted.

Unfortunately, Jay Naidoo couldn't seem to get his RDP kite airborne and went off to become a telephone operator. The RDP disappeared from the politically correct glossary to be replaced by 'black empowerment'.

Black empowerment works on simple, demographic principles and states that if, for example, black women constitute 40% of the population, this should be reflected in the workplace.

This is the government's latest social engineering fad and it goes a long way to explaining why mysterious new companies with apparent untold wealth and a politically acceptable public face have been popping up like Namaqualand daisies.

White businessmen have realised that to stand any chance at all of benefiting from government largesse, they will need to change colour, or at least appear to change colour, which is precisely what some of them have done.

If you're going to succeed in this game the first thing to do is to register a company with an appropriately African sounding name. Then find a black businessman who is prepared to sit on the board, preferably as chairman, for a fee of not less than a million a year.

When you have done that you can start putting the white management in place, complete with share incentives and option schemes. You will need to make some affirmative appointments for cosmetic reasons, so make sure that you have enough office space and some vague, meaningless job titles to hand out. A plentiful supply of executive accessories like cellphones and luxury cars help too, I'm told.

A combination of some creative accounting and a couple of understanding pension fund trustees and, hey presto, you are on the acquisition road to untold wealth. If you can reverse into a listed company so much the better.

At the moment every fund manager worth his citizenship wants some black chips in his portfolio at a price-earnings ratio of 40 because he thinks that once the exorbitant fees from government contracts start rolling in, the price will be justified. It's not difficult to predict that many personal fortunes will be made by those who have had the savvy to become chameleons. Whether their investors will do as well remains to be seen.

*

I read with delight that the National Symphony Orchestra has decided to take on the SABC over its ill-conceived decision to cut costs by dumping the NSO. I am unreliably informed that the orchestra is to embark on a course of industrial action which will include a 'go slow' during any pieces marked allegro, a 'down bow' policy from the second violins during works by Mahler and a compensation demand from the percussion section for 'repetitive stress syndrome'.

2 March 1997

Hold on to your homburgs – Bullard is voting for the ANC

If there was a general election tomorrow, I would vote ANC without any hesitation. I realise that this will come as something of a surprise to those readers who think that I dress in khaki shorts and spit-braai giraffes every weekend. It will come as more of a shock, I suspect, to members of the ANC and, in particular, government ministers for whom, I am told, the *Out to Lunch* column on a Sunday morning is the worst possible digestive accompaniment to eggs, bacon and coffee.

In fact, I fully expect this statement to cause mass resignations and disarray within the ranks as party officials analyse this most unlikely support base and wonder what they can possibly be doing to attract such undesirables. Today Bullard, tomorrow Eugene Terre Blanche: 1999 hangs in the balance.

As a migrant worker travelling under the protection of Her Britannic Majesty, I cast my first South African vote in the election of 1994. I was immediately attracted by many of the policies of the Soccer Party, but felt the party leadership lacked the necessary *gravitas* to guarantee future prosperity. After all, there is much to be said for hanging around with a loosely rolled zol in one hand and playing Bob Marley at the opening of parliament but it wouldn't look good on CNN.

I decided in the polling booth to switch my allegiance to Tony Leon's Democratic Party, mainly because they had canvassed me more efficiently than any other party but also because I thought they stood an outside chance of playing a part in the democratic process.

Although the DP fared badly in the general election, they have more than made up for their low numbers in parliament by asking precisely the sort of pithy questions to which we need answers. The National Party, by contrast, have proved absolutely hopeless in opposition and one can only pray that the party either finds something useful to do or disintegrates.

I have to confess to having a fairly low opinion of politicians in general believing them, rightly or wrongly, to be principally motivated by self-interest.

Preferring a system of 'guilty until proven innocent', I see no reason why they should be entitled to our automatic respect simply because they happen to have chosen a job that few of us would wish to do. Given the arrogance and inflated egos that seem to be inseparable from politics, it is hardly surprising that politicians are voted among the least trustworthy individuals in most parts of the world.

The refreshing thing about the ANC is that, at the moment, it is unencumbered by pomposity and egotism. President Nelson Mandela doesn't need a Ruritanian guard of toy soldiers in plumed helmets and white gloves to announce his presence. Unlike some of our African neighbours, politicians do not yet roar down the motorways, sirens screaming, escorted by gangs of heavily armed outriders wobbling around on improbably powerful motorcycles.

If anything, our top politicians are rather too casual, which perhaps mistakenly conveys the image that they are not taking things seriously enough. Although I admit to having been critical of this laid-back look in the early days, I much prefer it to the past, when politicians felt unable to appear in public without a homburg and a huge bunch of flowers in their lapels.

Few professionals would put in the hours or be willing to work for the sort of money that a cabinet minister gets paid, so one has to assume that those who do so either cannot get a job in the private sector, or they sincerely believe that what they are doing will improve the lives of others and change South Africa for the better. Since we have seen an exodus of about 70 MPs, many to the more verdant pastures of capitalism, I think we can safely assume it is the latter.

Whether or not you believe that they are doing an effective job, you would be hard put to question the commitment of most of the men and women holding cabinet positions, particularly in the case of the Water and Land Affairs portfolios. In sharp contrast to the previous government, there seems to be a genuine attempt on the part of the ANC to move towards open and consultative government, and that is why they would get my vote. Now perhaps they could devote more attention to transparency and accountability.

16 March 1997

'Sellout' cat has confused pigeons all aflutter with conspiracy theory

I was very amused at the brouhaha following my comments on the ANC two weeks ago. Indignant readers accused me of being a sellout, saying the only explanation is that I must have been 'got at' by the new black owners of the *Sunday Times*. I am ashamed to admit that my knowledge of corporate matters is virtually non-existent and I could probably name more breakfast cereals than I could name black directors of Times Media. There has never been any attempt to influence my copy and the only time something is removed from an article is when it might land me in court for defamation. The most unexpected response came from my old chum, David Gleason, who flatteringly devoted his entire Torque column to suggest that I was a few sandwiches short of a picnic. In the article I said that if a general election were held tomorrow, I would vote ANC. The key word is 'tomorrow' – I can't vouch for my affections in 1999.

However, unlike Gleason I believe that the ANC today is very different from the ANC of a year ago and that a new pragmatism has emerged, probably because the government realises that the gaffes of the past year have cost the country dearly. Unlike David Gleason, I don't believe affirmative action is an important issue. It is a largely discredited employment policy which insults talented black management by implying tokenism and places unqualified people in jobs they are incapable of doing. Logic tells me that the system is clearly unworkable and will eventually burn itself out. It was obvious that the public service would employ more black faces under the ANC, just as the previous administration created jobs for unskilled Afrikaners. As an aside, my own experience is that the new incumbents are far more courteous and helpful than their predecessors.

Gleason claims that he couldn't vote ANC because he doesn't know what the party stands for and doubts whether they do. So what major party does know what it stands for? Some of them don't even seem to know what they stand against!

As evidence of the ANC's confused policy-making, Gleason cites the example of the party's recent attempts to centralise power. As he correctly points out, two provinces have 'delivered sharp rebukes to the men who fondly think they run the show from the President's kitchen'. That looks encouragingly like the democratic process at work to me and surely should be cause for celebration.

Financial markets have been particularly robust this year, in sharp contrast to a year ago when the ANC was busy unwittingly sabotaging the economy. I surely don't need to point out to the publisher of a financial journal that the relative strength of the markets and the ANC's economic policies cannot be divorced. Foreign investors evidently believe the government is serious about cutting wasteful expenditure, growing the economy and keeping a watchful eye on its indebtedness. Maybe they are right, maybe they are wrong, but at least they are putting their money in SA markets.

Exchange controls are just another way a government interferes with an individual's personal freedom, in this case where to leave his after-tax income. Gleason has been rightly critical of them, so I hope he will remember who imposed them when the ANC dismantles them.

Perhaps David Gleason and I use different dictionaries, but my comment that nobody could doubt the commitment of the ministers of Land and Water Affairs could hardly be described as 'panegyric', particularly considering my damning comments about all politicians earlier in the article. Many people will remember that, under the previous government, the post of Water Affairs was used as a shunting yard for downwardly mobile defence ministers and had very little to do with water at all.

It is very easy and fashionable to trash the government week after week, but I believe that if this column is to have at least a modicum of credibility then praise must also be given when due. We live in a stunningly beautiful country which has emerged from four horrific and oppressive decades with remarkably little bloodshed. Tourists are visiting, significant foreign investment is poised to come in if we send the right signals, property is cheap, food is plentiful. In the words of Harold Macmillan: 'You've never had it so good.'

30 March 1997

Rich and powerful cosy up over lavish dinner while voters wait for bread

Try as I may (and believe me, I have put a lot of effort into this one), I cannot for the life of me understand why anybody in their right mind would pay R250 000 a couple just to rub shoulders with the great and glorious of our land and boast that they had supped on Robben Island with Hillary Clinton. Am I missing the point? Was the food so spectacular, the conversation so scintillating and the wines so rare that people were prepared to dig deep into their pockets for this never-to-be-repeated opportunity? I somehow doubt it.

I read in the *Sunday Times* last week that the names of the prominent businessmen who attended this decadent affair were leaked despite assurances that they would be kept secret. Why, if you have nothing to hide, would you wish nobody to know that you are prepared to spend R250 000 on a dinner for two on a former penal colony?

After all, South Africans aren't usually so modest when it comes to flashing their wealth about. One probable reason for this coyness is that it wasn't actually the guests who paid but the shareholders of the companies they work for. After all, businessmen are shrewd creatures. They know that, when it comes to putting their hands into their own pockets, they can find at least 101 better uses for R250 000 than dinner with the world's most successful futures trader and her toothy kid. However, if you can wangle it through the books as a legal expense and do a bit of political influence peddling into the bargain, why not?

Of course, the organiser of this lavish thrash, Ahmed Kathrada, dismisses as ludicrous any suggestion that businessmen could be attempting to buy influence. For me, this removes about the only valid reason to attend. Fortunately for the ANC, many of their supporters do not have access to the media, otherwise they would be asking why their leaders are swanning around on Robben Island enjoying expensive meals while they wait for houses, jobs and health care. Isn't life rough when you are merely a voter?

*

I was interested to read last week that the outlook for the Johannesburg CBD is brighter as a Malaysian property group prepares to spend R4-billion on upgrading and revitalising about 40 hectares of inner city property around the Carlton Centre.

Over the past few years accounting firms, merchant banks and law firms have been scrambling to get out of the inner city in the hopes of finding better conditions in the northern suburbs.

The Johannesburg CBD became more and more dilapidated, restaurants closed, crime rose and for a while it looked as though the city would be left to the mining houses and big banks which have all built splendid head offices and can't really consider moving.

In addition to the Malaysian investment, several major retail groups have also invested substantially in the CBD.

Now, paradoxically, the very places that many companies escaped to, looking for a better quality of life, have become just like the old city centre. Rosebank, for example, is no longer the upmarket shopping area it was five years ago.

The few pavements that actually remain are unusable because they are blocked by hawkers.

Oxford Road is the almost exclusive preserve of drug dealers and prostitutes, and in the parking lot outside the Constantia Centre vagrants harass shoppers and urinate in the gutter.

Our only hope is that the Malaysians will do such a good job that everybody will leave Rosebank and move back to Johannesburg.

*

Some years ago the medical profession gave the wine industry a boost by publishing an article in *The Lancet* which said that red wine drinkers had been found to have far healthier arteries than non-red wine drinkers.

A red wine a day keeps the coronary away. The only problem with using this very pleasant method to protect your heart is that you may well be putting a few other organs under pressure in the process.

So good old killjoy science has come to the rescue and you will shortly be able to buy a capsule which contains all the things in red wine that are good for your heart without actually having to risk a hangover just to keep healthy.

With any luck this will have an effect on wine prices and by the next Nederburg Auction red wine prices will be back at affordable levels.

4 May 1997

Winnie and the dastardly plot to import 30-million anti-ANC voters

Just when you thought that Winnie Madikizela-Mandela was about to be consigned to the scrapheap of political history or doomed to become an answer to some obscure Trivial Pursuit question, she has bounced back by winning the ANC Women's League five-furlong handicap at Rustenburg this week.

Although she romped home by several lengths, it turned out to be rather a one-horse race with Health Minister Nkosazana Zuma not even coming under starter's orders and the other horse, rank outsider Thandi Modise, trotting past the finishing post after most of the punters had already left the course.

Zuma's failure to even start the race will come as a disappointment to her ANC owners and trainer who had high hopes for her this season, particularly as it was Zuma who was a key figure in trying to topple Winnie two years ago. With the big race of 1999 fast approaching, the ANC would have preferred to have someone less accident-prone (although only marginally so) as president of their Women's League.

As things stand they will now have to be nice to Winnie, whose voice will be even more strident at ANC national executive committee meetings. Just in case anybody thought a year or two of political obscurity may have mellowed her, Winnie was quick to prove nothing has changed, and she is just as embarrassing and muddled as she ever was.

Winnie sees in every newspaper article about her a sinister plot to deprive her of the power and privilege she loves and abuses so enthusiastically. How dare the press draw the attention of mere taxpayers to the fact that she is unable to account for her spending sprees as deputy minister? How dare they say she doesn't pay her bills? 'Which black person doesn't have a problem with a bond?' she asks fatuously. 'I am proud of my poverty,' declares the woman who used to jet overseas on unauthorised trips at the drop of a hat and who was once reputed to spend R20 000 a month on cosmetics.

If the accusations in the press are so ludicrous, then all Winnie has to do is give straight answers to straight questions. However, directness has never been her forte and so she assures us that she has instructed her lawyers to deal with the issue – something we will await with interest. For a woman who claims she can't pay her bond, Winnie is spending a lot of money on legal fees.

While the rest of the ANC top brass now understands the economic and social importance of preaching reconciliation and nation building, poor persecuted Winnie can evidently think of nothing intelligent to contribute and so reverts to populist fire-side stories.

Last week had her babbling on about how the 'enemy and spies' are putting 'a daring plan together' ahead of the 1999 election. Exciting stuff. Although she refused to elaborate (presumably another job for her hard-pressed lawyers), she has accused the Department of Home Affairs of issuing forged documents to 'illegal immigrants' from Asia and Europe who are able to afford the R250 000 kickback necessary. This dastardly plan is being hatched by opponents of the ANC who apparently intend to 'import' enough voters to guarantee an ANC defeat in 1999.

So if the roads become a bit congested in the next year or two it is because the enemies of true democracy have issued about 30-million people with forged immigration documents. On the other hand, just think what this will do for depressed property prices!

Winnie has never had a high regard for the principles of either political or financial accountability because she believes that they were introduced by racist white bigots to stop people like her having fun. Neither does she have much regard for courts, which she uses at her convenience, depending on whether she is the plaintiff or defendant.

Winnie is not, and never has been, a great fan of freedom of speech, particularly when she is the topic of conversation. At the Women's League conference last week she gave a sinister warning that if the media persists in printing these absurdities about her private life, 'we, the women, will find a solution to closing you up'. I don't know what she means, but I am not taking any chances and am avoiding contact with women football players carrying boxes of matches and car tyres.

8 June 1997

Master of the photo opportunity sees the writing on the wall

One of the least surprising pieces of news in the past few weeks is the decision by Tokyo Sexwale to give up politics and search around for a well-paid niche in an empowerment company.

There are plenty of theories on offer as to why Tokyo feels the need to move on. One is that his progress up the ANC ladder has been frustrated by the dapper Thabo Mbeki, who probably doesn't like the fact that he wears silly shirts to work. Another rumour is that he cannot get on at provincial level with many of his colleagues and, more particularly, that he doesn't see eye to eye with the energetic and focused Jesse Duarte.

I suspect that the real reason for his departure is far more mundane. It has become obvious that Tokyo Sexwale has proved a complete disaster as the head of South Africa's power-house province and it is no longer possible for either the ANC or the man himself to pretend otherwise. The unfortunate and long-suffering residents of Gauteng, and more particularly those in the Johannesburg area, have spent the past three years watching their province become a giant rubbish tip. Residents who are used to paying for their amenities had their rates increased dramatically so that enough money could be raised to cover the shortfalls caused by those who have never paid for, and have no intention of ever paying for, their amenities.

We appear to have no cogent building or planning strategy in Johannesburg, with the result that once-tranquil residential areas are being invaded by business. Apparently it takes so long to get building permission under the new administration that most developers just go ahead anyway, which is probably why the northern suburbs look such a mess. The result is that residential property values have plummeted in Johannesburg with desperate sellers often having to rent their properties out simply because they cannot find buyers. Three years ago when the ANC came to power there was euphoria, with property prices rising to anticipate the foreign investment that should have started to pour into the province.

The worst problem though has been the tidal wave of crime and the increasing disregard for the law among previously law-abiding citizens, based presumably on the premise that if you can't beat them, join them. Red robots are now a mere traffic advisory; a warning that there is an intersection ahead. If you don't feel like stopping or if you think that the road is clear you can ignore the red light and drive on without any fear of a fine.

If there is no convenient parking exactly where you want it then feel free to double park, park in a no-parking zone or, better still if you have one of those rugged 4x4s, mount the pavement and leave your car there. Too bad if the pedestrians can't get past.

These relatively minor infringements are happening every day and where are the traffic police? Rather than risking the wrath of the taxi bully boys and winding up at the wrong end of an AK-47, they are busy ticketing safe targets like housewives for speeding offences on suburban back roads.

Even in New York it is illegal to have a pornography store within a specified distance of a school. Not in Rosebank though, and if porn isn't your thing then why not pop along and buy one of the many illegal narcotics freely available at the Constantia Centre just 300 metres from a police station.

How is it that the spaced-out zombies that stagger out of the clubs in this area early on a Saturday morning seem to be visible to everybody but the police?

It is impossible to ignore the fact that this decline in standards and quality of life has happened during Sexwale's term of office. Although he was undoubtedly a popular choice when elected, most people's perception is that the Gauteng leader has a rather high leisure preference and would rather turn up at social functions, sip wine with the great and good and attend expensive dinners on Robben Island than roll up his sleeves and attempt to sort out Gauteng's problems. A master of the photo opportunity and the sound bite, he has promised us much and delivered practically nothing. Now he has eventually decided that he is not up to the job, only one question remains. Who gets the keys to the BMW 740?

13 July 1997
'Let them eat cake' is the message from the empty benches of parliament

MPs may soon be voting themselves a 15% pay increase for ordinary MPs and a 12% increase for cabinet ministers. This would bring the annual package for a rank-and-file MP to R239 642 and a minister would receive a package of R474 713.

These figures obviously do not include all the freebies that go with the job such as the many international 'fact-finding' tours politicians feel obliged to organise for themselves on our behalf, generally to the world's more glamorous spots. Naturally it would also be quite unreasonable to expect an MP to make a long first-class flight to a hostile environment like New York without taking along at least one member of the family for company. It is also widely accepted that, because of the punishing workload, a politician's digestive system becomes very delicate, with the result that the body can only absorb the finest wines and easily digested food like caviar and pâté de foie gras. How things have changed.

Not so long ago I can remember Jay Naidoo standing up at one of those proletariat gatherings he used to love attending and telling the assembled masses that it was scandalous that anybody should earn more than R200 000 a year while the poor foraged around in the dirt looking for old chicken bones to gnaw on. Such traitorous enemies of the class struggle should immediately be slapped with a penal income tax rate to help them atone for their anti-social behaviour. Now poor old Jay is earning more than twice the offending amount, which is presumably why he has become so quiet of late. After all, it is rather difficult to confront the previously disadvantaged and still maintain your struggle credibility when your salary is pushing half-a-million a year.

Unfortunately, the sensitive matter of a politician's remuneration invariably prompts snide comments about a government gravy train, particularly as public servants have been told there will have to be a freeze on pay rises because there isn't enough money to go round. Few people would argue that a competent cabinet minister should be paid a proper executive salary and a package of R474 713 is hardly excessive when compared with private sector packages. However, the fact that a handful of disinterested, layabout politicians will receive R239 642 just for the privilege of biding their time until 1999 is scandalous; particularly as some of them don't even bother to attend parliament. Rather than waste taxpayers' money for another two years, surely it would be better to kick the freeloaders out of parliament straight away and only remunerate those politicians who are actually doing any work.

*

The financial markets have a saying, 'When America sneezes, we all catch cold', meaning that when US financial markets go into free fall, then other world markets are sure to follow, because the US is the biggest kid on the block and what he says goes.

The US's global influence extends way beyond financial markets, though, and what is hot in the US today will almost certainly be hot in SA tomorrow. The latest fad to hit the US's big cities is the cigar bar – which is quite extraordinary considering the recent settlement with the tobacco companies, who have had to stump up roughly $368 billion to compensate smokers who started puffing before the days of government health warnings and claim they never realised it was the cigarettes that were making them cough their lungs up every morning.

Cigarette smoking is now banned in all public areas of New York, and wherever you look in Manhattan there are sullen little huddles of cigarette smokers who have been banished from office blocks to satisfy their craving on the sidewalk where they pose no threat to delicate air-conditioning systems and where healthy, non-smoking citizens can look at these pitiful, addicted creatures with disdain and loathing.

Meanwhile, I am delighted to say, cigar smokers seem to have avoided the unwelcome attentions of the health fascists and are subject to none of the opprobrium suffered by their downmarket fellow puffers. Thanks to the existence of cigar bars, they can spend a pleasant few hours in a haze of blue smoke while attractive waitresses bring them well-mixed martinis. Now that the SA government has slavishly followed the US's persecution of smokers, maybe somebody will have the courage to start the first local cigar bar.

24 August 1997

A railway station with a history of open windows and slippery floors

Politicians love renaming things. It gives them a nice warm feeling inside and makes them appear decisive.

It is also a wonderful way of passing the hours while they are planning their next foreign fact-finding tour or trying to summon up the energy to get on with some of the more tedious and unglamorous tasks of government, like creating jobs and putting roofs over people's heads.

Some renaming seems to have been quite arbitrary. For example, I never quite understood why Transvaal had to be renamed Gauteng, unless it was to create employment in the number plate and road-sign manufacturing sector.

Anyway, I expect it gave Benny Alexander (who was such an enthusiastic renamer that he even renamed himself !Khoisan X) a few months of taxpayer-sponsored employment before he washed his hands of politics and leapt into the welcoming arms of capitalism.

One of the reasons for giving places new names is to eradicate painful memories of the past, and one can quite understand why the new government would not wish to make use of airports named in honour of previous oppressors. So I was very surprised that it had taken the government so long to rename that symbol of the apartheid era, John Vorster Square, a building with a dismal history of open windows and very slippery floors.

Unfortunately, the renaming committee must have been going through a period of creative constipation because they have managed to come up with one of the dumbest names I have ever heard. John Vorster Square will now be known as Johannesburg Central.

Can you imagine how many foreign tourists are going to go there expecting to catch a train to Cape Town, only to find themselves having their request for two return tickets laboriously taken down in crayon by a semi-literate desk sergeant?

I wonder whether this confusing name change isn't just a clever ploy by new cop supremo Meyer Kahn to motivate the force. All that business about owning the process, whatever that means. We all know by now that the police are a little shaky in certain essential skills, like keeping dangerous criminals where they should be kept – locked up in a cell.

Many manage to walk out of the charge office unchallenged. Even this month's public enemy number one, Gorilla assailant and alleged rapist Isaac Mofokeng, managed somehow to get hold of a saw and climb through the removed bars of the exercise yard roof to make his escape.

All of this is very bad for the image of the police because it makes them look incompetent and lazy when, in fact, they are probably just very unlucky.

So the idea of renaming John Vorster Square and making it sound like a railway station is really just a clever way of ensuring that there are always plenty of people milling around, and if a couple of convicts escape you can easily replace them with a couple of tourists and who will know the difference? The important thing is to always have the cells full just in case the media decide on a surprise visit. The other nice thing about a bustling police station is that it gives the impression of business as usual, as well as providing a variety of interesting people for the station staff to interact with. This is particularly welcome when so many prisoners are escaping, thus depriving the police of much-needed company.

*

In a couple of weeks we will know whether Cape Town will be hosting the 2004 Olympic Games. Although we are up against some stiff competition, there seems to be a growing unease that Cape Town might just win on novelty value.

It will be the first time the Games will be held on the continent of Africa and this offers great attendant commercial possibilities. As we get ourselves horribly into debt, kind foreign bankers will step in to lend us expensive money for the next 100 years.

The Olympic media machine has done its best to brainwash us and appeal to our rainbow patriotism with slogans such as 'If Cape Town wins, we all win'.

This is pernicious nonsense, because the truth is that if Cape Town wins then only Cape Town wins. For the next seven years money will be pumped into upgrading the Olympic city and its infrastructure while the rest of the country is allowed to slide even further into Third World squalor. All this to impress an expected foreign tourist invasion that will last a mere six weeks.

14 September 1997

Never mind the Olympics, Cape Town is playing

I just happened to be in Cape Town on the day they announced the winner of the Olympic bid for 2004.

It was an interesting evening and, as you may have already read, the city was racially divided with two potential celebration parties ready to roll.

One was at Cape Town's Grand Parade and was attended almost exclusively by what Western Cape Premier Hernus Kriel sensitively called 'people of colour', many of whom had obviously been bussed in for the benefit of the TV cameras.

The other party was held at the Waterfront and was patronised mainly by what I suppose we would have to call 'people of neutral tint'.

Some of them had quite expensive-looking tans – but these days that doesn't count.

It's what is underneath that is important and the Waterfront brigade were, by and large, intrinsically achromatic.

The *Cape Argus* attempted to wring a front-page story out of this the following Monday by saying the existence of two parties highlighted the glaring divide between rich and poor, as if this were in some way a great revelation.

Anyone who has looked out of the window of a plane landing at Cape Town international airport or driven along the N2 between Cape Town and the Stellenbosch offramp would have been aware – long before an Olympic party – of living conditions that are a world away from those in Clifton and Bantry Bay.

Apart from a desire to find the Mercedes parked safely where one left it, I imagine the reason many chose to party at the Waterfront and not at the Grand Parade is precisely the same reason the same people choose to build a multimillion-rand holiday home on the Atlantic seaboard and not on the Cape Flats – exclusivity.

What now? Should we perhaps levy an extra tax on those disgusting capitalists who keep expensive coastal holiday homes and use them only for two weeks of the year? Should we force them to allow the homeless and the destitute to use these properties while they are back in Johannesburg making even more money?

Maybe the provincial government could try to deter foreign buyers from making homes unaffordable for locals by adding a 100% surcharge and distributing it to the poor.

I have little doubt that ideas as barmy as these (and probably barmier) will surface as we approach the 1999 elections and unscrupulous lefty politicians exploit our failure to win the 2004 Olympics as further evidence of the great racial divide.

Fortunately those in command of the Western Cape at the moment seem to understand on which side their bread is buttered.

They know that Cape Town, and by extension SA, will fare much better by making itself attractive to foreign investors.

Poverty is not going to disappear overnight and neither is crime, so Gauties rushing to the Cape to avoid horrendous crime figures may be jumping out of the frying pan into the fire.

What Cape Town does have though, and which seems completely lacking in Johannesburg, is the promise of a better future.

As Johannesburg disappears under a pile of its own uncollected filth, Cape Town, already blessed with golden beaches, Table Mountain and stunning countryside, is striving to be the preferred destination of tourists and foreign investors.

Olympics or not, it has a better chance of becoming a world-class city than any other in SA. As that happens, and jobs and wealth are created over the next few years, the divide between rich and poor will narrow. And by the time the next Olympic bid is announced, everybody in Cape Town will be driving Mercedes-Benzes and parking them safely at the Grand Parade – which will leave the rest of the country wondering where it went wrong.

*

Attending a party to celebrate winning the bid for Olympic city is rather pointless if somebody else wins. So seconds after Athens was announced the victor, the phones started ringing in Waterfront restaurants to cancel bookings, and the exodus began, causing sufficient traffic congestion to convince even the most committed pro-bidder that Athens was probably a wiser choice.

Meanwhile, at a restaurant in Constantia there was great revelry as stoic Capetonians successfully tried to disguise the grief they must have felt at losing the chance to be host.

21 September 1997

Losing parliament could have a silver lining for Western Cape

Even after it was announced that SA had lost the Olympic bid, money was still being squandered in what looks suspiciously like an attempt to spend the full budget before the sponsors ask for some of their cash back. Within days, and possibly even hours, the large billboards which had attempted to convince us that 'if Cape Town wins we all win' had been redecorated with an equally large poster featuring two broken plates as the zeros in the 2004 and a self-congratulatory pat on the back for all the hard work that Chris Ball and Co had put in, together with a warm message for Athens. This is all very sporting, but one wonders what the point is. Are we going to continue putting signs along the highways for the next few months until the R96-million sponsorship money runs out?

Now all the Olympic nonsense is out of the way Capetonians are able to focus on the other big issue which concerns the city. Will parliament move? There is understandably a fair amount of hand-wringing at the prospect of losing some of the world's leading free spenders. After all, with the politicians gone, who will buy all those expensive German limousines? How many bottle stores will be forced to close without the regular departmental booze orders and I've heard that all those luxurious new hotels that have been springing up in Cape Town, hoping to make a living out of hosting extravagant government shindigs, are biting their knuckles.

One proposed alternative location for government is somewhere called Midrand which, for those of you who don't know the area, used to be the large tract of bushveld between Johannesburg, the dynamic city of gold, and Pretoria, the not so dynamic city of grey shoes and compulsory moustaches.

This area has now been 'developed', which is a euphemism for saying that someone has bought up lots of cheap land. Thanks to the complete absence in Gauteng of any discernible building policy, they have been allowed to erect huge, ugly warehouses, conference centres and charmless office blocks and now urgently need tenants or, better still, buyers. Admittedly, although the area looks like a waste land, it is already apparently thriving despite the fact that it is not served by any adequate public transport from either Pretoria or Johannesburg.

That won't be a problem for too much longer because the developers are now blitzing the area with nasty-looking townhouses which people will be forced to live in if they are going to work in Midrand. I have no doubt that if parliament decides to move to Midrand (at the taxpayer's expense) many a developer's dream will be answered.

Now, I'm not for a moment suggesting that there is anything untoward or financially dubious about a bunch of politicians deciding to move from one of the most beautiful situations on the planet to somewhere in the middle of the bundu; it's just that, given their propensity for the sort of fancy footwork worthy of Fred Astaire, we should keep an eye on them.

Meanwhile, Capetonians should not be asking themselves what happens 'if' parliament leaves Cape Town; they should already be eagerly making plans for 'when' they leave and urging them to do so as soon as possible. The short-term benefits of having parliament in Cape Town are far outweighed by the long-term benefits of running them out of town. For a start, there would be no more disruptive marches on parliament to ruin the tranquillity of the mother city and no need for the great unwashed to hang around the gardens protesting.

In fact, Cape Town would be a far nicer and healthier place without the pervasive cloud of sleaze and corruption that inevitably hangs over any city frequented by politicians and the sycophantic reptiles who dance to their tune.

Once parliament has made up its mind to leave Cape Town, Plan B can be put into action. It's quite apparent that the only thing holding back the Western Cape's metamorphosis from African basket case to African economic miracle is the impediment of being shackled to the rest of SA. An independent Western Cape with its own free-floating currency, attractive tax incentives for foreign investors and stringent immigration policies is the only logical solution given the self-destructive course the rest of the country seems to have chosen.

26 October 1997

Stals and his devious deputies pull the wool over miffed traders' eyes

Rather like sex, the anticipation of a Bank rate cut is often more exciting than the actual cut itself.

However, far from being pleased at Chris Stals's sudden surge of generosity, traders I spoke to were rather miffed, and with good reason. Only last week, Stals was intimating that a Bank rate cut was some way off and two of his deputy governors repeatedly stated that the central bank would have to be in possession of some encouraging economic data before they even considered requisitioning the 'Drop Bank Rate Now' forms from the stationery office. That wouldn't be until at least the end of the year, they told us. So just when we all came to believe that the governor and his deputies were men of steel, they dropped the rate.

Having cried wolf once more, it is going to take ages before the financial markets trust them again. Of course, the fact that the drop in Bank rate has failed to affect the financial markets is proof that it is becoming less and less important. All the calls for decisions on the Bank rate to be taken away from the Reserve Bank and debated by a gigantic committee made up of vested interests such as trade unionists, politicians and freelance free-marketeers will become quite pointless when money market rates are left to find their own levels early next year. The price of money will be determined simply by demand and supply and Bank rate changes will finally become depoliticised.

*

Many of my fellow scribes were lured to the recent Michael Jackson concert by the promise of free tickets and the prospect of nursing a glass of the amber liquid in one or other of the corporate boxes.

Fortunately, I received no such invitation, which saved me the trouble of declining. Quite why this strange creature holds such a fascination, I cannot imagine.

The appalling high-pitched nasal whining which he passes off as singing and that absurd dance, which looks as though he is trapped on an airport travelator going the wrong way, should be enough to put any sentient carbon-based life form off.

His popularity has been waning around the world, which is probably why he is in SA; a continent he couldn't previously visit unless he was wearing a protective surgical mask. In the US, for example, there is still some considerable concern over child molestation allegations which seemed to be magicked away by a substantial payment to the child's parents.

When Jackson was here, he lost no time in surrounding himself with pre-pubescent children, flying out his previous wife while leaving his current wife at home.

He strutted around the place dressed in the sort of military finery favoured by South American dictators.

As if this wasn't enough, his publicity machine erected a gigantic grey statue of Jackson in Sony's front garden in Dunkeld, Johannesburg.

There were horrible rumours that the statue had finished its useful life and would be left in darkest Africa as a permanent reminder that Jackson had graced these shores.

Happily, this is not the case. I telephoned Sony, which confirmed that Wacko had been dismantled in the past few days and crated back to his owner.

Frankly, I am surprised the thing lasted so long in Jo'burg without being swiped but, there again, thieves never actually steal the things you want them to steal.

The prospect of a gigantic statue of the gloved weirdo staring across the Bompas Road intersection and into the British Consulate is not one that Cecil Rhodes would have relished.

Just as nobody will admit to having supported apartheid, no one I have spoken to is prepared to admit that they like Michael Jackson's music, which is hardly surprising because everything he sings sounds the same. They just wanted to marvel at the stage show which would seem to suggest that people would be happier watching lots of flashing lights and smoke machines without actually having Jackson on stage at all.

They can't be serious. Having missed out on Jackson, I am pinning my hopes on being offered tickets to see that popular female singing ensemble, The Spice Girls. I don't like to grovel, but if you can manage a backstage pass then so much the better.

2 November 1997

Winnie still savours the sweet scent of survival

Do you remember the poor? All those bedraggled-looking individuals who queued for hours in the hot African sun to vote back in 1994 in the hope that a fresh, democratically elected government would bring with it a new and better life.

The sort of people who live in shacks on the banks of the Jukskei and whenever it rains and the river floods they have to change their postcode. Well, don't worry too much if you have forgotten them because they are likely to make a dramatic appearance next year as we approach the 1999 election.

Having looked after themselves remarkably well over the past few years and milked every cent out of black empowerment deals, it's time once again for politicians to start babbling on about the plight of the poor in the hope of catching their votes.

I suspect that what the poor would be more interested in hearing is how some of their former leaders have managed to become fabulously wealthy.

The mining industry is about to shed thousands of jobs, yet recently 'empowered' black businessmen apparently live a life of unparalleled luxury. Whatever happened to all those socialist principles?

Even union leaders have become recreational socialists and developed a taste for fine wine, cigars and short gourmet trips to France, just so long as they can manage to get back to Johannesburg every so often to lead the workers in the struggle against capitalist oppression.

As a ruling party, the ANC is in the enviable position of having no serious opposition.

The NP seems to be reinventing itself as a new touchy-feely, caring organisation. Interestingly though, only one person in five I asked could tell me the name of the new party leader.

The strange liaison between the odd couple of politics, Bantu Holomisa and Roelf Meyer, still has to come up with an original policy document and appears to be little more than a final resting place for sacked members of the ANC and disenchanted Nats.

It would be a great pity if the DP, the most active and intelligent of the government opposition parties, stopped exposing government profligacy, but it might be too much to expect that they would present a real challenge to government.

So, paradoxically, the only opposition to the ANC is the ANC itself. Although the organisation is understandably keen to play down stories of ideological differences, the recent Damascene conversion of Peter Mokaba to capitalism is hardly likely to sit well with the party's rank and file who can barely afford the price of today's lunch.

Personally, I am delighted that Mokaba is finally saying something sensible. Unfortunately it is not me that Mokaba needs to convince; it is the time-warp stragglers from the SA Communist Party and the economically illiterate members of his own party.

However, hard lessons about reality and admonishments to work harder and become globally competitive probably won't go down well with an electorate who were led to believe that, within weeks of the 1994 rainbow transition, their miserable lives would be changed forever.

The sort of questions they will be expecting answers to are where are the houses, the jobs, the hospitals, the schools, and the land they were promised?

The ANC has realised that delivering the goodies as a government is a far cry from promising the goodies as a campaigning party, but the balancing act between social upliftment and neo-Thatcherite economic policy is a difficult one.

Enter Winnie Madikizela-Mandela, the famous baby-sitter and deputy president-in-waiting. If there is one thing designed to send a shiver down the spines of the ANC hierarchy and foreign investors alike, it is the recent coverage of a turbaned Winnie addressing the million-woman march in Philadelphia.

The sisters had asked Winnie to give the keynote address, apparently unconcerned that she still has to explain a few legal inconsistencies back home.

No matter. With a superb sense of irony Winnie told the mob that they have a shared responsibility to save the world from violence.

'Amandla,' she shouted to the crowd at the end of her speech. 'Amandla,' they shouted back, uncertain whether this was a rallying cry or a new fragrance from Chanel.

16 November 1997

Hypocrisy and greed lurk behind labels of 'empowerment' and 'affirmative action'

The University of Cape Town Breakwater Monitor study on employment equity has discovered (surprise, surprise) that naughty whiteys are using black front companies and hiring 'ghost' black directors and managers to win contracts. I've often wondered whether one day I, too, could get paid a vast amount of money to conduct a study such as this and come up with the bloody obvious.

Long ago I predicted that precisely this type of thing was likely to occur once the dreaded affirmative action was allowed to become the vogue business practice. What I failed to predict, though, was that anybody would actually bother to conduct a study on the matter and appear surprised at the findings.

Not surprisingly, affirmative action has since been found wanting, largely because it is a wishy-washy notion that amounts to little more than reverse racism or black tokenism, depending on your point of view.

The fashionable business buzzword of the moment is the equally ghastly 'empowerment', which trips lightly off the tongues of black and white businessmen alike. Rather like upliftment, it is a word which is so gushingly politically correct and pious that it immediately masks all sorts of dodgy dealings, scams and sharp practices. Who, after all, would be brave or foolish enough to question any business whose apparent selfless dedication to the community and the oppressed comes so high on their mission statement?

The nauseating aspect is the hypocrisy of it all. People who not so long ago gathered around the boma fire at exclusive game lodges to swap racist jokes now ask us to believe that their waking hours are crammed with pure thoughts about how to improve the lot of the previously disadvantaged. Stick the official government empowerment label on your product and sit back and watch the money roll in. As the next election looms, empowerment is being disingenuously offered to the increasingly disenchanted black community as a cure-all wonder drug. Suitably vague and open to various interpretations, it is intended to imply that there would be jobs for all if only the selfish whites would squeeze up and make room. Worse though, it is presented in such a way as to suggest that no effort on the part of the empoweree is necessary. No skills need to be learnt, no boring days need to be spent in classrooms and no real qualifications are required. It is the government's decree ... you will be empowered.

I mentioned a few weeks ago that I had never, in 25 years in financial markets, seen so much easy money made. I wasn't referring to the buoyant (at the time) equity market. I was thinking more of the enormous amounts of funny money that seem to be conjured out of thin air. Many of the smart deals that allow a young banker in his early thirties to earn a salary of R10-million a year have been cleverly designed to circumvent the taxman. The government doesn't seem too concerned about this for some reason, presumably because the chums of politicians are doing so grandly out of the practice.

While I would never dispute that it is every taxpayer's right to use any legal means to deprive the taxman of money, I have to question the long-term effect, and probably even the short-term effect, of such thinking. Is the government really serious about upliftment? Is it even serious about an equitable tax system? If so, why does the Finance Ministry apparently condone business practices which are detrimental to the fiscus?

It may be very smart to use a series of trusts and offshore companies to deprive the taxman of his rightful due, but the problem is that the tax burden then falls on an ever-dwindling number of companies and individuals. Meanwhile, the unemployment figures rise, crime soars, healthcare and education standards deteriorate and there is no money left to spend on non-essential services such as repairing roads and clearing garbage. Edward Heath coined the phrase 'the unacceptable face of capitalism' in the 70s.

We now have such a culture of greed in this country that it is easy to forget that the majority of citizens don't even have the essentials for the most basic existence. The question is whether the majority of the poor will be content to live alongside the majority of the rich for the foreseeable future without showing the odd sign of envy. My guess is that they will not.

28 December 1997

Being a counter-revolutionary has its attractions

In his recent SABC interview with Allister Sparks, President Mandela described the media as part of a counter-revolutionary conspiracy trying to destabilise the government.

As he has spent the greater part of his life as a member of a counter-revolutionary conspiracy trying to destabilise past governments, I guess he should know what he's talking about.

I imagine the accusation is meant as an insult but I rather like it. It's certainly more glamorous than describing oneself as a journalist, even if it is a bit of a nuisance when it comes to filling in those official forms that ask your occupation.

It also opens up a host of possibilities. The first that comes to mind is not having to shave. No self-respecting revolutionary is clean-shaven, as anybody who had a Che Guevara poster on their bedroom wall in the 60s knows. It is also revolutionary chic to wear one's hair slightly long. This suggests that, because you are constantly avoiding the attention of the security police, it is difficult to get to a hairdressing salon. I expect I can also dispense with suits because real revolutionaries don't wear suits. According to Hollywood, they wear frayed sweaters, jeans, T-shirts, old army fatigues and, in winter, a woolly balaclava. They also stay up all night in restaurants smoking strong French cigarettes, drinking coffee and discussing how to overthrow the government.

From now on this column will be written on an old typewriter in just such an establishment during the hours of darkness. The final copy will be entrusted to a messenger who will have to dodge through enemy lines to get it to the *Sunday Times* in time for publication. I might even write it in code.

The other wonderful thing about being a member of a counter-revolutionary conspiracy is that we can give ourselves aliases and form strangely named little groups with other like-minded revolutionaries. Carlos the Jackal would probably never have been as successful if he had used his proper name. I have decided to call myself Dennis the Meerkat and am in the process of forming an extremist splinter group called 'the jolly hot December cocktail bar crawlers liberation army'.

When the pubs run dry on a hot day we are going to phone radio stations and claim responsibility. The only things we are a bit shaky on are the more traditional terrorist skills such as blowing up public places full of innocent people, but I guess there are plenty of members of parliament who could advise us how best to go about this.

*

With a superb sense of irony, the State President chose the Day of Reconciliation to slag off whites, the media, big business, opposition parties and just about anybody who happens to disagree with the ANC's rather unique brand of democracy. This Mugabe-esque display of paranoia didn't go unnoticed by the foreign press (also sadly run by whites and therefore unreliable) who wondered whether this wasn't the beginning of the final downhill slide for SA Inc.

As we all know, politicians have a very inflated sense of their own importance. With the party rank and file bashing on the door asking when delivery on last election's promises can be expected, it's not surprising the government, who appear to have looked after their own interests rather well, are looking for political scapegoats.

If one returns to the corporate analogy, SA Inc is actually owned by the shareholders (the taxpayer), and politicians are simply managers employed by us to run the business. If there is any haranguing to be done it should be the shareholders telling the managers they are doing a lousy job. Next thing they'll be suggesting a whites-only rights issue.

4 January 1998
Viva global domination and afternoon naps

South Africans who tuned into the Breakfast Club on SABC 2 last Tuesday in the hopes of being entertained or educated would instead have been treated to the painful sight of fellow *Sunday Times* columnist Zakes Mda and I attempting to do press-ups in the company of three very fit gym instructors.

I managed about four and had blurred vision and palpitations for the rest of the day. Zakes appeared to do rather better. But since my colleague could be described as being a 'circumferencially challenged' person, I am not convinced that his stomach ever left the floor even though his back was seen to be moving. Anyway, as I explained on the programme, Zakes and I are creative artists and can't be expected to be athletic into the bargain. He does at least have the excuse that as a television critic he has to sit in an armchair all day watching the box and scribbling notes for his column.

This was my second appearance on the show in a week, which means one of two things. Either the SABC is thinking of turning me into a serial, or all the real celebrities are out of town this month. I have a nasty feeling it is the latter. I also managed to get onto Nigel Murphy's radio programme a few weeks back and, as discerning Cape listeners may know, I do a regular slot for Kfm on a Friday morning.

Maybe it is the prospect of finally being in a position to demand an upgrade on SAA, but this sudden media exposure has gone completely to my head. As a result I am going to form a new political party this year just so that I can keep appearing on television like all the other politicians. I have decided to call it the Siesta Party. Central to the party's beliefs (apart from world domination) is that the entire country should close down for a sleep between 2.30 and four every afternoon. If you've ever watched the television relays from parliament, you'll know that this policy has already been endorsed by the ANC.

The party also plans to divide the country into different time zones and give each province a separate currency. This will stimulate internal trade and will enable us to make a comparative study of how economically viable each province is. Provinces that don't turn a profit will be unbundled and offered for tender to the highest bidder. This could mean, for example, that Mpumalanga gets sold to the Malaysians (if it hasn't already been) who will be able to enjoy a much healthier, smog-free environment than they do back home. The party will throw its weight, and taxpayers' money, behind the bid for the next winter Olympics with Ogies as the preferred location.

As far as medical health is concerned, the Siesta Party acknowledges that it will be difficult to undo the damage that four years of ANC meddling has inflicted on the country and so we will wash our hands entirely of any obligation to provide even basic health care. Instead, we will introduce a sickness tax to deter the public from becoming ill. Education is another minefield where the party will wish to avoid any responsibility so we will simply continue with the ANC's policies.

A new commission called the Lies and Blame Commission will be set up with a brief to investigate all the sanctimonious twaddle that has been peddled as part of the healing process over the past few years. As no amnesty will be available due to the current world shortage of that particular commodity, the whole point of the commission will be to see who can accumulate the most air miles. The winner becomes archbishop.

Finally, the party will give full consideration to land rights on an equitable basis. Every time you buy a box of the new, nutritious breakfast cereal Siesta Flaky Corn, you will have the chance to win a land reclamation token. Just collect five of these tokens and you could be well on your way to the Free State farm of your dreams. Unfortunately, the competition is not open to anyone who is not a member of the Siesta Party.

11 January 1998

No room for an orgy but your R1m Clifton box says you've made it

Johannesburg over the New Year holiday period was nothing short of disgraceful. Rain, rain and even more rain. I blame the ANC, but I expect they will deny responsibility as usual and tell us that it was all part of a counter-revolutionary plot by the media designed to destabilise the government; an accusation that implies the government is stable in the first place, which is clearly far from true.

Anyway, I decided that it was time to escape to Cape Town which has been baking in temperatures more usually found in the Kalahari. That's what National Party efficiency does for you. Fortunately, most of the lemmings have now left and it was actually possible to drive into the Waterfront, buy a few essential items and drive out again without getting caught in a 5km traffic jam. That, of course, is the beauty of a flat in Clifton at Christmas time. The beach is on your doorstep, but you don't get caught in traffic jams for the simple reason that it is impossible to even get into the main traffic flow in Victoria Road. The congestion saves you a fortune in entertaining costs because whenever you invite people round for seasonal drinks you know they are going to have to park in Green Point and walk the rest of the way. This way you can hand out invitations liberally, knowing that only the most dedicated freeloaders will turn up.

Apart from the pleasure of having about 500 people babbling into their cellphones on the beach in front of your window every day, what is it that makes people want to spend Christmas in an apartment on Clifton beach? The short answer is exclusivity. Everyone knows that only the very rich and successful can afford to pay well over R1-million for a sea-facing apartment which is so small that even a simple orgy of more than three people becomes impossible, with stray legs crashing into wardrobe doors and knocking over the designer Italian chairs. However, tiny or not, the Clifton apartment announces to the world that you have arrived. The problem with Clifton's beaches is that they are public and so a lot of hoi polloi turn up every day trying to give the impression that they belong there. What distinguishes the real Cliftonian from the day-tripper poseurs is possession of the combination code for the gate which separates the vulgarity of the public beach from the exclusivity of the beach-front apartment blocks.

The riff-raff can only watch in wonder and envy as their superiors carefully wash the sand from their toes and pad up to their individually decorated apartments for more vintage champagne. Just for fun they might drape a banner over the balcony with the words: 'I've just made R6-millon on my share options.' High visibility is, after all, everything and what's the point of having all that newly acquired wealth if you can't tell everyone?

As it is virtually impossible to leave the building because of all the holiday traffic, days are spent aimlessly commuting between the apartment and the beach to top up the suntan and network with fellow power figures. This is a good time to reflect on the triumphs of the past year and to address the more important questions in life such as: 'How can I make even more money and who can I screw in the process?'

This week the Clifton beaches were almost deserted. The blinds were drawn in most of the multi-million rand apartments and the dreadful yuppies with their warbling cellphones and designer labels had thankfully returned to Gauteng.

Two of the chief attractions of Clifton, I am told, is that the beaches are protected from the wind and the bathing is safe.

Apparently sharks won't go near the place; they can't stand the competition.

One of the problems with buying an expensive upmarket property on the Atlantic seaboard is the quality of your neighbours.

In the good old days one was fairly assured of meeting a similar class of person if one had spent several million on a house and about the same again to do it up. Now, instead of hobnobbing with fellow captains of industry and commerce, one is likely to find that the neighbours are either shifty-looking European tax fugitives or local drug lords.

The trick, I am told, is to make your house clearly identifiable so rival gang leaders don't firebomb the wrong house at three o'clock in the morning.

1 February 1998

Clinton should have stuck to vacuum cleaners in the Oral Office

There is apparently no truth in the rumour that the White House Oval Office is to be renamed the Oral Office. I expect that joke has already been cracked, but just in case it hasn't, remember you read it first in the *Sunday Times*.

Poor Bill Clinton looked decidedly ruffled on television last week as a new wave of sexual allegations kept the world's media amused and boosted the gold price, in the process breathing life back into many of South Africa's marginal mines. The case actually has very little to do with Clinton's alleged penchant for pre-dawn steamy telephone chats (at least that's safer than pre-dawn nuking raids on Libya) and the occasional pre-summit blow job from raven-haired lovely Monica Lewinsky.

Indeed, Clinton's whole term of office has been riddled with rumours of sexual dalliance. Paula Jones, who may just be a small-town girl greedy for rather more than her allotted 15 minutes of fame, has repeatedly accused the president of demanding oral sex from her, back in 1991. The real issue, or so the lawyers would have us believe, is the fact that Clinton allegedly told young Monica to lie to the investigators into the Jones allegations and say that she had never had a sexual relationship with him.

The only problem was that somebody called Linda Tripp, who purported to be a close friend and confidante of Monica's, secretly recorded their private conversations while she listened to Monica's accounts of her alleged sexual activities with the leader of the free world. Being an upstanding American, she handed the tapes to the FBI with never a thought for commercial gain. Tripp seems a singularly nasty piece of work. She has already blabbed to the investigators about another woman, Kathleen Whilley, who has also previously testified that she was a victim of unsolicited sexual advances in the Oral Office. In fact, I shouldn't be at all surprised if, before too long and with a little prompting from the FBI, many more female White House staffers suddenly remember that they, too, have been improperly propositioned by the president at some time.

But why all the fuss and why now? Ever since Clinton came to power his name has been linked with sleazy property deals back in Arkansas and he has always been suspected of being a serial philanderer.

He's only following in the footsteps of President John F Kennedy. So the American people are hearing nothing they didn't either already know or suspect. The paradox is that, despite being an alleged low life, Clinton has led the US into a period of almost unparalleled prosperity and peace.

Being the disposable consumer society it is, the US now evidently feels that Clinton has fulfilled his purpose and should be put out with the trash. The Americans only have themselves to blame. After all, if they had any real doubts about Clinton they surely wouldn't have voted him in for a second term. However, a potential impeachment and possible prison sentence demonstrates to the world that a highly moral society like America won't put up with any hanky-panky from its presidents. The hypocrisy is quite nauseating isn't it?

*

As one of the growing band of men who have 'come out of the pantry' and admitted to being a 'house-husband', I was fascinated to read of a study by sociologist Jean Claude Kauffman, who suggests that repetitive activities such as dusting and vacuuming are erotic experiences for many women. Apparently women were never intended to go out and get careers, which is why so many of them have become disenchanted with their lives. If they had spent more time doing the dishes and ironing they would all be wearing Mona Lisa smiles, Kauffman would have us believe.

Valerie Swales, a lecturer at Portsmouth University, goes even further. She considers the performance of housework comparable to the sex act itself; 'their repetitive nature is similar to the orgasm'. One can but speculate about her sex life.

The study concentrates on housewives and may, of course, just be part of a chauvinist plot to get women back to the sink. Now we need a similar study on men. For example, I suspect if men found housework sexually arousing the Oval Office would have been full of vacuum cleaners instead of young, kneeling women. Personally, I have never been sexually aroused by housework, but maybe I've been going out with the wrong sort of household appliance.

8 February 1998
Accountability takes a back seat in the BMW as leaders take wrong turning

My hopes of winning a Pulitzer prize were dashed last week when Mzi Khumalo abruptly resigned from the board of JCI, thus depriving many shareholders of the lively annual general meeting they were so much looking forward to as compensation for having been taken for a downhill ride for so long.

For poor Khumalo it would have been rather like being a Christian in a den of lions. I am reliably informed that, in those barbaric days, appearance fees for Christians were so appalling that Christian vs Lions' games were often cancelled until some bright Roman had a great idea. Instead of paying the Christians to attend, why not just drop them in the den and see how things pan out?

This proved extraordinarily popular and gate takings went up immediately with the added advantage that you didn't have to pay the Christians anything.

However, I digress. The plan was that I should attend the annual general meeting in order to bring readers of this esteemed publication a ring-side view of what was expected to be one of the livelier AGMs of the year. Unfortunately, but understandably in the circumstances, JCI hadn't on this occasion made special provision for press seats. In fact, they made it quite clear that unless we were shareholders we would only be welcome to attend the watered-down press conference at 1 pm, by which time the blood would have been mopped up.

Plans were at an advanced stage for me to gain entrance to JCI disguised as a tea-lady and then to crawl through the airconditioning ducts above the auditorium with a powerful directional microphone and a fibre optic camera which I was to lower slowly through one of the grilles in the auditorium roof. Khumalo's decision not to become food for lions saved me the bother. Anyway, I already had a far more tempting prior engagement.

In the company's heyday it was very fashionable to own one share in JCI. The reason for this was quite simple. JCI was known for offering the best shareholders' lunch in the world. It apparently knocked anything the five-star hotels could offer into a cocked hat and the price of a single share was more than compensated by the sumptuous annual feast. The lunches probably stopped when the gold price fell in the early eighties and the only good reason for owning one share in JCI these days is that you would have lost half as much than if you had owned two shares.

The last annual general meeting was a sad day for a once proud company that has played a major role in the history of South Africa. Certainly, the share price wasn't helped by the falling gold price, but it is the tales which have emerged over the past few months of the ex-chairman's complete disregard for good corporate governance that worry me.

It is impossible not to compare the microcosm of JCI with the macrocosm of South Africa.

Johannesburg, as those of us who are unfortunate enough to live here can testify, is a city in sharp decline. It has now become virtually impossible to drive a Lamborghini Diablo down Jan Smuts Avenue without hitting potholes and damaging the expensive bits underneath.

Apart from the appalling condition of the roads and pavements, very few traffic lights work and the traffic police seem strangely reluctant to pull over vehicles that are clearly unroadworthy.

In short, there are no rules and anarchy reigns. The reason for that is that the politicians responsible seem to feel that, once elected, they are answerable to no one and their main purpose in life is to drive as expensive a car as they can wangle at ratepayers' expense while doing as little as possible in return. In other words, there is the equivalent of no corporate governance at local government level.

At the national level, the situation is even worse. Here it is permissible for a Member of Parliament to lie to parliament, to obtain a false driving licence, to be a convicted criminal and to ignore normal tender procedures without any fear of job loss. The public outcry when politicians are caught behaving improperly is met with accusations of racism.

While that remains the accepted form of behaviour, we can hardly expect the principle of accountability and good governance to trickle down from our country's leaders to the newly empowered corporate sector.

15 February 1998

Oh for an honestly naughty politician with a decent housing policy

I had high hopes that we may become a tabloid society at last. However, our very own, home-grown sex scandal involving FW de Klerk had a relatively short news shelf life.

Compared with Bill Clinton, who has parried allegations of sexual misconduct for most of his term in office, FW limps in a very poor second, barely managing to remain on the local front pages for a week and only appearing as a minor news item on the inside pages of foreign newspapers.

The Clinton story, by contrast, has dominated the world's press.

News magazines have devoted several pages to a full rundown on who's who in Zippergate as though they were characters in a long-running soap opera which, in a way I suppose, they are.

It is quite bizarre that US threats to bomb Iraq have virtually been ignored by a public who are far more interested in whether Monica Lewinsky played the pink oboe in the Oval Office.

Still, that's the power of the press for you.

I guess that once the cameras and lights are all set up and the make-up girls have finished dabbing powder on to Saddam's sweating face, then we can all sit back in our armchairs and tune in to CNN later this month for a missile eye's view of the destruction of Baghdad.

Heaven forbid the American public having to think about more than one major issue at a time.

Of course, the FW story never had great potential for tabloid longevity. It was doomed from the start.

The only surprise was that, while we all believed FW was trying to forge a new alliance with Nelson Mandela and build a rainbow nation of equal opportunity, his mind was on other things.

Otherwise, all that happened was that De Klerk, while enjoying the hospitality and patronage of an extremely rich Greek businessman, decided to steal his wife.

Most yacht owners are fairly particular about who they invite aboard.

After all, yachts aren't cheap these days and you don't want people walking down the gangplank with bits of valuable electronic equipment or solid brass shower heads swiped from the master suite.

However, the disappearance of the odd monogrammed fish knife is an occupational hazard, particularly when you invite film stars on board.

The hapless Tony Georgiadis probably felt even the fish knives were safe with those nice De Klerks until he went for a short walk on his yacht and found, to his horror, that his honoured guest had 'gone below' in more ways than one.

Entering a room on one of the lower decks, he apparently discovered his beautiful wife in the arms of his trusted guest, discussing empowerment no doubt. I imagine the atmosphere at dinner that night was tense.

The question the radio talk shows and newspapers have been posing is: Do we have a right to know these things and to pry into a public figure's private life?

The answer is a resounding yes. Politicians delight in our adulation and we are expected to turn up and applaud them at political rallies or, at the very least, hang on to their every word during television news broadcasts.

They are not shy to tell us how to live our lives and to claim that they represent family values, honesty, integrity and all those good wholesome things.

So, when we find out that their own sordid lives are rather removed from what they expect from the rest of us, we have every reason to crow and bay for blood.

The fault lies in a system that makes unreasonable demands on mere mortals.

We expect our politicians to be paragons of virtue only because they tell us that they are so.

Wouldn't it be refreshing if a political candidate stood up before the next election and detailed his wild and varied sex life, told us that he had inhaled frequently and deeply and that he often drove the wrong way down one-way streets with an open bottle of whisky between his knees.

However, despite these minor human failings, he would go on to explain that he had a neat line in housing policy and would have everyone in their own home, with water and electricity connected by 2004.

The only flaw with this Utopian scenario is that firstly, politicians tend to believe their own hype and secondly, most of them can't distinguish between right and wrong anyway.

22 February 1998

Do-it-yourself cloning kits could cause a rift in the nuclear family

We may not be able to provide basic primary health care in this country but, if recent newspaper reports are correct, a Johannesburg fertility clinic has the expertise and equipment to replicate genetic material and create human clones.

Dr Mohamed Cassim is currently preparing an application to the University of Witwatersrand's ethics committee for permission to go ahead with cloning.

If he gets the thumbs up he will get to work on four Gauteng women who are so desperate to have children they will allow Cassim and his team of ovarian opportunists to create replicas of themselves or their husbands.

Apparently this cloning lark is no big deal. Cassim reportedly said: 'Getting the genetic material into an egg is easy ... my son could do it.' If it's as easy as that then I wonder whether the best-selling toy next Christmas won't be a home cloning kit? School kids will be able to replicate their best friends in the comfort of their own bedrooms.

While the moral and philosophical arguments against cloning have already been spelt out, nobody has really considered the practical implications. If the cloned child can be a replica of either the mother or the father, who gets to choose?

There's much to be said for the gene pool, even when you're only dipping into the shallow end. A child that is exactly like one of its parents is likely to prove exasperating for the parent it replicates.

Take wine gums for example. Not many people like the green ones, but I do. At the moment, wine gum consumption in the Bullard household is an amiable affair, with me giving up the orange ones in exchange for the green ones. The distribution of the other colours then simply becomes a matter of wine gum detente or who can chew faster. Enter junior, a cloned replica, and before too long we will be fighting over the green wine gums.

Then there is the problem of airports. Heaven knows, it's bad enough trying to recognise somebody coming through international arrivals as it is.

Once cloning has really taken off and we are into third-generation replicants, we'll presumably need a bar code scanner to recognise our relatives at Johannesburg International.

The official view of the Health Department appears to be that cloning is illegal in terms of the Human Tissues Act. In addition, Health Minister Nkosazana Zuma is wisely sidestepping comment on the issue, presumably on the sound principle that she has already courted enough controversy for one term of office. The last thing her career needs now is the scandal of Sarafina Sarafina Sarafina, a new musical extolling the virtues of cloning.

Most significantly, though, the hue and cry over Cassim's proposed experiment ignores one important fact: cloning is already here in SA and has been practised for years.

Anybody who studies old videos of National Party conferences couldn't fail to notice that, not only was everybody dressed identically, right down to the homburgs and the ludicrous flower arrangement in the lapel, but they even said the same things.

Could the Nats have been the result of some ghastly uncontrolled scientific experiment, I wonder?

However, evidence of widespread cloning in SA goes beyond mere politics.

Whether it's in the leafy suburb of Constantia or among the sterile, labyrinthine shopping centres of Johannesburg's northern suburbs, it's impossible to ignore the fact that thousands of bejewelled women with identical platform shoes, designer handbags and nasal accents are all shopping in identical stores with cloned men who drive the same type of car. Spooky isn't it?

*

Now it's becoming more widely known that I am no longer gainfully employed in the financial markets, I am starting to receive invitations to freebies.

Last week several busloads of scribblers with nothing better to do were whisked off to the revamped Mount Grace in Magaliesberg. The main part of the hotel caught fire last year and has been rebuilt in local stone, but this time round it has a tin roof and plenty of ashtrays.

Upon arrival, a waiter with a lone dry martini on a salver stalked me, greeted me by name, offered me the glass and hoped that it was mixed to my specifications, which it was. If that happens every time I visit a Grace hotel, I fear my plans to become teetotal will have to be postponed.

1 March 1998

No such thing as a free wooden lizard in the business forest

According to the recently published register of members' interests in parliament, Water Affairs and Forestry Minister Kader Asmal was given a carved wooden lizard by Indonesia's forestry ministry. This may, on the surface, appear to be an innocent gesture of friendship, but it has sinister undertones.

The Indonesian forestry ministry doesn't really have much to do since it managed to burn down most of its forests last year. Clearly, it is eyeing global opportunities and looking around for other countries' forests to reduce to ashes. Despite Indonesia's appallingly corrupt and nepotistic political system (paradoxically, precisely the sort of thing the ANC fought against when in opposition), the SA government evidently feels that these are people with whom we should be doing business.

There is a well-known saying in business: there is no such thing as a free wooden lizard. Asmal would do well to remember that when he privatises the forests.

The publication of the register of members' interests, in which MPs are required to disclose any gifts received with a value of R350 or more, is intended to be a serious document created to give the electorate the impression that we are being ruled by people with only the most noble motives. Unfortunately, its release just over a week ago leaves me with the uncomfortable feeling that this is just another ruse on the part of the government to persuade us that they are marginally more honest than their predecessors. Are we really interested in whether politicians receive T-shirts, cufflinks and pen-and-pencil sets while the more important issues of accountability and good governance are ignored?

Within a week of the list's publication, the *Sunday Times* had already revealed that seven MPs representing various parties were flown on a junket to Texas by Bell Helicopter. Surprisingly, none of them thought this worth a mention in the register.

Indeed, Tony Yengeni of the ANC defended the omission by saying:

'When I go on these trips I'm not going to a Greek island to lie on my back. It's work and I don't see any reason why I have to declare it.' Yengeni complains that he doesn't even enjoy the trips because it means that he has to be away from his family. He is, of course, completely missing the point.

Should a lucrative contract be given to Bell Helicopter in future we will be very interested in what, if anything, was agreed on the country's behalf by Yengeni and his fellow travellers while being entertained by that company. I don't think his enjoyment or otherwise is particularly relevant.

Without doubt, any register of members' interests is better than no register at all, and for that the ANC should be applauded. However, if the list merely becomes an annual diversion, designed to distract an electorate with an already short attention span from what is really going on in government, then it may as well be scrapped now. Democratic Party leader Tony Leon is absolutely correct when he says that unless the register is taken seriously by MPs it will amount to 'ornamental window dressing'.

What the register can never hope to do, though, is to disclose those many odd relationships in politics which allow relatives and friends of influential politicians to successfully tender for lucrative government contracts without ever having had any relevant experience in the area concerned. For that we need to open all government tenders to public scrutiny before a final contract is awarded.

In fact, the fewer secrets there are between government and the people the better.

The grand architect of the register of members' interests was, in fact, Asmal, one of the ANC's few performing assets and a man who sincerely conveys his commitment to open and clean government without sounding smarmy and hypocritical.

Evidently fired up with enthusiasm for the culture of disclosure, he is now suggesting that leading business people and newspaper editors perform the financial equivalent of 'the full monty' by revealing all. 'Why should they hide behind arguments for privacy when this is out of step with the age of disclosure in which we now live?' he asks.

Well, one reason is that, unlike politicians, they are not paid out of our taxes and do not rely on the electorate for their jobs. In the case of leading business figures, their financial positions are often published (to their intense embarrassment) by financial magazines. Newspaper editors, it is well known, are impoverished and merely devoted to printing the truth.

15 March 1998

Not even an apple for teacher puts diligent Trevor at the top of the class

Pity poor Trevor Manuel and Chris Stals. They have diligently handed their homework in on time. They have not been disruptive in class like some of their less disciplined fellow students.

They may even have managed to save some of their pocket money this term by visiting the school tuck shop less frequently.

So it comes as a huge disappointment that their end of term report from rating agency Standard and Poor's gave them only a BB+ with the teacher's note in the margin saying something like: 'Trevor and Chris have worked well together but need to try harder. Unfortunately the outlook is only stable at the moment and they must concentrate harder on economic growth next term. They sometimes seem to forget that there are other children in the class who are also keen to attract foreign investment. Unfortunately they lost marks last term on their Gear economic model which looked very good on paper but didn't actually work on parents' day. Trevor has become much quieter in class and no longer tries to make the other children laugh by using words like 'amorphous'. The Ritalin seems to be working.'

So it's a silver star and not a gold star and those of us who claim to understand these things are terribly disappointed.

This is the financial equivalent of being beaten by Tonga in the next Rugby World Cup and gives everybody the opportunity to wander around in a blue funk muttering about how the referee must be blind and biased.

Initial comment from the financial market placed the blame fairly and squarely with the teacher, Standard and Poor's, who were said to be 'at odds with reality' in one newspaper report.

That's the problem with the ratings business though; what is reality? One moment you are confidently giving a country like Singapore a tip-top rating and then along comes an Asian financial disaster and you are left with great splodges of *oeuf sur le visage* as they say in France. Investors are hammering on your door yelling, 'Oi squire, thought you said Singapore was safe as houses. I've just lost my yacht thanks to you.' So then you tread warily with a new kid on the block like South Africa and you upset the natives who have all borrowed money to buy government bonds in expectation of an investment rating continuing to fuel the bull market.

It's a lonely life in the ratings world. I don't expect they get too many lunch invitations.

The problem with asking somebody else to hold the looking glass while you say 'mirror mirror on the wall, who's the cutest emerging market of all?' is that the answer may not always be quite what you had in mind.

The easiest way to get round the problem is to get a new mirror, but there is a jealously guarded professional etiquette among mirrors which forbids one mirror to completely contradict another.

Standard and Poor's is only one of many rating agencies world wide. Have you ever wondered how they survive financially? I'll tell you. They charge people like the South African government money to tell them how financially healthy they are.

It's like a medical check-up. You presumably wouldn't berate your doctor for telling you that your blood pressure is too high or that the reason you can't heave your wheezing frame up and down all those steps is that you are a fat, burger-munching slob who should cut back to 50 cigarettes a day for starters.

For the same reason, we should not be upset with Standard and Poor's for its rating of South Africa just because it tells us what we do not want to hear. Even allowing for the fact that Standard and Poor's may be erring on the cautious side after the Asian troubles, we would be deluding ourselves if we believed they had been anything less than thorough.

The squeals of dismay seemed to come mainly from the bond market, which is currently thrashing around at levels last seen some four years ago.

Admittedly, the bond rates kicked up on the news but that was only because they were perhaps a little too low anyway.

What irked the bond traders is that the market is so long of stock that everybody is wondering who will buy the market down further.

An investment rating would have introduced new lambs to the slaughter, which is great for anyone looking to take profits. Now that Standard and Poor's has rained on the parade we will have to look for other reasons to be bullish.

29 March 1998

Checking for interns in the wardrobes and assassins in the palm trees

Little did I know when I booked to fly to Cape Town for the last week of March that the leader of the greatest nation in the free world would also be there.

I knew the trip was scheduled, but I assumed that a combination of domestic problems combined with the need to keep his finger on the pulse of Gulf War II would mean that US President Bill Clinton would be forced to cancel his hotel booking and lose his deposit.

The extraordinary thing is that very few Capetonians appeared to be talking about the visit. Indeed, one or two that I spoke to didn't even know that the Clinton circus was coming to town at all.

In a city where most people think Camp David is a gay friend of the American president, this shouldn't come as too much of a surprise. After all, there are far more important things to occupy the mind, like drinking cappuccino at trendy pavement cafés.

So Clinton's visit probably passed unnoticed by many Capetonians, particularly if they were unaffected by the traffic snarl-ups that these things cause.

Apparently the president was accompanied by about 800 fellow Americans. Many of them were here to look at business opportunities and to avoid the bad weather at home, but a good many of them were connected with the visit in an official capacity.

South Africans who complain about the extravagances of our own globe-trotting politicians and their entourages should hang their heads in shame at even mentioning the subject, because when it comes to hosing it against the wall the Yanks are in a league of their own.

All right, the US economy is so large that nobody really cares that much. What are a few billion dollars here and there?

Anyway, an official visit to Africa is a special case because it gives African-American White House staff a chance to discover their roots, something they all apparently like to do until they realise that they would probably be living in shacks with no running water if their ancestors hadn't been abducted by slave traders.

Still, it is a hell of a lot of people just for a two-day visit, so why are they here and what do they do for their money?

There is a suggestion that Washington was warned that Cape Town has some of the most beautiful girls in the world and the 800 travelling partners are simply here as witnesses to testify that the president didn't get up to any of his old tricks.

More realistically though, they are here to make sure Bill and Hill have a great time, don't meet any time wasters, don't get interviewed by right-wing extremists with an ulterior motive and get home safely.

That last one is very important, particularly as last weekend Cape Town provided the setting for a gangland gunfight not two kilometres from the hotel in which the First Couple stayed.

The advance guard have apparently been here for months, much to the delight of a certain hotel group.

They are the security people whose job it is to make sure the phones work, that there are no listening devices hidden in the shower heads and no interns hiding in the wardrobes.

There is also a special contingent of highly trained interior decorators whose job it is to redecorate, at the American taxpayer's expense, any room where the president or the first lady might linger for longer than 10 minutes. They picked this habit up from Hollywood where film stars are notorious for gutting entire hotel floors and having them redesigned to their own peculiar specifications.

With any luck this idiosyncrasy won't be picked up locally, although I wouldn't put it past Winnie to try.

There was a suggestion that the US security people wanted to seal all the manhole covers in Cape Town and dig up the palm trees lining the drive to the Mount Nelson just in case Iraqi hit men were hiding in them.

Even Table Mountain didn't escape the attention of the men in black who thought that the top of the mountain was flat enough for hostile helicopters to land and asked the Cape Town municipality to make it more mountainous during the president's visit.

The refreshing thing about living in a new democracy is that we haven't yet discovered crass commercialism.

Nobody has rushed out a special commemorative wine called 'Oral Sensation', there are no souvenir Clinton visit T-shirts with the slogan 'Bill blows into Cape Town' and no tacky coffee mugs with smudgy pictures of Madiba and Bill. More's the pity.

12 April 1998

Ladies and Gents, at last the full spectacle of military 'intelligence'

Someone once remarked that the words 'military' and 'intelligence' are a contradiction in terms. The recent goings on in the South African National Defence Force seem to support the notion. Early in February, if press reports are to be believed, General Georg Meiring allegedly handed the State President a report which suggested his government was about to be overthrown.

Meiring is head of the defence force, and I assume that when a president is given detailed plans for his imminent dispatch by such an authoritative source, he would have no choice but to take them seriously.

After all, Meiring is not really in the business of sketching plots for Frederick Forsyth novels. Under normal circumstances, the head of state would have hastily found a reinforced concrete bunker and stayed there with a few trusted colleagues until 'troops loyal to the government' had managed to round up the suspects and beat a confession out of them, before impaling their severed heads on the spiked railings of the presidential palace as a warning to others.

However, in this case, no one reacted at all and the first the public learnt about the planned overthrow was in a newspaper report some weeks later. Strangely, no one seems remotely concerned that there has apparently been a plot to topple the democratically elected government. More pertinent is why the most senior and experienced officer in the defence force would present such a ham-fisted attempt to give a nice old gentleman like Mr Mandela the willies.

I have often said that living in SA is rather like being trapped in a Gary Larson cartoon. Is there a more surreal scenario than the president referring an urgent report on a plot to oust his administration to a commission for verification? And when the news of the intended coup was finally leaked, it made zero impact.

Nervous foreign investors did not pull large sums of money out of the country, and the rand remained stable. All of which suggests that President

Mandela was probably right to ignore the report in the first place. That's assuming he even read it.

There is a suggestion that the president finds affairs of state rather tiresome these days, and he was busy flicking through the QE2 cruise brochure for 1999 while Meiring's file lay unread on the coffee table. It wasn't until one of his cabinet colleagues began looking for a place to put down his mug of tea without leaving unsightly rings on the presidential Sheraton that the file was rediscovered – between a copy of *Loaded* magazine and a subpoena from Louis Luyt. Only at that point, I believe, was the file opened and read, at which point everybody present fell about laughing.

Meiring is a physicist by training and this shows in his choice of characterisation. A few rands invested in one of those correspondence courses that teach you how to write would not have gone amiss. After all, who in their right mind would believe that Robert McBride, Winnie Madikizela-Mandela and Bantu Holomisa have the organisational ability (let alone the motivation) to overthrow a hot-dog stand, let alone a government.

McBride can't even conduct an independent investigation into cross-border gun running without getting himself arrested for the very crime he claims to be investigating.

Winnie is far too busy caring for the poor and spending R20 000 a month on cosmetics to want to smudge her mascara in a botched coup attempt.

And poor little Bantu Holomisa is now out of uniform and fully occupied with collecting membership subscriptions for his ailing United Democratic Movement. Add to this that the sole source for the report was an alleged police spy who is currently sojourning with friend McBride in a poorly ventilated Maputo prison, and you have a comedy of errors which suddenly makes the Mossad look rather efficient by comparison.

The problem is, where to now? If Meiring really has circulated a fake report to spook the government into thinking there is going to be a coup, it suggests there are other parties who wish to destabilise the government.

So, paradoxically, the report might be correct, but for all the wrong reasons. If Meiring and other 'apartheid era' defence personnel are cashiered, they are likely to wander off into the wilderness bearing grudges and plotting real coups.

Surely it's better to have them inside the tent pissing out rather than the other way round. The answer is to keep them on and tell them to catch up with the filing.

26 April 1998

Sorry Jani, I don't fall off horses and my underpants ain't got no holes

Some claim imitation is the sincerest form of flattery. Even so, I think I can do without it in this particular case. Last week I received an e-mail from an observant reader drawing my attention to excerpts from Jani Allan's column on the MWeb Internet site.

Jani Allan, as some of you may recall, used to be the star columnist on this newspaper until she went to interview Eugene Terre'Blanche and found herself smitten by 'the blue flames of his blowtorch eyes' (copyright Jani Allan).

Unfortunately bombs soon started going off in her proximity as is often the case when you hang around with loonies. Things eventually got a bit hot for Ms Allan and she was spirited away to the UK, where it was felt she would be safer. There she amused us all and took some media pressure off the royal family by unsuccessfully suing Channel 4 television for defamation.

Finding little demand for her talents, Jani eventually returned to South Africa to an uninterested public who had clearly completely forgotten her. She subsequently discovered God and the experience was evidently so meaningful that she felt compelled to share it with the rest of us in an interview. Whether God was quite so enthusiastic at finding Jani was never recorded.

Now she is back in the media swing with a radio show on Cape Talk and a regular column and chat forum on MWeb.

On 14 April Ms Allan published her column for MWeb's Lifestyle page on the Internet. One of the topical stories she quite naturally chose was the Georg Meiring case. However, it was the content that my reader found interesting, as did many of my colleagues at the *Sunday Times* when we called the page up on the Internet.

In her piece Ms Allan mentions, among others, Frederick Forsythe [sic], the QE2, troops loyal to the government rounding up the usual suspects and impaling heads on spiked railings, and she winds the piece up by asking why she feels as though she is trapped in a Gary Larson cartoon.

All these references appeared in my column which was published two days earlier on 12 April. It is hard to imagine that such an eclectic set of ideas and phrases would have been used by two unconnected writers within such a short space of time. The coincidence is simply too great.

As any columnist knows, knocking off several hundred words to meet the weekly deadline is not always easy. Sometimes one feels inspired and dashes the thing off in forty minutes, leaving the rest of the day free for frivolity. On other occasions it takes days. I have literally cried with frustration staring at a blank computer screen for hours while trying to think of a topic. Eventually an idea forms itself into words and another week's anguish is over.

But even in the most extreme case of writer's block it is unforgivable to crib somebody else's work and present it as your own. In journalism it is known as plagiarism and ranks as an even greater sin than deliberately misreporting an event. Plagiarism is theft of intellectual property and when the plagiarist is remunerated for somebody else's work then the sin is compounded.

If you are intending to filch somebody else's material it is normal to allow a decent period to elapse – say 300 years. To borrow liberally from an article that is a mere two days old and still warm seems the height of folly. Clearly Ms Allan believes that so few people read the *Out to Lunch* column that she would be likely to get away with it.

I am told by my colleagues at the *Sunday Times* that I should not feel particularly singled out for attention. Ms Allan has apparently been caught out for plagiarism before. It seems a great pity that a fellow scribe should be so short of original thought that she is reduced to reproducing other people's work (sometimes without even bothering to change the word order) as her own and then dishonestly adding the words 'copyright Jani Allan'.

An interesting theory from a psychiatrist suggests Jani may be infatuated with me and this is simply an awkward way of attracting my attention and opening a dialogue. In other words, the plagiarism was so obvious that she intended it to be noticed, tipped off a friend to alert me to it and is waiting for me to react.

Sorry to do this, Jani, but I have to tell you that I am probably not your type. My eyes are dark brown, I don't fall off horses but, more importantly, my underpants are all in good repair.

3 May 1998
Warning: too much time on the phone with psychopaths causes racial hatred

One of the few advantages a regular newspaper column affords its author is the opportunity to ridicule one's readers week after week.

It's an extraordinary symbiosis, that of columnist and reader, but one has to be careful not to abuse the privilege of always having the last word.

Jon Qwelane, who writes a splenetic Saturday column for the Independent group of newspapers, is a respected journalist and broadcaster. Sometimes I love what he writes, at other times I find him infuriating – but I never find him boring.

Qwelane's stock in trade is industrial-strength controversy and the postman doubtless staggers under the weight of the sacks of hate mail he receives every week. In the past two weeks he has had a man called Roger Sinclair firmly in his sights.

Mr Sinclair (who writes from that bastion of white privilege, Parktown North) had the misfortune to have a letter published in the *Saturday Star* in which he had the temerity to refer to 'isolated' incidents of racially motivated violence and, as evidence of the spirit of reconciliation, mentioned his efforts in helping his domestic worker acquire her own home.

In the first of his diatribes, Jon labelled Sinclair a 'guilt-ridden conservative-liberal English-speaking type' and mocked his attempts at helping his domestic worker own her own family home as an act of 'conscience salving'.

Parktown North is not famous for its giraffe braais or mampoer festivals, and I happen to know that I am the only person in the neighbourhood who regularly wears khaki bush fatigues while on blockwatch.

So the description of Roger Sinclair as a conservative-liberal (surely a contradiction in terms?) is ludicrously inappropriate, even though it is causing much mirth among members of the International Wine & Food Society where Sinclair holds the rank of Grand Imperial Wizard and regularly dresses in white bed sheets and pillow cases with small eye holes cut so that he can keep an eye on the evening's sacrifice.

As far as guilt is concerned, the nearest Roger Sinclair has ever come to guilt is emptying the dregs of a bottle of good burgundy into his glass before anyone else gets the chance. Even then, it was only fleeting guilt.

So we can dismiss Jon's exaggerated description of Roger Sinclair for the artful prattle it is. He is clearly trawling for new readers. Sinclair correctly uses the word 'isolated' to describe racial violence but as his letter was published at the same time as the horrific Benoni shooting of a six-month-old black child by a white man, Qwelane mischievously usurps that emotional incident to suggest that all whites, given a gun and a conveniently located group of unarmed black children, would tighten their fingers on the trigger. Unless crime statistics are being horribly suppressed, we know that is not the case.

I have no problem with Jon Qwelane's regular use of his weekly column to lambaste what he calls 'arrogant' whites; I am sure he finds it as therapeutic as I find writing about shamelessly corrupt black politicians.

Where Qwelane loses the plot, though, is to take his readers' comments out of context and present them as evidence of the irrefutable racial hatred he imagines to be all around him.

However, it is through his comments about Sinclair's attempts to help his domestic worker own her own home that Qwelane reveals an unenviable bitterness. He says Sinclair appears to think this 'epoch-making' and that the world must know about his 'belated generosity'.

'What the dear man forgets,' he loftily pronounces, 'is that the right to shelter is exactly that – a basic human right, not a privilege.'

Precisely, Jon. So what on earth are people like Roger Sinclair and many others doing foolishly wasting their hard-earned taxed income helping blacks to own their own homes when the popularly elected government should be providing them free of charge anyway? Despite Qwelane's jaundiced view, I would suggest it has very little to do with conscience salving or post-colonial guilt.

On the contrary, I suspect that, beyond the racial hatred that Jon Qwelane sees all around him, there are people of all colours getting on with their lives and trying to help their fellow citizens.

Perhaps poor Jon has spent too many lonely nights cooped up in a radio studio listening to the nocturnal ramblings of the gallimaufry of insomniacs, psychopaths and assorted loonies who have nothing more constructive to do with their lives than phone radio call-in programmes.

My advice is to get out and meet some real people, Jon.

17 May 1998

Creating desirable winter homes for rats and an undesirable city for humans

Gauteng Premier Mathole Motshekga's greatest asset seems to be his name. Few whites can even remember it, let alone pronounce it, with the result that, until recently, relatively few people have been aware of the lousy job he is doing running the richest province in South Africa.

His predecessor, Tokyo Sexwale, was far more visible as a leader. Completely and utterly useless maybe, but at least we knew who was supposed to be in charge and could pronounce his name. We could phone his *Talk to Tokyo* show on Radio 702 and whinge about the litter and crime. It made us feel good even though we suspected that Sexwale's main reason for being in the job was the high social visibility it gave him.

Tokyo seemed truly happy only when he and his wife were schmoozing with the rich and famous at northern suburb parties, nursing gourmet canapés in one hand and a Paris goblet of boxed wine in the other. Unfortunately, the same enthusiasm could not be detected back at the office where the minutiae of provincial government clearly bored Tokyo to distraction.

Alas, the burden of holding public office finally become too much and Tokyo, like many others, cashed in on the current empowerment craze and took his talents to the private sector where he will be able to watch the price of his share options rise while somebody else does the work.

When the time came for the election of a new premier the name Amos Masondo was put forward as the ANC's favoured candidate. Little was known of Masondo apart from the fact that he was said to have had a charisma bypass.

Motshekga was the people's choice and it was a minor triumph of democracy that the people's choice triumphed over the rubber-stamped candidate.

Of course, this has little relevance for whites who feel their interests are no longer represented either at local or provisional level. Their view is that the voice of minority white voter is so *sotto voce* as to be barely audible.

Still, that's democracy for you. Like it or not we have to live with it, even if we are forced to watch the city of Johannesburg crumble before our very eyes as a result.

Although I have no doubt they will be back with their hands outstretched in the traditional pose at Christmas, I haven't seen a street sweeper in my area for months. The rubbish bins outside Standard Bank in Jan Smuts Avenue have been overflowing for weeks and down Seventh Avenue there are great piles of garden refuse, rotting food, old posters and possibly even the carcasses of dead animals piled up next to a bus shelter. Even though the dustmen pass by once a week, nobody has attempted to clean the area which will shortly offer a desirable winter residence for rats.

We are told that the municipality is about to spend R2-million upgrading Zoo Lake, but paradoxically there is no money to replace broken bulbs in traffic robots and to repair roads. My wife was involved in a car crash at Easter and is now hobbling about on crutches with a broken foot. The car, which was a write-off, aquaplaned during a heavy rainstorm. It wouldn't have done so had the storm drains not been packed tight with uncollected rubbish. In the US the municipality would face huge legal damages but in Johannesburg we have come to accept such things because it is pointless to expect First World standards here.

Turning back to the provincial rulers, the early days of Motshekga's reign don't fill me with hope. His name is linked to all sorts of strange deals and he has been accused of enriching himself with donor money and nepotism among other things.

An ANC internal commission found no evidence of Motshekga's guilt but that is hardly convincing. You may remember that the ANC tried a similar stunt when Reverend Allan Boesak was accused of having his finger in the cookie jar; employing an unknown lawyer to tell us that there was no case to answer. So much for the due process of the law!

Interestingly, the ANC has used the same 'struggle accounting' defence to explain a missing donation of R630 000 from the Irish agency, Trocaire.

The fact that no donor agencies followed up their suspicions with specific allegations cannot be taken as evidence that they were happy with the situation. They may have decided that it wasn't worth the bother.

Meanwhile, an apparently unrepentant Motshekga still presides over the country's most important province, even though his own party has damned him as a disastrous manager.

7 June 1998

Will that be economy, business class or the hanky panky section, sir?

According to last week's *Sunday Times*, it would appear that SA Airways is now featuring 'live sex' in an attempt to attract passengers back to the ailing national carrier.

It sounds like a great idea to me and could work rather well. After all, nobody travels on SAA for the food, so sex seems a reasonably good way of passing the time on a long international flight, particularly if you have seen all the movies on circuit.

The story involved flight SA233 from London to Johannesburg. Two passengers boarded the flight in jovial mood and carried on drinking. They became rowdy and the cabin crew eventually refused to give them any more to drink so, instead, they decided to have sex in full view of the other business class passengers. This was extremely considerate of them because it left the toilet free.

The *Sunday Times* teasingly said the names of the two passengers were known to the newspaper but didn't actually publish them. There is nothing more irritating than running a raunchy story with the identities of the main characters protected.

So, thanks to some nifty work with a penknife blade on journalist Roger Makings' filing cabinet lock, I too know the identities of the couple and will be contacting them to ask what they did with the seat belt buckles during sex.

According to Leon Els, SAA's senior manager for corporate relations, the airline doesn't plan to take any action against the copulating couple, which implies SAA condones such behaviour.

In fact, I am reliably informed that they see huge marketing potential in this and will shortly be running a new TV ad to the tuneful backing of *Come, fly with me*. The ad will announce the launch of the 'Hanky Panky' class section of the aircraft.

Passengers will be given a new look 'bawding pass' and offered a couple of Viagra pills with their champagne as they settle into their seats.

In keeping with the re-branding, out goes the current in-flight magazine with its unpronounceable title, pages of dreary maps of the world and boring articles by underpaid freelance journos in search of a travel freebie.

Instead, the new in-flight magazine, 'Mile High', will feature hints on the most appropriate sexual positions for airline travel (remember, the aisles must always be left clear) plus useful articles such as '101 erotic things you can do with the bread roll they gave you at dinner'.

On flight SA233, the cabin crew were 'goggle-eyed and didn't know what to do'. A little re-training will sort this problem out and in future cabin crew will bring around a selection of battery-operated sex aids and rubber wear during the flight and will be encouraged to offer customer-friendly comments such as 'may I lend a hand?' to passengers travelling alone.

Cabin crew will be expected to join in the fun on long-haul flights. This will make a pleasant change from their usual game of hiding the drinks trolley or skulking in the galley during the movie to indulge in their own selfish sexual gratification.

Even the pre-flight safety checks are likely to be updated. Instead of the predictable 'in the event of a change in cabin pressure oxygen masks will be released from the panel above you, etc, etc', we will now have 'in the event of a change in libido, fruit-flavoured condoms will be released from the panel above you. Once you are wearing yours, please assist other passengers who may be struggling to put theirs on. Bonking is not allowed when the "no bonking" light is on. Ensure that your tray table is stowed and that you are in an upright position before having sex. Some electronic devices and loud moans of ecstasy may affect the flight crew on this flight. If in doubt, consult a member of the cabin crew'.

Not surprisingly, rival airlines are eagerly watching developments at SAA and even Richard Branson is reconsidering the legal ramifications of using the name Virgin – unless he can guarantee a regular supply, that is.

*

One of the more profitable businesses to be in at the moment seems to be something called 'micro-lending'. As I understand it, this enables you to lend black people money and to charge them a much higher rate of interest than you could get away with if you lent the money to white people.

Apparently they don't mind paying because they treat the high interest payments as an 'overhead'. That's presumably because they are too trusting to realise what rate they are being charged. Let's hope, for the sake of the lenders, they never find out!

14 June 1998

Serious training needed to get into shape to not run the Comrades

I am not running the Comrades marathon for the tenth time this year. While others set off on this suicidal mega-jog at some unearthly hour, I will still be tucked up in bed awaiting the welcoming smell of fried bacon and eggs and freshly brewed coffee, which serves as my normal wake-up call.

Then, after breakfast and an invigorating shower, I shall put on one of Wagner's lighter albums and settle down to my morning cigar and a good book while I contemplate which wine to open at lunch.

This strikes me as a much better plan than spending most of the day running from somewhere you didn't want to be to somewhere you don't want to go on the off chance that you will get a medal to commemorate this folly.

The conscious decision 'not' to run the Comrades for the tenth consecutive year is not at all the same as simply having no interest in running the race. Rather like training for the Comrades itself, it is something that needs to be worked at.

Long ago I started training on the shorter races and the so-called 'fun runs'. I would get an application form, fill it in and deliberately not submit it, knowing that if I could somehow avoid the smaller and less important races I could surely strive for greater things.

It's surprising how, with the right training and a positive mind-set, the body can tolerate the pain and disappointment of not being at the starting line on the morning of a long, boring road race. I was fortunate enough to be able to afford the services of a superb personal trainer who insisted that I stick to his rigorous programme. 'You're never going to not run the Comrades if you don't do exactly what I tell you,' he explained in what I assumed at the time to be a solecism.

On the first morning of training he turned up with two six-packs of beer, a bag of beer-flavoured chips and a couple of raunchy videos. He then announced that if he couldn't get me into shape not to run the Comrades then his name wasn't Arnold Schwarzenegger, which it definitely wasn't anyway.

Apart from making me lie around on the couch doing strenuous beer-opening exercises for what seemed like hours on end, my trainer also insisted that I learn to 'hop'. He would toss me the TV remote control and when he said the word 'hop' I had to switch channels.

I also became aware that correct eating habits were an essential part of my training if I was to not run the Comrades competitively. Carbo-loading is vital to build up the necessary flab, but all the advantages of a good carbo-load are completely wasted if you walk to the takeaway, so we used Mr Delivery to send the pizzas.

This year I am in peak form, and I know I will walk not running my 10th Comrades. After all, I already have the Two Oceans and The Argus under my belt, so what's a piddling 90 kilometres?

*

If I get out of this mess, I will never take the name of Jay Naidoo in vain again. I promise not to make fun of his silly suits, to accuse him of being a recreational socialist or to confuse him with the one who works for Nedlac.

Last week I went to my post box but found it locked. I enquired at the counter and was told it was because I hadn't paid the rental. I explained that I normally got a reminder form but hadn't had one this year, so could I have one now please? The staff were extremely courteous and sympathetic but, unfortunately, the post office didn't have any rental forms, so my post box remains locked. My car licence renewal reminder is still in there as are my credit card accounts, along with investment letters warning me of the imminent collapse of the stock market, royalty cheques, Viagra trial offers and any other post that hasn't already found its way into the Braamfontein Spruit.

This lockout can only result in chaos. With my luck, I will almost certainly get arrested for driving an unlicensed vehicle, be unable to stand bail because my cheques will bounce and end up having all my credit cards cancelled for non-payment.

*

The rumour that Cape gangster Rashied Staggie is planning to move from Cape Town to Johannesburg is not all bad news. Staggie is, after all, a businessman and must expand his empire if the opportunity arises. Apart from introducing some competition into the lucrative areas of drug dealing and prostitution, Staggie and his fellow free-spending gangsters could give a much-needed boost to house prices in Johannesburg.

5 July 1998

It's time to stop beating our breasts and start working for the future

Theresa Oakley-Smith, writing in the *Sunday Independent* a few weeks ago, has suggested that it would be rather jolly if all we 'ordinary' whiteys got together and apologised to our fellow South Africans for apartheid and all the horrid things that made life so beastly for people with slightly darker skins in our dim but not so distant past.

Oakley-Smith is frightfully keen that everybody plays this time and that nobody goes skulking behind the bicycle sheds refusing to say sorry as has happened before.

What she has done is to draw up a plan. She suggests there should be a national day of reconciliation (who knows, maybe the headmistress could give the school a half-holiday) by which time everybody should have collected a piece of paper and a pencil from the stationery office. On that piece of paper they must write out an apology to black South Africans for the evils and injustices of apartheid and then they must write down how much of their pocket money they are prepared to give to help pay for the psychological damage.

Oakley-Smith will be prefect in charge of the project. Besides, she knows all the right buzz words. The first thing to do is to put together a committee of suitably guilt-ridden whites drawn from all sectors of the community. The committee will then 'formulate a vision, a business plan and a plan of action culminating in a series of events designed to allow white South Africans to write messages of apology in a variety of forms'. When they have all been handed in, Oakley-Smith will stick them carefully in a scrapbook and present them to that nice President Nelson Mandela or any other black politician who happens not to be on an overseas, taxpayer-sponsored freebie on the great day. At this point, a golden light will shine around Oakley-Smith's head and she will be carried up to the heavens on a winged chariot drawn by rams. Yea, and all the people of South Africa shall live in perfect harmony forever after; for it is written. That, at any rate, is the general idea.

If Oakley-Smith wishes to dress in sackcloth and ashes and publicly flagellate herself because of the unfortunate paleness of her skin, that is her prerogative.

Unfortunately, I must decline the invitation to join her. As far as I'm concerned I have absolutely nothing to apologise for. As a law-abiding, tax-paying resident of this country, I have chosen to remain in South Africa and support the new democracy, only to be rewarded with high interest rates, a worthless currency, collapsed health and educational systems and a government too terrified or inept to deal with the country's growing crime and corruption problems.

I would suggest to Oakley-Smith that she remove herself for a while from the cosseted, risk-free world that she inhabits and sniff the air of reality. Most white people still running businesses in South Africa today survived despite, not because of, apartheid.

What particularly maddens me about this admission of guilt drive of hers, though, is that all the real villains of the apartheid era have negotiated amnesty for themselves and are living off their ill-gotten gains.

Constant calls by professional bleeding hearts like Oakley-Smith for apologies and compensation do absolutely nothing for this country. They merely encourage people to continue to think of themselves as victims and to believe that they are entitled to compensation.

It is now over four years since the first democratic election and yet the past is still conveniently blamed for the country's woes. If I understand Oakley-Smith correctly, she suggests that anybody with a white skin who happened to work hard and accumulate wealth prior to 1994 owes it all to the inequities of the apartheid system. She cannot be serious! Isn't it time we grew up in this country and stopped expecting whites to carry on treating their fellow South Africans like idiot children?

Oakley-Smith calls herself a management consultant in organisational change and diversity. I can't help thinking that she could make herself far more useful by pointing out to the previously disadvantaged some of the obligations of the new democratic South Africa.

Maybe she could explain that 'empowerment' doesn't actually mean sitting around waiting for free handouts. Perhaps she could explain that the reason foreign investors are selling the rand is that, thanks to the culture of entitlement, we are looking more and more like a basket case. It's not apologies we need, it's a work and service ethic.

12 July 1998
Wanted: bright lad for top bank job. No experience necessary

Obviously, there is less to this central bank governor business than meets the eye. There we all were thinking that this is a highly specialised job calling for nerves of steel and a thorough knowledge of the machinations of the global markets, not to mention years of banking experience, when all you really need is a year's training.

Of course, the governor in waiting will have to sharpen up his dress sense. None of this traditional costume and shirts with no collars stuff. Central bankers are expected to look the part, particularly when they gather at the annual International Monetary Fund conference and swap George Soros jokes.

The decision to announce the appointment of Labour Minister Tito Mboweni as Chris Stals's replacement as Reserve Bank governor last weekend was intended to calm the markets. Unfortunately it didn't. Bond market rates immediately soared about 1% while the rand continued its free fall against the dollar and sterling, although things improved once traders realised the sky wasn't about to fall as well.

This is all rather unfair on poor Mboweni, who is probably the best man for this thoroughly unpleasant job, although the puddle of available talent from which to draw a new governor is hardly impressive. Apart from having had the misfortune to attend the University of East Anglia, an area notorious for its cold winds, mustard factories and weak beer, he seems to have all the right credentials. Certainly, he is a political appointee, but anybody who seriously believed that the next Reserve Bank governor would not be a political appointee is living in a fantasy world. After all, what do you think the Broederbond governors of the past were if not political appointees?

What Mboweni does bring to the party is youth (he is a fresh-faced 39-year-old), political credibility and self-confidence. Fears that he will simply become a puppet and toe the ANC party line are, I believe, unfounded. The realities of the job are such that Mboweni cannot afford to ignore the world's financial markets and the enormous influence other countries now have on SA's affairs. In his own words, 'It is a tough call.'

A worst-case scenario would have Mboweni artificially dropping interest rates to stimulate the economy and win plaudits for the ANC. This would be tantamount to printing money, resulting in a short, euphoric period of low interest rates swiftly followed by the sort of rampant inflation that the Latin American economies experienced during the eighties. The rand would become worthless (it's only relatively worthless at the moment) and the government would have no option but to re-impose exchange controls.

Hopefully, Mboweni has the savvy not to be tempted into that quick-fix solution, much as some of his political colleagues might wish it. Besides, he will also be working closely with the now respected Department of Finance triumvirate of Trevor Manuel, Maria Ramos and Gill Marcus, whose free market principles are no longer in question. Despite an unfortunate early start, Trevor Manuel has turned out to be the best finance minister this country has ever had.

In case you are gagging on your morning coffee and croissants at this comment, I hardly need remind you that it was not the National Party that relaxed exchange controls.

However, Mboweni's strengths as central bank governor lie in his struggle roots. Just as Manuel has the political credibility to point out to organised labour the economic facts of life, so will Mboweni need to explain the role of a central bank to the economically ignorant ANC rank and file, many of whom have convinced themselves that Mboweni will be giving away free money once Stals hands over the keys to the vault next year.

Whether or not you like the news that Mboweni will be the next Reserve Bank governor is irrelevant; it is a *fait accompli* and one either has to live with it or leave the country.

The renewed assault on both the currency and the bond market early last week will undoubtedly be attributed to last weekend's announcement. It may have had a little to do with it. I believe the writing has been on the wall for the rand for some time now; it's just that we were too complacent to read it. Part of Mboweni's job will be to clean the wall and hopefully Stals will leave him with a few useful tips for central bank governors before he retires.

One of these should be 'don't venture an opinion on the direction of the financial markets during a crisis because you will almost certainly be proved wrong'.

19 July 1998

British Airways decides it is simply too British for its own good

British Airways have announced that they are to re-train their cabin crews to make them 'less British' and 'more informal'.

This is apparently the latest stage of the company's strategy to market itself as a global airline. British Airways has already infuriated regular passengers by removing the easily recognisable Union flag and painting the tail fins of its aircraft in various ethnic designs.

This is all very well for a rainbow nation like South Africa because our bona fides entitle us to ethnic designs, but a British Airways Boeing with an Ndebele tail fin looks quite ridiculous on the tarmac at Heathrow under a perpetually grey summer sky. Instead of filching other nations' cultures, why couldn't they have used their own ethnic groups as inspiration?

Perhaps a pair of Doc Marten boots crunching into a Frenchman's head to commemorate the England football hooligans' victory at Marseilles? Or maybe the Spice Girls, those articulate commentators on every aspect of life in Cool Britannia, could each have a plane named after them, with pictures of them cavorting in skimpy clothing painted on the tail fin. I quite like the idea of flying to London in a Scary Spice 747. It's a pity that Ginger Spice has now left the group to begin a solo career because I think a full-length reclining figure of her would look rather fetching painted down the side of an aircraft.

Apart from slavishly following some hare-brained re-branding strategy recommended by the shiny-suited marketing trendoids in search of a fat fee, British Airways appears to be telling the travelling public that it no longer wants to be thought of as British. This is a great mistake because the airline will lose the identity it has built up so successfully over the years and become just another flying taxi service.

The company argues that 40-million people fly with them each year and by 2000 fewer than 20% of its passengers will be British. Quite why that should be a good reason to go for brand anonymity escapes me. After all, if you insist on being served goat's head soup on board and want sword swallowers instead of in-flight movies then choose another airline. British Airways claims that many passengers have told them that the stewardesses are 'too aloof'.

These surveys are often conducted at Heathrow after a British Airways flight has landed. Someone comes up to you with a clipboard while you are waiting for your luggage and fills in a customer satisfaction questionnaire.

If a male passenger has just spent 12 hours in the air fantasising about tearing off the cabin attendant's clothing and having passionate sex with her, it's quite understandable that he will describe her as 'too aloof' – particularly if all she gave him was another cup of coffee when he said he needed something hot and sweet to help him through the night. It is well known that gorgeous British Airways stewardesses are constantly being propositioned by libidinous passengers hoping to join the mile-high club, so a bit of British reserve probably comes in quite handy.

However, British Airways management think they know best and have started a new training regime called Kaleidoscope. The course is designed to encourage cabin crew to bring more of their own personality to the job. They will be encouraged to make more eye contact, give friendly taps on the shoulder and 'spend more time crouching beside passengers'. This can only end in tears. For example, if the guy in seat 36D gets more eye contact during the flight than me and I suffer a loss of personal self-esteem as a consequence, will British Airways provide a counselling service for me on arrival?

This tapping and crouching business is all very well for the Yanks, but we Brits don't want complete strangers coming up to us halfway through the movie and tapping our shoulders for no apparent reason.

I also sincerely hope the cabin crew will be issued with fluorescent hats to wear while they are crouching in the aisles. There is nothing worse than tripping over a crouching stewardess on your way to the toilet.

The stewardesses are also being trained to study their passengers and adapt their personalities to suit the clientele. This could be quite complicated in a plane full of people each with their own separate and widely differing personalities. Maybe instead of First Class, Business Class and Economy, British Airways should split their aircraft into Cheerful, Miserable Sod and Manic Depressive class. That way at least the cabin crew have the advantage.

16 August 1998

Looking for short, fat white men to make up quota in basketball team

Two years ago in this column, I mocked Sports Minister Steve Tshwete by suggesting that his must be the cushiest job in the Cabinet. All he was required to do, I insensitively suggested, was to travel around the world at taxpayers' expense, cheer the national team at major sporting events and attend a stream of riotous parties.

One has to admire his energy and enthusiasm, although I am bound to say that the minister is somewhat fastidious when it comes to choosing those sporting events to which he is prepared to lend his support.

While waiting to board a flight to London last year, I met the proud, green track-suited members of the SA underwater orienteering squad in the bar at Johannesburg International. They were off to some remote Eastern bloc country to take part in the Underwater Orienteering World Championships and believed they were in with a good chance.

'Where,' I asked, 'is Minister Tshwete?' Perhaps he had been delayed in the traffic. Anyway, rather as the Arthurian knights left a seat empty at the Round Table, we bought an extra beer just in case 'he' appeared. Sadly he didn't, and our dejected underwater champions boarded their flight without the minister's benediction.

For the uninformed, underwater orienteering involves swimming around in the murky depths of a lake and finding your way from one point to another with the aid of a compass. As a spectator, it's rather difficult to cheer the national team because you are securely rooted to the muddy bank of the lake while they are underwater and, therefore, completely invisible from the shore. The only thing they can hear is the sound of their own air bubbles so any amount of lusty shouting is a complete waste of time.

For similar reasons I suspect, television coverage of underwater orienteering events has been scant (even on satellite TV), thus denying an entire generation the pleasure of watching people grope their way through pond weed from one part of a dark lake to another. If darts can make it onto television, then why not underwater orienteering?

One reason is the problem of lighting. The water is so murky down there that, no matter how strong the lights, anything more than three metres away becomes a shadowy blur. This has obviously affected sponsorship too because companies don't want to throw millions of rands at sports sponsorship if the company logo is invisible. Maybe there is an opportunity for tobacco sponsorship here?

However, the main reason that television companies, corporate sponsors and the Sports Minister have ignored underwater orienteering is that it is a thunderingly dull, mind-numbingly boring activity which urgently needs an injection of vitality from someone with some imagination and commercial savvy. What about introducing nude underwater orienteering for a start? Then throw some dangerous eels and sea serpents into the lake just to make things more interesting. Within months, I reckon I could make underwater orienteering one of the highest-earning sports in the world. I confidently predict that, before long, mothers will be cancelling their daughters' tennis lessons and sending them underwater in search of fame and fortune.

The other reason that Tshwete didn't make it to the airport to wave goodbye to our sub-aqueous heroes that day is that they were all white; although when they're underwater you would hardly know the difference. Because of the repressive apartheid era, blacks were denied the opportunity to fall into a deep dark lake and swim from one place to another underwater unless they had the approval and support of members of the security forces. Now, thanks to provisions in the Sport and Recreation Bill, all this is likely to change. Sports administrators and selectors will face prison sentences if SA sports teams don't reflect the demographics of the country.

The Bill is still being studied by legal experts who are expected to add amendments. Perhaps one of these will be a clause which says that, even if the selectors have picked a team that reflects the rainbowness of the nation, if the team loses the selectors should have their personal assets seized and redistributed to disappointed fans. Repeated offences would result in the selectors being fed to hungry crocodiles.

I strongly believe this landmark legislation will set a world trend. Already, I am told, the Harlem Globetrotters have been instructed to include more short, fat white men in their team.

23 August 1998

Roll up, roll up, comrades – borrow from me and make me rich

Paradoxically, more white people have made themselves millionaires under the ANC since the 1994 elections than ever managed to do so under National Party rule. Not bad, considering that the ANC came to power espousing socialist and communist ideologies.

Another interesting feature of the SA economy under the ANC is that it is now perfectly acceptable to exploit poor blacks, provided you have a black shareholder at your side.

In the run-up to the election, any suggestion that black people should pay a higher rate of interest than whites would have been met with howls of protest. In fact, when the ANC came to power, the suggestion was that the banks should have a two-tier rate of lending, the lower rate applying to previously disadvantaged borrowers who would be subsidised by a higher rate charged to ordinary borrowers. For sound business reasons, that didn't happen, although a couple of banking groups did go through the motions of pretending to want to lend money to people who hadn't a hope of repaying.

These days nobody pretends any more and micro-lenders are doing a roaring trade offering small amounts of high-interest money to people who wouldn't be able to qualify for a loan elsewhere. Even young Mark Thatcher seems to have jumped on the bandwagon, although I suspect that lending money to people who carry guns for a living is not a very smart business move, especially when you try to get them to repay their debts.

Nearly all the loans are rolled on a monthly basis, which means the borrower almost certainly has to re-borrow to pay his interest, plus borrow a bit more to keep pace with his outgoings. That way he remains a loyal customer of the micro-lender, who is guaranteed to make a small fortune, providing his default rate remains fairly low.

Enter a black empowerment group who, instead of saying: 'Hey, whitey, you're exploiting my brother,' takes a good look at the profits rolling in, licks its corporate lips and thinks to itself: 'Exploitation be damned, we're talking serious money here. Give me some shares please.'

The irony is delicious. Towards the end of the year the ANC will be rallying the rank and vile and preparing them for the 1999 election. So as you sit back and listen to all the cant and pious rhetoric which will spew from the politicians' mouths, you can console yourself that this is just politics and it will be business as usual next May.

*

Another feature of the economy I find fascinating at the moment is the stratospheric price:earnings ratios of some of the recent listings on the JSE.

More conservative investors have been known to grumble that these companies are a flash in the pan and one should stick to blue-chip quality. This is partly because, for many people, it is extremely difficult to invest in a company that was formed in a pub five weeks ago, has no product, no profit record and where the managing director is still using acne cream and only shaves every second day.

A share p:e of 500 tells you the company is expected to maintain its current profitability for the next 500 years. Name me a quoted company anywhere in the world that has been in business with an unbroken profit record for that long.

Better than that though, go back to the year 1500 and list ten major developments in that time which might have affected business thinking. Then include the odd world war to upset the smooth flow of business and you will begin to realise how utterly lunatic a p:e of anything much beyond 30 really is.

Even information technology stocks have started to look rather pedestrian against some of the shares in the banks and financial services sector. Either some of these companies have discovered how to turn base metals into gold or investors have gone mad. To expect a company to sustain earnings for the next half millennium in a business as volatile as financial markets seems to be rather optimistic.

What we are being asked to believe is that, despite increased competition and the opening up of the market to foreign banks, the cake is growing and the slices are even more tasty than before. Spherical objects to that one I say. When newly listed financial groups have a market capitalisation higher than that of a group like Barlows, the alarm bells should be ringing. The problem is that no fund manager can afford not to support these new issues if he is to remain competitive. The question is ... why?

6 September 1998

Queuing up for bar code democracy is a taxing business

I am still the proud owner of an old-style identity document, the one without a bar code. According to recent media reports this will disenfranchise me when the general election takes place next year. Another two million people are also expected to be affected, so I don't feel particularly victimised.

Apart from the certainty of the ANC's losing my valuable vote, this surely calls into question the morality of a government who sends me a tax return every year and regularly siphons off large chunks of my salary without my approval. After all, a basic premise of democracy is that there should be no taxation without representation – so if I am turned back at the polling station maybe I should, in future, return all correspondence from the Receiver with the words 'not known at this address' scrawled across the envelope.

Although the identity document I carry is perfectly legal and allows me to open a bank account, it is apparently not good enough for the government.

Bar codes are all very well for packets of corn flakes but I haven't yet worked out why one needs one in addition to having to provide a passport-sized photograph, fingerprints and what have you.

What does the bar code actually say anyway? Suppose it is an encrypted message that reveals one is in the habit of writing newspaper columns that criticise the government's complete inability to grasp economic fundamentals. It all looks very sinister and Orwellian to me.

My decision to make do without a bar-coded identity document is more a matter of logistics than non-conformity, though. We appear to have a government which is under the impression that its citizens have unlimited time and are able to queue for hours for an official document.

This is probably true of around 70% of the population, but unfortunately the rest of us have to work to keep the politicians and their lackeys in the grand style to which they have become accustomed. Because the queues are so long and the service so inefficient, most employees need apply for a day's leave just to get a new identity document or a driving licence.

Of course, queuing for an entire day is no guarantee of success. Many people spend a whole day waiting for one of these documents only to be told to return the next day.

For those who are self-employed the problem is even worse. Every hour spent in a queue is an hour of lost earnings. This government-enforced lack of productivity means less money trickles back into the economy to create new employment. Maybe somebody could explain this basic economic principle slowly and clearly to our politicians before the jobs summit in October.

*

It was no coincidence that the stock market crumbled the week after I wrote about the absurdly high price:earnings ratios of some shares in the information technology and financial services sector.

This is, after all, a highly influential column although it was hardly an earth-shattering revelation. What surprises me is that it took punters so long to realise that they were being sucked into a classic investment bubble.

Now, of course, there are plenty of disillusioned investors wandering around nursing wounded wallets and telling anybody who is interested how much they have lost over the past few weeks.

It's difficult to be sympathetic. If you can sell a share for ten times what it cost you within a few months of buying it and you don't, you are either incredibly naive or incredibly greedy.

What will be interesting to see over the next few months is how many investors borrowed money to ride the bull market in hyped stocks. The so-called 'empowerment groups' are a case in point.

As previously disadvantaged South Africans they presumably had no money to start with. So it's fair to assume they either received generous donations or borrowed money. And as business is not generally a philanthropic operation, let us assume they borrowed the money to make their investments, the lender perhaps taking comfort in the fact that the growth in the investment would more than cover the loan.

When these loans were originally made most people expected interest rates to fall. As we all know, they haven't and so empowerment groups now find themselves in the uncomfortable situation of paying at least 7% more for their money while their investments have fallen by at least 50%. I wonder what they'll tell their investors.

13 September 1998

The mystery of South Africa's invisible white stinkwoods

It is surprising how many things you can blame on the dreaded apartheid era if you really put your mind to it. I wouldn't be in the least bit surprised to read one day that the reason the taste in chewing gum disappears after the first two minutes is due to apartheid.

You may not know it, but we recently celebrated Arbour Week in this country. Unfortunately, the excitement of the occasion was overshadowed in the press by plummeting stock markets and tedious reports of the collective wisdom of the Non-Aligned Summit.

So, few of you will know that Water Affairs and Forestry Minister Kadar Asmal delivered a speech announcing that by planting trees South Africans could attempt to redress some of the problems caused by apartheid. Actually, the minister didn't deliver the speech himself. It was read on his behalf by forestry conservation director Dr Jabulani Mjwara during Arbour Week celebrations at the Ivory Park informal settlement in Midrand. (Asmal was probably behind the parliamentary bicycle sheds at the time puffing on a cigarette.)

The minister's speech quite rightly said that planting trees was a good thing and called on all members of society to plant as many trees as possible so they can cut them down again and use them for firewood or log cabins at a later date. However, one comment in the report particularly caught my eye. It's not clear whether this was part of the honourable minister's speech or *obiter dictum* from Dr Mjwara. Anyway, somebody said that 'historically, South Africans had not had a culture of planting trees'. Clearly one cannot let a comment like that pass without ridiculing it.

According to reliable reports, backed up by aerial photographs, Johannesburg is one of the most wooded cities in the world. The tall things with green bits sticking out of them on the slopes of Table Mountain look pretty much like trees to me as well. Mpumulanga is full of planted forests, parts of KwaZulu-Natal are a jungle and even the Free State can boast the odd sheltering bower.

So where did they all come from if nobody's been planting them? Well, of course, many of them are indigenous so nobody can take any real credit, but what about Johannesburg which was a dusty plain 100 years ago?

As a keen follower of the breathless botanist, David Attenborough, I now know that plants seed themselves in a myriad different ways. For example, sycamore trees have little helicopters that whirr gently down to the ground carrying the seed with them but they don't generally have the energy to travel across continents on the wind. Other trees rely on small furry animals carrying the seeds to receptive new soil. Perhaps the oak trees that line the streets of Stellenbosch are the result of a super breed of European marathon squirrels which jogged across the continent of Africa with their little cheeks full of acorns. Then again, according to Attenborough, our avian friends play a crucial role in the propagation of forests by swallowing seeds with the fruit of the tree and later excreting the seed wrapped in its own mini manure pack. If we are being asked to believe that Johannesburg's trees are purely the result of bird droppings, then I would have to say that is so much shit.

Why can't the minister come clean and tell the truth? The fact is that trees were planted, but apparently by the wrong sort of people. For example in the older northern suburbs of Johannesburg like Parkview, Parkwood, Saxonwold and Parktown North, once the mining houses had finished scrabbling around in the earth unsuccessfully looking for seams of gold, they would have the areas proclaimed townships. They would then make a gift of trees to the new suburb, which explains why there are so many plane trees in Parktown North and jacaranda trees in Parkwood.

In fact, there has been no shortage of tree planting by white South Africans, which explains the proliferation of nurseries around the country. The minister now wishes to redress any apartheid imbalances by encouraging blacks to also plant trees. This is to be welcomed. In some government departments, equality is being achieved by reducing the level of service to a pitifully uniform lowest common denominator. If Water Affairs and Forestry took that line they would be chopping down trees in formerly white suburbs to make them as barren as the townships. There's only one thing that troubles me. Are we in for an affirmative tree policy? Must we replace our white stinkwoods with black wattles?

20 September 1998

Intelligent leaders should wipe the egg off their faces and apologise

The leadership of the ANC is exhibiting disturbing signs of paranoia. A fortnight ago the South African Chamber of Business (Sacob) released its business confidence index, which showed a 12-year low of 86.2 points, down 4.1 points from the previous month.

Deputy President Thabo Mbeki, immediately sensing a sinister white plot to destabilise the government, swung into action, slamming Sacob for apparently ignoring the views of black business. 'Whose confidence does it reflect?' he questioned. 'It certainly does not reflect black business confidence.'

Since this extraordinary outburst there have been several erudite letters to the business newspapers explaining that the index is made up of 13 sets of economic data – one of them being the rand/dollar exchange rate. It's rather difficult to see how this could be racially skewed to reflect the views of whites only.

Then there is the Consumer Price Index, a measurement of domestic inflation that is handed out every month by a government agency. Is Mbeki suggesting that the information from the Central Statistical Service is inaccurate or that there are two inflation rates, one for whites and another for blacks? Surely not.

The list goes on, and the only indicator that could possibly be interpreted as reflecting the views of whites is the '12-month outlook of manufacturers on skilled and unskilled employment as reflected by Sacob's manufacturing survey'. Paradoxically, this is one of the four positive influences on the index during the month Mbeki complains it is unrepresentative.

At this point I must come clean and say that, until last week, I too was a little hazy as to what actually made up Sacob's business confidence index. Admittedly, I didn't think Raymond Parsons rang around a few white business friends once a month to ask them how things were going and whether they were thinking of emigrating. I imagined it must be a bit more sophisticated than that.

However, my ignorance of such matters is immaterial. After all, I am not expecting to become the state president next April. Nor do my words, influential though they undoubtedly are, get quoted quite as widely as Mbeki's.

It would have been intelligent for a man who read economics at university to have investigated what actually went into the business confidence index before commenting. And having opened his mouth only to find his face covered with fresh, runny egg it would have been even more intelligent to have admitted ignorance and offered an apology to Sacob, whose credentials he has called into question.

Instead, Mbeki ploughed gamely on and threw his weight behind a black business confidence index launched by the National African Federated Chamber of Commerce and Industry (Nafcoc) at its annual conference at Sun City. It will be interesting to see what Nafcoc includes and what it leaves out of its index, bearing in mind it dare not come out with anything that could be seen as negative lest it incur the wrath of the government.

The other issue at stake, though, is whether anyone will believe a positive Nafcoc index against a negative Sacob index. But one thing is certain. There will be enormous mirth among foreign investors who will continue to withhold investment from this country until our politicians can demonstrate that they can behave more like adults and less like petulant children.

*

When the going gets tough, the tough get going. Not if they are real South Africans though. President Nelson Mandela's criticism of those leaving SA for what many perceive to be greener pastures has predictably caused something of a stir.

It is inevitable that the comment should be directed at white South Africans for the simple reason that these are the people with internationally marketable and transferable skills. Unfortunately, the same cannot be said for the sort of people pouring across our borders into the country. An indicator of a free and confident economy is mobility of labour.

SA has elected to be part of the global village, so our politicians mustn't whinge if they find they cannot keep talent. What they should do is address the reasons for emigration and make it more attractive to remain in the country. That does sound like an awful lot of hard work, though, doesn't it? Certainly more effort than convening another pointless summit or renaming a provincial hospital after a struggle hero.

11 October 1998

Watch out smokers, the Drag Squad will put you behind bars in a puff

Faced with a spiralling crime problem which threatens to destroy the very fabric of our society, I see government has finally decided to bite the bullet and implement a policy of zero tolerance by introducing Draconian measures to stamp out one of the greatest scourges of our society.

Yes, dear reader, it will soon be illegal to smoke in public. I hear that a crack new division of the South African police has been set up and that hand-picked officers are undergoing specialist training before being released onto our streets. The Drag Squad, as they will be known, will be in constant two-way radio contact with one another and have been trained to react to a reported crime within seconds. They will be armed with fire extinguishers and fresh-air sprays, and after arresting the foul villain and dousing his cigarette in foam, they will attempt to freshen the area as part of a public service so that decent law-abiding folk can enjoy it.

It is already anticipated that hardened criminals could attempt to avoid arrest by cupping their hands over a lighted cigarette in an attempt to hide the burning end from the police. In smoking parlance this is known as the FW de Klerk position. They will soon realise that they are up against a superior adversary. The training the Drag Squad receives naturally includes detection skills. They have been instructed to look for shifty-looking people loitering around street corners with smoke coming out of their nostrils and to listen for telltale coughing fits.

Once the suspect is sighted, he will be kept under surveillance until he eventually gives in to temptation and takes a long drag. Only then will they move in. Police tracker dogs are also being brought into the crackdown, known as 'Operation Stub-out', and are being trained to smell a smouldering Cohiba at 100 metres.

Backing up the uniformed officers of the Drag Squad is a small group of plain-clothes detectives, all of them former 40-a-day men. Their job will be to conduct on-the-spot breath tests to see whether a member of the public might have just had a crafty smoke. They will then check the video records from hidden surveillance cameras for evidence which could lead to an arrest and prosecution.

Lieutenant Phil Terre-Tippe of the Drag Squad also told me it could be illegal to solicit or to use language 'likely to cause a combustible tobacco substance to be incinerated'. Previously innocuous phrases such as 'Have you got a light, mate?' should now convey to law-abiding citizens the message that a crime is about to be committed and that a police officer should be called immediately. Worried human rights lawyers have suggested that, in their enthusiasm, the police might be tempted to lay traps for unsuspecting smokers, such as leaving packets of open cigarettes on bars.

The fine for public smoking is R200 at the moment, with a prison sentence for those who are either unwilling or unable to pay, although public floggings and the severing of fingers have been suggested for repeat offenders.

Clearly the SA government, as always, has its priorities absolutely right. It is staying soft on hard crime because it knows it hasn't a hope of winning the battle. Even if the police do manage to arrest criminals and they actually go to prison before escaping from police cells, you can be sure the President will let them out again as a birthday present to the nation.

So the ANC have done the only logical thing. They have criminalised a formerly legal activity knowing they will be able to face the SA public ahead of the election and say with some degree of honesty that they are winning the fight against crime. Quite why the government is wasting taxpayers' money by introducing legislation to stop people from enjoying a legal substance like tobacco in public, instead of concentrating police resources on getting illegal substances like cocaine off the streets. remains a mystery.

Maybe they just have too much time on their hands.

*

Continuing with the theme of political correctness run amok, I was amazed to see that Gauteng education MEC Mary Metcalfe has apologised to the parents of those four little darlings for the humiliation they experienced after their thieving offspring were asked to apologise for pinching food and money from the school tuck shop. In my opinion, a theft of R48 000 is a serious crime, not a childish prank. To allow the culprits to remain at school and not prosecute them is a clear indication that the ANC supports the crime initiative.

1 November 1998

Get involved – or stop whinging about the decline of our cities

I attended the annual general meeting of my local residents' association last week. The group represents five areas in Johannesburg's northern suburbs and the purpose of the association is to voice residents' concerns, to liaise with local councillors and, where possible, with representatives from municipal departments.

The latter is not so easy because, even when meetings are set up and confirmed, the local official often fails to turn up, probably preferring to visit the BMW showroom to select his new free car.

The issues raised are the usual ones: business developments encroaching on residential areas; unauthorised use of residential properties for business purposes; brothels in the neighbourhood; poster pollution; unrepaired roads; increasing crime and so on.

The meeting, held on a Saturday morning, drew about 20 people from perhaps more than 3 000 represented households. My immediate knee-jerk reaction was to put this down to apathy. On reflection though, I realise this was extraordinarily arrogant of me because it made the assumption that my fellow residents feel the same way as I do about the deterioration of services and general decline of our neighbourhood.

Obviously they do not – otherwise they would have given up an hour and a half to make their voices heard. When local officials ask who the residents' association represents and are shown the attendance register for the annual general meeting with a mere 20 names, they can be forgiven for letting out a howl of derisive laughter and dismissing the association as little more than a minority of whinging malcontents.

A couple of weeks ago I was the guest speaker at a luncheon at the Inanda Club. I gave my normal gloomy outlook for the country and encouraged everybody to stock up on canned fruit, chemical toilets and water butts, in addition to keeping a few razor blades handy just in case it all became too much to bear. When it comes to scenario planning, my high road makes Clem Sunter's low road look like a cliff-top stroll.

As my speech was much too short, I was asked to remain at the podium to while away another fifteen minutes, answering questions from the floor. One of these concerned the demise of Johannesburg and I was asked what, in my opinion, could be done about it.

As I hadn't the faintest idea what the answer was, I found myself slipping into auto-babble mode and discovered, to my delight, that I would make an excellent politician – I gave a five-minute, impromptu answer to the question without offering any solution whatsoever. Actually, that's not strictly true. I did make a suggestion but realised that it was so unorthodox and wildly improbable as to be instantly rejected. I suggested that it would help if people took some interest in local affairs and become more involved in keeping their immediate environment clean. For example, if everybody took down posters outside their properties, posters would no longer be regarded as an effective advertising medium.

Surely it's not too much to ask residents to clear up litter in the street outside their homes. They do in First World countries but in SA it is obviously regarded as demeaning for a white person to be seen picking up rubbish in the street. This attitude has to change. Local government finances are in such poor shape that all but the most essential services are likely to be scrapped before long. You can score 200 points in your I-Spy book if you spot a street cleaner these days.

Hiding behind security fences and electric gates pretending the outside world doesn't exist is one way to handle the problem but it doesn't offer any solutions. Whether or not you are in the habit of paying your rates, the quality of life in the suburbs will continue to deteriorate as long as people refuse to acknowledge that the problem is theirs and attempt to do something about it.

For example, if you cannot be bothered to give four hours a month to drive around your suburb on blockwatch, you mustn't complain if car thefts in your neighbourhood rise. If you have no interest in taking part in the many community policing forums that exist, preferring to leave it to someone else, you are not entitled to complain about rising crime.

And if you can't even be bothered to support your local residents' association by attending a short meeting once a year, then you have absolutely no right to expect things to get better. The greatest strength the ruling party has is knowing it has a small and apathetic opposition.

22 November 1998

Please don't mention Julius Caesar – I could be traumatised for days

As Oscar Wilde remarked, 'there is only one thing in the world worse than being talked about, and that is not being talked about'. So, it was with a mixture of disbelief and amusement that I read the Human Rights Commission's case against me.

Eventually, I decided that either it was an elaborate practical joke or business was a bit slow on the human rights front and poor Barney Pityana was casting around for something to occupy his day. Human rights commissions usually concentrate on serious issues like unexplained death in detention, poor prison conditions, police brutality and child abuse.

Clearly nothing like that is happening in SA at the moment and the HRC has been forced to spread its net and concentrate on more subtle human rights abuses such as subliminal racism in the media.

The accusation is that I am guilty of using hate speech in this column. My accusers are two organisations I have never heard of, one calling itself the Black Lawyers' Association and the other the Association of Black Accountants. Their case against me is so flimsy that even the HRC (which, one suspects, had already made up its mind that I was guilty) realised that they would be wasting time and money pursuing it and eventually declined to investigate the complaints.

One example the complainants chose as evidence of 'hate speech' was from a column written earlier this year during the Clinton visit which mocked the yearning of many African-Americans to return to Mother Africa; an idea they find very attractive until they realise that, had their ancestors not been abducted by slave traders, they too could be living in a tin shack with no electricity or running water. According to my accusers, this comment was deeply offensive to many Africans who still bear the scars of those traumatic times a few hundred years ago.

Strangely enough, when the article was published it provoked absolutely no reaction, so I must assume that the thousands who found the article so 'deeply offensive' suffered in noble silence. Not to be outdone when it comes to claiming to be a victim of a cruel history, I too bear deep scars of the Roman invasion of my country of birth and am still trying to come to terms with straight roads, baths and linguini. It's a long healing process and it doesn't help when people insensitively mention the name Julius Caesar.

The HRC invited me to defend myself, which I declined for several reasons. Firstly, the supporting evidence was so appallingly contrived and rambling that it was impossible to determine what exactly was being complained about and therefore to answer any charges. Secondly, the complaint came not from individuals but from two amorphous organisations which had been used to hide the true identities of the complainants. Finally, even if I had been able to answer the accusation of the Black Lawyers' Association and the Association of Black Accountants, I would not have done so because my conscience forbids me to have any dealings with racially exclusive organisations. Since the key entry requirement for both organisations would appear to be a black skin, I must assume that both are in contravention of our new constitution which, as I understand it, prohibits discrimination on the grounds of race and colour. It is a strange irony that I should be accused of hate speech and racism by two groups which practise racial segregation.

Although the complaints specifically against the *Mail and Guardian* and the *Sunday Times* will no longer be investigated, the HRC has nevertheless decided it could be onto a good thing and has declared that it will launch a general investigation into racism in the media. It seems particularly concerned with what it calls subliminal racism. This is racism that is so subtle that only highly trained members of the HRC are able to sniff it out. Because nobody can actually define what constitutes subliminal racism, the HRC will be able to strut around for months pretending to investigate something that nobody understands. Nice work if you can get it.

Meanwhile, the HRC can busy itself with some examples of overt racism in the media. For example, the *Madam and Eve* cartoon strip continues to portray black domestic servants as lazy and cunning. Perhaps it's time to round up Messrs Francis, Dugmore and Rico for a nice quiet chat. Then there's the editor of the telephone directory who insists on calling one of his books 'White Pages'. You can't get more subliminal than that.

29 November 1998

If you don't know Led Zeppelin, you're too young to handle my money

It seems that barely a week passes without a new bank or financial services company bursting onto the scene.

One would have thought that the sector was a little overcrowded at the moment, but that doesn't seem to deter them. There are evidently still plenty of people around who think anything to do with financial services is a licence to print money.

In the aftermath of this year's equity market crash, shares in selected financial services companies recovered particularly well, although they are still well off their pre-crash, magic mushroom levels. Those that haven't recovered probably never will – which is hardly surprising bearing in mind some of the dogs that managed to stray onto the JSE board this year.

Amid the frenzy of a bull market and on the promise of a fast buck, it was staggering how many private investors pumped money into some of these ventures without reading the prospectus carefully or occasionally tempering their enthusiasm with a good dose of cynicism.

Judging by some of the share prices, the madness continues. As a retired financial markets man I have to confess to being totally unconvinced by all this breezy optimism. I believe that more participants leads to more competition which means tighter margins. That presumably leads to lower profits unless turnover can be boosted. That normally means increasing market share, which is difficult to do if you don't have any market share to start with.

New banks and financial services companies normally come to the market in a haze of PR gobbledygook, blathering on about how they are offering a unique service, tapping into foreign expertise and focusing on becoming a niche player.

They may have succeeded in pulling the wool over many an investor's eyes in the early days, but there are now so many banks squeezed into the same space that it can scarcely be called a niche any more. Besides, if a niche banking opportunity was that profitable you can bet the established banks would have either concentrated on it already or will muscle in on the territory pretty soon. New ideas don't stay new for long. Corporate banking is all about knowing what deals are floating around the marketplace and bankers are notoriously nosy when it comes to finding out what the competition is up to.

I am told that one leading bank in Johannesburg regularly phones top restaurants to see which of their competition have booked for lunch and then dispatches a spy to find out who the guest is and, better still, pick up snippets of conversation. Bank luncheon rooms are regularly 'swept' for listening devices after some were found in a boardroom a few years ago.

Bearing in mind increased competition, a drop in deal turnover, high interest rates, bad debts and the appallingly slow pace of the government's privatisation programme, one wonders how some of the niche banks and financial companies can afford to open their doors every morning?

The answer, I suspect, is that they are doing very little apart from operating a meagre and rather uninspiring treasury function, waiting for an empowerment opportunity to be tossed their way and dabbling in the sort of deals that have already been turned down by the more successful merchant banks. Meanwhile, swanky new head offices are being built and there are all the signs of another looming banking crisis as it becomes more and more difficult to get straight answers to simple questions such as 'what do you actually do?'

*

Another area of apparent growth is in the fund management business. Not only are there already a bewildering number of unit trusts to choose from but new asset management companies are also springing up like daisies.

Many claim to give a highly personalised service to private clients who are offered 'tailor-made' portfolios to suit their individual requirements. In a business where profits are purely generated by commission, it is obviously in the interest of fund managers to move clients in and out of stocks as often as they can get away with it, so you may find your portfolio tailor making frequent and unwelcome alterations to your bespoke investment.

However, the major problem with fund managers today is how young and fresh faced many of them seem to be. My general rule of thumb is if they can't name all the members of Led Zeppelin and say which instruments they played, they are too young to be trusted with my money.

6 December 1998

A panic button for Joe Modise could save us all a lot of money

Having finally committed ourselves to R30-billion worth of new weaponry over the next few years, we may yet find our gleaming fighter aircraft sitting idle on the runway and our redundant subs bobbing disconsolately about on the water in Simon's Town, assuming that somebody has remembered to tie them up. The Pretoria High Court, in its wisdom, has ruled that members of the armed forces can join unions and engage in collective bargaining with their employers which, in this case, is the government.

Admittedly, the decision may still be overturned by the Constitutional Court but that will depend on whether or not the armed forces are deemed to be an essential service under the Labour Relations Act. Currently the Act precludes members of the armed forces and the intelligence agencies (yes, apparently we really do have them) from joining a union and enjoying the right to strike because they are deemed essential services.

If the Pretoria decision is upheld then the obvious solution would be to disband the defence force and save ourselves a lot of money because, by implication, they would be non-essential. An alternative defence strategy for the country would then have to be considered.

Personally, I am in favour of outsourcing on something like this. It seems crazy to have all those soldiers hanging around on full pay just in case Lesotho decides to strike back. The whole problem with the perception of the armed forces is that they are not really doing a proper job unless they are out killing people or defending dams in distress. Dressing in battle fatigues and monitoring queues of old people trying to register for the election next year is hardly job satisfaction.

So what the government should probably do is take a tip from Johannesburg's northern suburbs and engage the services of a reliable armed response company. Very few of us want or need a security guard on the property all the time but when we hit the panic button we like to know that somebody will leap over the wall and pepper the retreating backside of the guy filching our TV with buckshot.

The macro version of this would be for Joe Modise to have a panic button which he could push whenever he felt the country might be threatened by invasion, whereupon the armed response control room would phone to ask if this was a genuine call or whether one of his colleagues had mistaken the panic button for the BMW remote control.

Joe would then give his secret code number and armed troops would be swiftly dispatched to deal with insurrection, revolution or illegal smoking in whichever city had the red alarm light flashing. We would pay only a small monthly fee and the purchase and maintenance of equipment would be the problem of the security company. Obviously a full-scale engagement would mean we'd have to chip in for the cost of ammunition. Here again, rather like medical aid, we could elect to go for 100% cover (the enemy gets completely obliterated) or 70% cover for a lower monthly payment (the armed response is limited to land attack and the restoration of essential services like shopping malls, cigar bars and cult cinema complexes).

Given this country's penchant for industrial action, though, the more likely outcome if the Pretoria ruling is upheld would be the creation of a more militant military. For example, prior to an act of engagement, contracts would have to be negotiated and a fair wage for a fair day's slaughter would have to be hammered out around the table before we could go to war. A knee-jerk reaction to invasion without going through the proper channels could have potentially disastrous effects.

War is a notoriously unpredictable occupation and no respecter of the average working man's day. Do we, for example, have to pay time and a half for night attacks?

Should we not be negotiating tea breaks every two hours or 30 rounds of ammunition, whichever is the sooner? To ignore these fundamentals of good management is to invite trouble. Without them we could easily be facing industrial action such as a 'shoot-to-rule' where only limited rounds are fired at the enemy until workers' demands are met. Then there are the important peace-time issues of whether the uniform is funky enough and the whole matter of why tanks can't be fitted with more comfortable reclining seats, pink fur on the dashboard and a sophisticated CD sound system with booming bass speakers.

24 January 1999

Life's a blast in Cape Town in the aftermath of New Year bomb

I have been putting a lot of effort into the new lifestyle choice that I mentioned in last week's column.

Clearly not a man who is afraid of a hard day's leisure, I have been rising just as the sun appears on Lion's Head and driving round the mountain to the coast for a gentle walk along the beach, starting at Clifton and moving along to Camp's Bay. Then it's back home for a triple St John's Wort on the rocks and a couple of thousand words on the computer before lunch.

The bottom line (as we say at *Business Times*) is that I am feeling very chipper and tremendously happy with life.

According to my astrologer all this happiness will end mid-February and I will be back to my normal, brooding, subliminally racist self; the one that matches the Identikit pictures that have been issued to the crack investigating officers of the Human Rights Commission as they wade through mountains of SA publications frantically searching for examples of racism to prosecute. Just to be sporting I've decided to co-operate with them and have suggested that if they take the first letter of the third paragraph of every column published over the past five years and rearrange some of them, they might spell the dreaded 'n' word.

One of the great pleasures of being in Cape Town this time has been the easy parking and accessibility to the V&A Waterfront. As you've no doubt read, tourists and most of the locals have been steering clear of the place since the New Year's bomb blast, with the result that it is virtually deserted. Not only can you get a table at any restaurant you wish but the waitress with attitude now has to serve you with a smile because she needs the tip. She also knows that her chances of breaking into an international modelling career have been greatly diminished because model agency heads are too jittery to visit the Waterfront. It may also be something to do with the security video cameras installed throughout the Waterfront which could capture on film the regular cocaine deliveries that seem to keep the fashion business going.

Paradoxically, the Waterfront is probably safer now than it has ever been because there are Casspir loads of cops at all the access points conducting random searches. This seems to have escaped most Capetonians who are now rushing off like panicked lemmings to shop in crowded and unguarded shopping centres that have yet to be bombed.

One good thing to come out of all this, though, is that it is a potent reminder of what things will be like if we don't get our tourism act together by getting tough on crime. Maybe big business will stop sucking up to politicians and put some pressure on them to perform. Maybe pigs will fly.

Cape Town even has a new tourist attraction to rival Table Mountain. As you drive along the R310 to Stellenbosch you pass the Spier Estate.

In the old days Spier used to produce the definitive foul pinotage and many wine enthusiasts keep a bottle handy to show their friends what a really disgusting wine should taste like. Mercifully the quality of the wine has improved and the estate now features, among many other facilities, an amphitheatre which brings culture to the philistine Capetonians during the summer months.

The only thing that destroys the classy, upmarket image is a cluster of gold statues that looks from the road rather like a nine-piece, all-girl singing group. Opinion is divided as to the 'naffness' or otherwise of the nine painted muses. Staff at Spier are loyal people and will only say that 'you get to like them eventually', but they are apparently known as 'Dick's chicks' below stairs.

The Italian attitude to statues is that they should be spread throughout gardens rather than lumped in one place which makes them look like the rich man's equivalent of garden gnomes. The origins of the statues of the nine daughters of Zeus are lost in the mists of time, but rumour has it that Spier's owner was approached by a shady looking character in London's Petticoat Lane who offered to throw in a Royal Doulton tea set if he took all nine off his hands. Other equally improbable stories say that the statues came from a mail order firm in Alabama called 'Muses-R-Us' and were originally black but had to be resprayed for the sensitive Cape Town market. At night they are illuminated and look like nine saintly manifestations.

All we need is a few tears and some miraculous cures and Spier could become a place of pilgrimage. Now that ought to be good for tourism in the Western Cape.

7 February 1999
Now that SA has democracy, the people couldn't care less

When I was a young boy, my mother wouldn't let me leave the dinner table until I had eaten all of my vegetables.

I grew up in an unenlightened, pre-Dr Benjamin Spock, post-war rationing environment and my parents felt that if you asked for something to be put on your plate you should eat it, although it was my mother who was left to enforce the policy. This she did by alternately threatening to serve the food at every future meal until it was eaten or appealing to my better nature by explaining how fortunate we were to have food on the table and how one potato could feed a family of starving Africans for a year.

Even at the age of five I didn't believe the official statistics and the stalemate continued until my younger brother was old enough to sit at the family dinner table. He ate everything and would quite happily let us load our steamed cabbage, parsnips and Brussels sprouts onto his plate in exchange for a share of our pocket money. Of course, if I was an American I could now sue my mother for a vast amount of money to compensate for the mental damage and trauma of my youth. I mentioned this to her recently until she mumbled something about updating her will and I swiftly dropped the topic.

All of this is rather like democracy in South Africa. Just a few years ago, everybody wanted platefuls of it. But now that they've got it they no longer seem to want it. The ANC would have us believe they struggled against an unjust and oppressive regime to bring freedom and democracy to the people. They must be wondering why they bothered and didn't just hang around in exile pursuing academic careers and enjoying visits to London theatres.

Judging by the recent voter registration, the people couldn't give a damn about democracy. They tasted it some five years ago, thanks very much, and it was very nice but they don't think they want any more, particularly if it means queuing for a bar-coded identity document. This rather lackadaisical attitude to our new-found freedom hardly fills me with confidence for the future of our young democracy.

All over Africa people are butchering their fellow citizens in the name of freedom and in Zimbabwe the despotic Mugabe is busy attaching electrodes to the testicles of anybody who happens not to like the way he is running the country into the ground.

Do we care? Apparently not. We can't even be bothered to register to vote a popularly elected government in once every five years. This sends several messages, the most significant being that relatively few people are interested in who runs South Africa so why bother with all the expense of elections? A country gets the government it deserves and such apathy inevitably leads to dictatorship.

Another possible reason for the woeful lack of interest is the commonly expressed belief among the rank and file that the ANC has been a bit of a disappointment. Since it seems inevitable that the ANC will get re-elected anyway, what's the point of voting?

The real cause for concern though is that the low electoral registration means that, whatever the result, half of the population will complain that the government is not popularly elected or legitimate. I am told that the figures are probably not much better in the US but there's no comparison. Americans have a strong currency and a sexual deviant for a president so, with all those diversions, why would anybody worry about bothering to vote?

Another huge question mark hangs over whether the ANC will get the majority it needs to push through controversial legislation. That's assuming that the ANC stays intact before the election. If I were a power-hungry junior politician, I would be thinking of splitting the party. Given the mood of the country, a pro-death penalty breakaway faction would cream votes away from the more staid elders of the party who steadfastly refuse to listen to their constituency's demands to get tough on crime.

All of this means that we are in for a fascinating year, but it doesn't really address the problem of whether the election (if and when it happens) can be called representative. I imagine that the insistence on bar-coded ID books will be dropped when the ANC fully appreciates the implications of the looming cock-up. The obvious solution is to allow only registered taxpayers who have been assessed within the past two years to vote. That way we could get the elections over in half a day.

14 February 1999

If we're scraping the bottom of the diplomatic barrel, send me to Cannes

Thanks to a free press in SA, the consul-general designate to India, Ramesh Vassen, will not be taking up his post.

Although the *Sunday Times* reported just over a fortnight ago that the Foreign Ministry's *crème de la crap* choice of candidate had been struck off the role of attorneys for helping himself to trust funds (also known as theft) in 1996, Foreign Minister Alfred Nzo staunchly defended his decision to appoint Vassen, suggesting that he was a good man who had paid the price for his dishonesty and should now be free to continue on his crony-sponsored career path.

Using the same logic, why not appoint convicted rapists, bandits, muggers and child molesters who have also paid their debt to society and happen to have a passing acquaintance with a cabinet member to high diplomatic positions? Collin Chauke for Chile maybe! The fact that Vassen hasn't actually been prosecuted for filching trust funds but has merely been censured by the governing body of his profession is simply his good fortune. Lesser mortals would have already appeared in court.

The extraordinary thing was that Vassen appeared on SABC on Monday morning looking peeved and protesting that he should still be offered the job and, indeed, would have been had not fastidious members of his profession cut up rough over his unorthodox use of other people's money to fund his lifestyle. This was not an isolated incident. On the contrary, according to reports, the Cape High Court ruled that Vassen had misused clients' money on dozens of occasions over several years. Vassen felt his contribution to the cause of human rights while a partner of our enigmatic Justice Minister Dullah Omar should mitigate this small oversight. This is clearly a subtle variation on the 'struggle accounting' defence employed by our old friend, Rev Allan Boesak (another friend of Dullah's).

The fact that Vassen has a somewhat bleary view of what is right and what is wrong should immediately sound alarm bells and raise public suspicion over the suitability of his appointment to anything grander than official souvenir ice-cream salesman to the ANC during the week of the election.

So much for Vassen. What is far more worrying is that our Foreign Minister also saw absolutely nothing untoward in appointing a man whose integrity is less than impeccable as our consul-general to India. Not only would this have put the Indian government in a hugely embarrassing position should they have been forced to accept his tainted credentials, but it makes SA look foolish in the eyes of the world. Perhaps Alfred needs a crash course in ethics. Or could it be that we have run out of honest envoys and are now scraping the diplomatic barrel? Are we now quite happy to put the telescope to our blind eye when investigating the backgrounds of potential plenipotentiaries in our haste to reward chums of cabinet ministers with a cushy, all-expenses-paid posting to some exotic location where they won't become a nuisance in the run-up to the next election?

Remember, had it not been for a vigilant press, Boesak would have been wining and dining in Geneva at our expense these past four years. The sad thing is that, while the ANC publicly espouses honesty and openness, it continues to try to pull the wool over the electorate's eyes by attempting to rush through the appointment of spivs and charlatans to grace-and-favour positions. The ANC has also shown very little enthusiasm for the work of the Heath special investigative unit, particularly when it affects one of its rising stars.

If the ANC has run out of scandal-free candidates for ambassadorial positions, I am quite happy to devote myself to the service of my country – providing I don't have to explain the government's occasional extraordinary behaviour.

*

It must have been a strange day of mixed emotions for Liberty chairman Donald Gordon when he chose to announce his retirement.

The 17% rise in the share price of the company he founded might have been good for his bank balance but it wouldn't have done much for his ego. My reaction on a 17% instant rise in NAV would be 'bugger the ego', but then I'm not Donald Gordon.

The question is: what will he do now? My guess is that, like the billionaire Bruce Wayne of Gotham City, he will keep an identical batsuit and batmobile in London and Johannesburg and devote the rest of his life to helping Meyer Kahn defeat crime.

28 February 1999

Who's going to take a black man trapped in white skin seriously?

In one of his most extraordinary outbursts to date, Zimbabwe's President Bob Mugabe has accused Cyril Ramaphosa of being 'a white man in a black man's skin'.

Clearly, surgery is far more advanced in Zimbabwe than we realised and, for all we know, skin transplants could have been taking place up there for years.

Maybe even Comrade Bob has a soft white centre, but I somehow doubt it.

Sifting through the content of his confused and paranoiac tirade, it seems what upset President Bob most is Cyril's close association with the wicked, white-owned South African media who have been spreading all these terrible rumours about him.

It's all absolute nonsense of course. Everything is going extremely well up in Zim as any of the residents of that happy country will gladly tell you, particularly if they have the cold muzzle of an army rifle nestling against their left temple when you ask them the question.

All right, things can get a bit uncomfortable if you happen to be white, a homosexual, a farmer, a journalist, a student, an academic, a judge or any combination of the above – but that's the price you pay for achieving the greatest good of the greatest number, as that old brainbox John Stuart Mill remarked. You can't please all of the people all of the time.

And, just because Zim's Foreign Minister, Stan Mudenge, blows Z$22 000 on a dinner for eight (including some very decent Nuits St George) while the government struggles to find Z$19 000 for emergency food aid to help 7 000 people in Bulawayo avoid starvation is no reason to suggest that Zimbabwe is a confirmed basket case with a tinpot dictator in charge.

The issues are totally separate. It's like comparing apples with atom bombs. Firstly, three bottles of Nuits St George wouldn't go very far among 7 000 people. Besides, why waste good wine on starving peasants when you have the expensively cultivated palates of Zimbabwean cabinet ministers ready to lap the stuff up? To even mention this is typical of the hostile, white media who want to see dynamic, forward-looking African economic powerhouses like Zimbabwe fail.

Comrade Mugabe also rants on about the source of Cyril's wealth, suggesting that it has been handed to him in a Faustian pact by evil white business in return for his eternal black soul. 'It's not really the wealth of the majorities,' chides Bob enigmatically.

So what is the wealth of the majorities, I wonder? Presumably the stash that Mugabe has allegedly salted away in foreign bank accounts while his country collapses around him would qualify as the 'wealth of the majorities'.

When General Noriega of Panama finally became too much of a pain in the butt, the Americans sent in troops to blast him with loud music until he finally gave himself up at the umpteenth high-decibel rendition of *Born in the USA*.

Perhaps our own Foreign Affairs department could be persuaded to do the same in the interests of creating stability in the region. We could send a fleet of blue Citi Golfs with boom boxes up to Chez Mugabe and blast him out with *Glad to be Gay*. The only problem is what to do with him once he gives himself up. Perhaps Evita Bezuidenhout should sit on his lap and give him lessons in tolerance and diplomacy.

This whole matter of whether Cyril is indeed a white man in a black skin made me wonder whether I am not, in fact, a black man in a white skin.

It's terribly inconvenient of course because when I am finally summoned to appear before Dr Barmy's inquisition on media racism I will, to all intents and purposes, appear to be white and, therefore, guilty but deep inside I know there is a black man struggling to get out.

I first became aware of this when I started walking around the house humming *Ol' Man River* and switched my beer brand to Carling Black Label. I've also been watching a lot of basketball on satellite TV and saying 'Yo' to people.

The whole thing came to a head, though, when I began mowing my own lawn. From that point onwards, there was no going back and I know that, were it not for the fact that I am trapped in this lily-white skin, I would almost certainly have been invited to go fly-fishing at Whiskey Creek and have joined the board of an empowerment company. When I think about it, I must be one of the most disadvantaged members of society. Who's going to take a black man trapped in a white skin seriously?

Still, I suppose it could have been a lot worse. I could have been a black woman trapped in a white man's skin.

7 March 1999

Let's not end up with only stale ANC portions on the menu

The latest thing at the trendier sushi restaurants is to sit at a food bar while a conveyor belt brings a selection of little wooden platters to you in one long passing piscine parade.

All the platters have coloured dots on them which represent different prices. So, for example, the white dots tell you that six pieces of cucumber and rice wrapped in seaweed and cut into cubes will cost you a mere R10, while the blue dots mean two pieces of raw salmon languidly draped over a ball of glutinous rice will set you back R16. At the end of the meal, the dot values are totted up and you get your bill.

It's rather like the luggage carousel at Johannesburg International arrivals hall, except that you generally don't have to wait as long for something to come by. When you see a piece of fish you like, you take it off the conveyor belt and eat it – which doesn't take very long because sushi or sashimi normally come in small, designer portions. Two bites and it's gone. So after the first bite you are already looking at the conveyor belt again like a predatory shark and waiting for something tasty to pass by.

It may be a laborious way of eating a meal but it cuts down on waitrons and means that they don't have to spend hours explaining all those unpronounceable names to neophyte sushiphiles.

I've often wondered about the etiquette of dining in such establishments. Should one, for example, allow the last of the fatty tuna to do two laps before grabbing it, thus giving other diners a fair chance – particularly if you have already wolfed down four platters already? Is it regarded as bad form to loudly exclaim 'the swine has taken the last California roll' when the person three seats away grabs the very dish you had your eye on before it has a chance to reach you?

Is it permissible to leave your bar stool and dodge between fellow diners to grab platters before they can get their greedy hands on them? Heaven knows, it must be difficult enough to persuade most people to eat raw fish anyway without having to burden them with a whole new set of social skills.

Most South Africans are still trying to learn rudimentary manners such as turning their cellphones off in restaurants.

With the psychology of sushi, there's an absorbing new study in human behaviour – a few grand of the government's money ought to be used for a research project. For example, assertive people will tend to sit as close to the chef as possible, so that they can get first choice of what goes on the conveyor belt. This means they can eat their meals in a fraction of the time those further down the food chain can, giving them time to go and find a real restaurant. These people most likely run their own companies and are what the recruitment agencies call 'self-starters'.

The ones who take something off the conveyor belt, look at it and put it back again are poorly informed and indecisive. They are the sort of people who haven't yet applied for bar-coded ID documents or registered as voters. They are probably employed as hairdressers or newspaper columnists.

The customers who eat their sushi and put the empty platter back on the conveyor belt are clearly refugees from the Brazilian Coffee Shop and are the sort of people who go to dirty movies with subtitles, believing them to be artistic.

Finally, there are those who know that the white dots on the colour-coded platters equal R10. They drop in to the CNA before a meal and buy a packet of white dots. At the end of the meal they can be seen scraping the blue and red dots off the platters with their fingernails and replacing them with white dots before asking for the bill. They are almost certainly either visiting MECs or educationalists from Mpumalanga.

The interesting thing is that such establishments only work if there are lots of customers and plenty of choice. Three people at a sushi bar is a disaster because nobody wants to take a plate of fish which may have been going round and round for hours. If it's the only thing on the conveyor belt, you either eat it or go hungry.

Which brings me to the comparison with the SA elections. If we are not vigilant, the only choice of party on the political conveyor belt will be a lone platter of stale ANC in years to come. A strong parliamentary opposition is essential for democracy, which is why it's important to have plenty of registered voters sitting up at the bar and lots of small servings of other parties on the conveyor belt as well. You don't have to pick them but at least you have the choice.

21 March 1999

Bigger than Tom Wolfe, bolder than all the kugels in Sandton

Out to Lunch is five years old this weekend. It first appeared in *Business Times* on Sunday March 20 1994, making it older than democracy itself in South Africa. Whether it is any wiser after all these years is a matter for speculation. This is the 244th column and a quick, back-of-the-envelope calculation brings the tally of words to around 160 000. This allows for the fact that, when the column was first published, it was a niggardly 450 words long rather than the roughly 820 words of shimmering prose that currently grace this page. I am told that the average novel has 400 words on a page so this means that, placed end to end, five years of *Out to Lunch* would fill exactly 400 pages.

It took the dapper American novelist Tom Wolfe ten years to produce his latest doorstop, *A Man in Full*, and since that passes the finishing post at just under 800 pages, I can justifiably claim to be a more prolific writer than Wolfe. Or perhaps not as lazy. The only problem with this claim is that Wolfe already has his name on the spines of heaven knows how many books plus he probably gets an advance fee of several million dollars from his publisher just to pretend he's thinking about writing a new novel.

I wish I could tell you that the process of producing a weekly column has become easier over the years but it hasn't. In this case practice does not make perfect. By Sunday evening I become extremely irritable and if the column hasn't been written by Wednesday evening I break into a cold sweat and seek inspiration in a glass or two of Chivas Regal twelve-year-old. When the column first began it was written as an extracurricular activity while I was busy running a bond option company with my then business partner, who I should credit with thinking up the title of the column.

She felt that it best expressed my laid-back attitude to life; something that was to rankle a few years later. Two years ago I went on a sabbatical without first checking that the knife drawer was empty and quickly found myself with rather more time on my hands than I had expected. Like Prufrock, my life had been measured in quarterly options close-outs for ten years; now it was to be measured in weekly deadlines.

Looking back over the past five years I can honestly say the only thing that really surprised me was the fact that anyone actually wanted to read the column in the first place. If I'd been a betting man I would have given it three months at most. In those early days it was a recreational diversion which allowed a closet journalist to sound off once a week in the pages of a high-circulation Sunday newspaper and get paid for the privilege. As I hadn't the faintest idea who read the column it didn't really matter what I wrote. Then came Sandton Square. Bereft of original ideas in the second week of my first slow-news December, I penned a scathing attack on Sandton Square and its denizens.

The following week the hate mail filled nearly the entire letters column, complete with a specially commissioned cartoon of a kugel hitting me with a handbag. I received hate calls at work which I taped on the dealing room recording system and listened to for weeks after. They gave me untold pleasure.

One caller was so incensed with the article that he threatened to come over and give me a good thrashing. As I don't usually indulge in S&M with complete strangers I suggested that we meet for a drink first. The bitch slammed the phone down. I think that was the turning point in the column. Not only was I thrilled that so many people had read the article but I was incredibly elated that I had ruined so many people's Sunday mornings. It's always pleasing when somebody takes the trouble to say they enjoy the column. Critical feedback is in short supply. Minor celebrity status also has its advantages and I now get greeted by name whenever I take my films in to be developed, although I am told that I still have a long way to go before I even make the socialites' B Reserve invitation list.

Perversely, though, it's the hate mail that I really enjoy. All those letters to the editor full of righteous indignation, calling for my instant dismissal from the *Sunday Times*. That is when I know that I have hit target. Far from ending my writing career, they have normally resulted in the column being extended or moved to a more prominent position, thus demonstrating that the *Sunday Times* is in tune with readers' wishes – although it may wilfully misinterpret them on the odd occasion.

18 April 1999

Workers no-balled but illegal Zaïrean basketball players get the red carpet

Illegal immigration is a problem that threatens to undo much of what the ANC has achieved over the past five years. It's not difficult to see why we are the destination of choice, compared with most of the African continent, as disillusioned trekkers arrive from the ragbag of basket-case countries to the north of us.

In central Africa there is precious little evidence of the 'African Renaissance' that Thabo Mbeki is always banging on about. Far from improving their fresco techniques, knocking bits of marble into statues of voluptuous women and getting up before breakfast to compose a symphony like that appalling little show-off Mozart, the folk from that part of the world prefer to wander around in badly fitting army uniforms, bury machetes in the skulls of those who annoy them and look for somewhere new to loot.

It's hardly surprising that the more cerebral survivors from that part of the continent take one look at the political and economic mess their countries have become under the liberation armies and decide to head south.

Even if, miraculously, peace were to suddenly break out in that part of the world, the damage that has already been done to those countries will ensure that they remain firmly part of the Third World for decades to come.

By comparison, SA must look like the promised land.

Predictably, the locals are less than enthusiastic about the arrival of their African brothers and sisters. Unemployment is sky-high and illegal immigrants are seen as parasites who compete with the locals for jobs, land, houses and any government handout that happens to be going.

Even those who arrive on SA soil and immediately set up as street hawkers have been made to feel unwelcome. This may be because they are showing a willingness to do proper work, which many unemployed locals find offensive.

The preferred method of survival in SA is to hang glumly around on street corners asking more industrious folk for money while offering absolutely nothing in return. At least illegal immigrants understand economic reality, which is why they often turn out to be much more reliable workers than local labour.

The problem is that they are exploited as a source of cheap labour while their presence theoretically denies locals job opportunities.

Fortunately, the intrepid Department of Home Affairs is galloping to the rescue. A particularly confusing (to me at any rate) policy document called the White Paper on International Migration seems to suggest on the one hand that immigrant labour should be discouraged, while at the same time insisting that immigrant labour should be paid no less than the SA wage for the job.

The policy document doesn't appear to address the real issue of illegal immigrant labour because illegals shouldn't be here anyway. Instead, what Home Affairs have managed to do is to come up with the extraordinary suggestion that employers should be penalised for having the cheek to employ non-South Africans, even if they do so legally. It is proposed that an extra payment should be made to government which would go into a national training fund.

This raises an interesting conundrum. Will the Department of Health have to pay the Department of Home Affairs for employing Cuban doctors?

The thinking behind this policy document is rather bizarre but we probably shouldn't be too surprised, as it comes from the Department of Home Affairs. It goes something like this. If illegal immigrants are to be stopped from sapping the scarce resources of our country, they must be discouraged from coming to SA. To achieve this, we will penalise those legal foreign workers who have taken the trouble to get their work permits in order, either by making it difficult for them to enter the country in the first place or by charging their employers a levy, thereby making their labour uneconomical. (Another fine example of government stuffing around with the free market system.) When they see how difficult it is for a foreigner to legally get a job in SA, any illegal immigrant will no doubt shrug stoically and wander back to the killing fields of the Congo.

None of this would be nearly as funny as it is were it not for the fact that while the Department of Home Affairs pretends to be concerned about the problem of illegal immigration, the director-general of that department, Albert Mokoena, is accused of issuing fake identity documents to Zaïrean and Zambian basketball players.

25 April 1999

Bringing some plummy eccentricity to our desolate political landscape

Poor Nigel Bruce, the only man who can claim to have edited every one of the country's financial weeklies (with varying degrees of success it must be said), is suddenly finding out that a career in politics opens your past to unwelcome scrutiny from the rabble.

That little comment about preferring not to be served by 'some surly tribesman with his thumb in the soup and eye on the clock' has come back to haunt him.

He was writing about white teenagers taking jobs in restaurants and said their willingness to serve in the hope of higher tips was a refreshing change and easily worth 15% on the bill.

The comment and ensuing discussion of Bruce's suitability as a parliamentary candidate have appeared in virtually every local English language newspaper and enjoyed more radio air time than they deserve. Thankfully I have been without a television these past two weeks, which has given me an ideal excuse to avoid such major world issues as Yugoslavia and Nigel Bruce's opinions on what makes the ideal waiter.

However, I read in Andrew Donaldson's column last Sunday that Bruce had gamely appeared on breakfast television to sort of explain and apologise for the comment.

I'm sorry I missed it. If I had known I would immediately have hired a television for that morning only. Apparently the apology was rather unconvincing and I didn't get the impression that Bruce's heart was really in it; rather like the bit in *The Wind in the Willows* when Mr Toad (a flamboyant character not unlike Nigel Bruce) is forced to promise Badger that he will never again be tempted to drive cars at breakneck speed on the King's highway. Toad's promise is soon broken and before long he has borrowed a large shiny automobile from the car park of an inn.

I couldn't understand why Nigel Bruce decided to apologise to the media for his comment, until somebody pointed out that this is the sort of thing you have to do if you want to get elected.

One of the features of our colourless democracy is that, officially, other people are no longer funny. We are not supposed to make jokes about other races or less fortunate individuals because the poor darlings might get upset and have to go for trauma counselling. We certainly mustn't get caught sniggering at other people's racist comments, even if they are funny.

As the basis of most good comedy involves making fun of human failings and using racial stereotypes to get a laugh, I predict we are in for a lean time. Does Manuel, the unfortunate waiter in *Fawlty Towers*, really imply that all Spaniards are incompetent idiots who can't even learn a simple language like English? Of course not.

I would guess that Bruce had his tongue in his cheek when he wrote the comment but, unfortunately, that is no defence when an election is looming. The Democratic Party is obviously trying hard to attract the elusive 'surly tribesman' vote and so a public apology was inevitable.

However, I suspect that it's not Nigel Bruce's views on waiters that are on trial in the media but the man himself.

To begin with, Bruce often dresses as though he has just stepped off a grouse moor. His tweed suits are impeccably cut and he clearly favours good quality cotton shirts, silk ties and expensive shoes. Since most of our male politicians seem incapable of tying a necktie and dress as though they are off to a casual lunch in a burger bar, such sartorial style could well be seen as threatening (although Thabo Mbeki, our dapper President in Waiting also favours expensive bespoke suits and handmade shirts). Why should it be acceptable for a black politician to power dress but not for a white one to do so, I wonder?

Then there is the problem of Nigel's plummy home counties accent which appears to worry some of my colleagues in the media. Unfortunately, this is an inevitable side effect of having lunch at 44 Main Street during his time as editor of the *Financial Mail*. If you spend a lot of time with people who speak strangely you often find yourself mimicking them involuntarily.

However, it is what is being said rather than how it is being said that is important and Nigel Bruce is an eloquent and well-informed debater who promises to bring some much-needed individuality and eccentricity to an otherwise dry and desolate political landscape.

2 May 1999

Bring out the cigars for Shilowa as the invisible man says goodbye

Some time ago I wrote that Gauteng premier Mathole Motshekga's main advantage in the job seemed to be that very few whites could remember his name and so personal criticism of him would be likely to remain minimal.

Now it's time to wave goodbye to whatsisname and burnish the BMW 740i for yet another incoming premier, Mbhazima Shilowa. Three in five years is pretty good going, and at this rate of attrition many more loyal party officials stand a chance of becoming premier of a province; a giant victory for the democratic process.

As far as Motshekga goes, I know it's bad form to kick a man when he's down but as far as I know he has never really been up, and I really can't afford to wait on the remote off chance that he might stagger unsteadily to his feet before I hurl a couple of critical comments in his direction.

If there was ever an invisible man, Motshekga was he. When he became a candidate for the position of premier after Tokyo Sexwale decided to seek his fortune in the private sector, Motshekga was already being dismissed as a man who had undergone quadruple personality bypass surgery. At the time the slur was blamed on certain of the ANC leadership, who didn't approve of Motshekga's candidacy in the first place, and who were thought to be spreading vile rumours to discredit the poor man. He did, however, enjoy the support of the townships and informal settlements and was swept to power when the ANC's internal democratic process was called into question. One might have hoped this would have been sufficient incentive to finally prove his critics wrong and spur him to get on with the job. One would have been disappointed.

Even following the decidedly lacklustre performance of his social butterfly predecessor, Motshekga failed to make any impression on the political scene in Gauteng. His early days in office were plagued by accusations of fraud and corruption. Motshekga's reaction to the stories was to deny everything, and an ANC commission subsequently cleared him of the charges. That's not quite the same as a court of law clearing him of charges, and we should remember that the ANC had also doubted there was a case against the errant cleric Allan Boesak.

We should also remember that a commission of enquiry is almost always appointed by a government as a first attempt to avoid acute embarrassment to itself. It is the commission's task to come up with all the tiresome pages of waffle to support the finding that suits the government of the day. This avoids the need to appear in open court and go through all that messy business of listening to evidence and calling witnesses who may have an unpalatable truth to tell. An 'in camera' hearing in front of a 'reliable' judge is also a neat way of shaking the media hounds off the scent.

There is nothing uniquely South African about this. It is a trick that most governments try and pull on their voters when they are looking after their own miserable skins. If it didn't work nine times out of 10, they wouldn't do it.

So, despite every advantage known to mortal man, Motshekga still managed to cock up the running of South Africa's most important province and, to the great embarrassment of the ANC, leaves an office on the verge of collapse.

This is why I was delighted to hear that Mbhazima Shilowa is taking over the reins. I no longer care whether the ANC's internal democratic process has been followed in the election of new provincial premiers. All I want is somebody I can believe in to lead Gauteng.

I have to say I preferred things when he was just plain old 'Sam' because I didn't have to keep checking how to spell his name, but he can call himself 'Gonzo the giant flying ptarmigan' for all I care, just as long as he gets on with the job. And I have every confidence he will. Shilowa has had a remarkable rise through the ranks of trade unions to the mainstream of politics. He is a skilled negotiator and a man who is unafraid of confrontation. He is also aware of the economic importance of the region, and I would be surprised and saddened if he didn't use his considerable influence to help encourage new business to the province.

Most important of all though is that Shilowa seems a reasonable and personable man. Those who know him tell me he has a wonderful sense of humour, a good singing voice and an appreciation of the finer things in life. If I weren't a journo and he weren't a politician I would probably send him a Havana cigar as a welcome present.

9 May 1999

Thanks to nice Mandela and dozy Nzo for saving us from being bombed

Professor Willie Breytenbach of the University of Stellenbosch has been studying his Nostradamus and has hit us with the terrible news – World War III is scheduled to begin in June or July this year, hopefully after the men's final at Wimbledon.

This casts something of a pall over my holiday plans for the latter part of the year. The problem is that Nostradamus appears to have a pretty good track record to date. He got the Great Fire of London spot on as well as apparently predicting the existence of Napoleon, Hitler, Pasteur and the Kennedy family. Unfortunately, he is a bit shaky on financial markets and failed to predict the global market meltdown of 1987 or the emerging market crisis of 1998. He hasn't been much help on the winner of the Durban July either.

So vague are many of Nostradamus's predictions, that cynics suggest it would be possible to connect a host of other actual events to them with the benefit of hindsight or skilful adaptation to the facts. They claim that the bearded seer was nothing but an old fraud who would have been reduced to predicting interest rates for a merchant bank if he were living today. Others say that he was writing symbolically, so a month of metaphorical time might really mean a month or a year of real time. Not particularly helpful when you are trying to pinpoint to the moment which flight to take out of Europe on your final visit to the continent.

Personally, I don't think it's worth taking any chances. If Nostradamus reckons that there will be a third world war before the end of the millennium, it's probably worth giving him the benefit of the doubt and stocking up on toilet paper, tinned food and whisky at the earliest opportunity. Obviously one could afford a more cavalier attitude to such predictions back in the swinging sixties because the problem was not so immediate, but with only a few months left I'm not so sure we can afford to be cocky.

Having been forewarned by the eminent professor, you're going to look pretty daft hanging around at Frankfurt airport waiting for a plane back to

South Africa while the public address system announces that all flights have been cancelled due to the four horsemen of the apocalypse cluttering the airspace.

I'm not even sure that you can pick up apocalyptic horsemen on a radar screen, and even if you could, you can't exactly contact them on the radio and ask them to fly a bit higher because you've got a KLM jumbo taking off on runway zero nine. Flying horsemen are no respecters of aviation law.

I was rather hoping that the worst that the new millennium could throw at me was a non-functioning computer. I have already made provision for that and stocked up on HB pencils and executive pads so that I can at least keep the weekly column going.

What I hadn't reckoned with was another world war. Not that I, or anybody under the age of 60 for that matter, has much recollection of what a world war is all about apart from what we have seen on newsreels and at the movies. I sometimes wonder if that is why our baby boomer world leaders are dropping bombs on Belgrade with such gay abandon. It's all been too easy for them. Things are fine as long as nobody shoots back but when the Millennium Dome gets flattened by a bad-taste-seeking missile it will be a different matter.

It's not all bad news though. When Nostradamus talks of a world war he is clearly only referring to Europe. Down here on the southern tip of Africa we will be miles away from all the carnage and collapsing renaissance architecture. Nobody is going to bother to send a missile down here. This is partly because of the fuel considerations but mainly because Madiba has been so nice to everybody over the past five years that everybody loves us.

He even appointed Alfred Nzo as Minister of Foreign Affairs. Poor Nzo has been criticised for being dozy and having no foreign policy but, with hindsight, the man has been a star. Our foreign policy is to have no foreign policy which means that we don't swagger around the world telling countries how to run their affairs. This is actually very clever because it means that we don't make ourselves unpopular. The result is that other countries are unlikely to bomb us when they are looking around for someone to have a world war with.

The only thing that really troubles me about Breytenbach's interpretation is that, in true Hollywood style, the Americans win the war. If you thought they were insufferable now, can you imagine what they will be like in 10 months' time?

16 May 1999

Liberals should not hang their holier-than-thou washing out to dry

There is something mildly repugnant about using a public platform to tell people how liberal you are. It's rather like bragging about how much money you give to charity. Liberalism, sexual predilection and charitable donations are intensely private issues and should, I believe, be a matter of conscience and not aired for public consumption.

Personally, I would hate to be known as a liberal because it conjures up horrific images of earnest men in baggy sweaters, corduroy trousers and leather sandals listening to their collection of old jazz records. Obviously Ken Owen has no such misgivings and is proud to peddle his 'more-liberal-than-thou' platitudes every week in his *Business Day* column, 'Dropping Off'.

Just for good measure, Owen also bores us with all the tedious detail of his humble origins, no doubt to add a bit of struggle credibility. In fact, he has been tugging at our heartstrings so much over the past few weeks that he runs a real risk of metamorphosing into a one-man comedy sketch. In his next column, I wouldn't be in the least bit surprised to read that he once lived in a shoe box at the bottom of a lake and was forced to eat handfuls of gravel.

Quite why Owen thinks anyone is remotely interested in how he would have voted had he not decided to go and sun himself in the south of France in early June remains a mystery. I can only assume that, like all columnists, he was casting around for a subject for his weekly contribution and decided, in desperation, to treat readers to his reasons for defecting from the Democratic Party, adding some personal invective for flavour.

If one were to measure journalistic impact purely on the weight of a mail-bag, he obviously did a good job. Even such Democratic Party luminaries as Helen Suzman were moved to pen a few lines of protest to the editor.

Owen's main objection to the Democratic Party appears to be that it still entrenches white privilege. This, incidentally, from a man who sails a privately owned yacht and lives in splendour in an exclusive, high-security complex near the Cape Waterfront. Obviously it's one thing to support the great unshod but quite another to run the risk of the buggers moving in next door.

Neither am I particularly impressed by the patronising little anecdotes describing how, against all odds, Liberal Ken fought the apartheid establishment and uplifted black journalists during his editorship of various newspapers. Are we really to believe that, without him, their talents would have withered and disappeared?

Some years ago, when I was still involved with the financial markets, I was invited to an editor's lunch at *Business Day* hosted by Ken Owen. I recall Owen, who takes pride in his poor social skills, ignoring all his guests except one. That was a Mr Louis Luyt, who was placed next to the editor at the lunch. Owen hung on his every word rather as an adoring groupie might hang on the incoherent ramblings of an ageing rock musician. Perhaps Ken still has one more pre-election surprise for us in his column. I think we should be told.

*

I suspect that a newly minted Order of Good Hope (Gold Class) has already been couriered to Yugoslav President Slobodan Milosevic – things are still a little too explosive in that part of the world to deliver it personally.

The revelation in last week's *Sunday Times* that 'Slobbo' has been secretly sending his family's stolen wealth to SA should come as no surprise. That, at least, explains why the rand has remained relatively strong over the past few months.

What did come as a surprise was President Nelson Mandela's obviously misreported comment that Milosevic would not be refused entry to SA should he wish to seek asylum. An unlikely statement indeed for a global icon better known for opposing human injustice.

I recently met someone who is trying to get a permit to work in SA. He has been offered a lucrative job in the financial sector and would be a valuable addition to the tax net. Unfortunately, he hasn't slaughtered half a million Albanians so his application is taking some time to be processed by the Department of Home Affairs.

But at least 'Slobbo' will have private means if he arrives in the country, so we are unlikely to find him waving us into vacant parking bays or standing at a robot with a piece of cardboard bearing the scrawled words: 'Unemployed despot. Please give food, job, money. God bless.'

20 June 1999

Mute cashiers at Pick 'n Pay can talk – they just don't want to

There used to be a quiz game on British television called 'Take your Pick', the forerunner to our own 'Money or the Box'. In the original, a man with a gong came onto the stage just before the main part of the show and contestants were asked rapid-fire questions by the quizmaster. If they answered either yes or no to the questions, they were gonged out and their bodies were fed to the vultures, while more fortunate contestants went on to win lounge suites and radiograms. The simple solution would have been to take the Fifth Amendment and say nothing but unfortunately the rules didn't allow that.

For some reason I thought of this last Sunday as I was shopping at Pick 'n Pay. For years I have been under the impression that the large supermarket chains have been doing their bit for equal opportunity by employing a quota of deaf-mutes at their checkout tills. I have become so used to saying good morning and not receiving any answer that there seemed to be only two possibilities. One was that I mysteriously become invisible whenever I have a full trolley of groceries in front of me. The other was that I was dealing with a hearing-impaired person.

So on Sunday I wheeled my trolley along to the checkout and bade the young lady 'good morning'. No response, so I assumed that I had picked the eight items or less deaf-mute queue again. Everything was rung up and a figure appeared on the cash till. As she didn't say 'that'll be R96 please and thanks for shopping at Pick 'n Pay', I took this as further confirmation of her infirmity.

The poor girl just looked at me with empty eyes and held her hand out while I counted the money for her. Then, just as I was trying to remember the sign language for goodbye and have a nice day, a miracle of New Testament proportions happened.

A fellow member of staff passed by and suddenly she was able to hear again and her tongue was no longer cleaved to the roof of her mouth. I congratulated her warmly on the return of her faculties but she just gave me a blank stare.

Am I being too fussy, I wonder, or are we entitled to demand a minimum level of courtesy from shop assistants? Maybe the majority of shoppers are perfectly happy to hand over their money to a company that clearly couldn't give a damn whether or not it gets their business. Unfortunately I am still a little old-fashioned about these things, so perhaps Pick 'n Pay should have a special checkout queue for those of us who still want to interact with real people.

Obviously we must expect to pay more because it's an expensive business retraining your staff and drumming the message home that it's the customers who pay their salaries. Who knows, if there were overwhelming demand from the public for good service and politeness, supermarket chains might even consider making most of their checkout lanes customer-friendly. They could then introduce special 'no chat' lanes for shoppers who just want to pay for their groceries and get out.

I mention all this because there has been a stunning reversal of fortune in two of Britain's high street stores. Ten years ago Marks and Spencer and Sainsbury's were seemingly invincible market leaders. As the pile on the carpet in the executive suite grew deeper, management distanced themselves from their customers as they drooled over the potential profits of their share options. They were arrogant enough to believe that no one had the muscle to topple them from their position as market leaders.

Today they are busy cutting head office staff and telling this year's graduate intake there will be no jobs for them at the end of the summer holidays. Survival is the name of the game and they are concentrating on getting back the market share they have shed over the years. The problem is once you have lost your good name it takes a long time to get it back again. Sainsbury's is clearly worried about its loss of market share to Tesco's and is rather bizarrely rebranding itself by changing its corporate colours and making all its staff wear baseball caps. Whether this will improve Sainsbury's market share is impossible to say but none of it would have been necessary if management had understood in the first place that consumers have choices.

11 July 1999

You can't fish and look at a computer screen at the same time

Nobody can accuse me of being a Luddite. When compact disc players first came out in this country back in the early 1980s I was right at the front of the queue. Never mind that we only had record shops in those days and I could only find three CDs that I actually wanted to listen to.

Admittedly, I delayed buying a microwave oven for a few years but that's only because, in those days, I had rather elevated opinions on how food should be prepared; the result of reading too many Elizabeth David cook books.

I still believe most food tastes better cooked the traditional way, but I have to admit that the microwave has its uses – particularly when you want to warm damp socks or reheat the Chinese takeaway that has been on the passenger seat of the car for the past 30 minutes as you struggle home through the traffic.

When the now ubiquitous cellphone eventually came to darkest Africa, I wavered for a short while. This was partly the fault of *Sunday Times* style guru Barry Ronge, who railed against them in one of his columns, suggesting that ownership of a cellphone marked one as a person of appalling taste.

Then I saw Barry in a restaurant using a cellphone. So I applied for one, and for the past five years I have been walking around like Wyatt Earp with my cellphone on my hip in its new quick-draw holster.

Today, the cellphone has become so common that function organisers are apparently being re-educated as to how to lay out place settings for all those lavish banquets the government loves throwing. The cellphone always goes on the left of the setting between the fish fork and the side plate. I'm told that there are some people who think the side plate is actually there for the cellphone and wonder what they're supposed to do with the bread roll.

Presumably it's only a matter of time before companies like Rosenthal design a dual-purpose side plate that accommodates both bread roll and phone in separate compartments. Then it's simply a matter of remembering to put the phone and not the bread roll to your ear whenever you hear *Ode to Joy*.

I also have a nagging suspicion that much of the research linking the use of cellphones to brain tumours never enters the public domain. There's simply too much money being made by the cellphone manufacturers and service providers to have a bunch of nerdy scientists spoil it all.

When we're all walking around with great lumps on our heads in a few years time we'll realise we should have taken more notice. At least we can console ourselves with the thought that we can join in a class action and sue the cellphone companies for inadequately warning us about the health hazards.

Where my latent Luddite tendencies do surface, though, is with computers, and particularly with the Internet. A few years ago I bought a new computer system with all the bells and whistles. I have all these little icons sitting on the screen inviting me to put together a slide presentation and offering to lay out a business letter for me but do you think I can find out how to double underline something in a letter?

My main complaint is that, although my computer does all I want, it is now hideously out of date (as it was three months after I bought it) and apparently needs more megs of RAM, whatever they might be. Nobody can explain exactly why this is necessary when it's working perfectly already but apparently I can't download things from the Net unless I have more drives or bytes or whatever they are.

When I asked somebody whether I could trade in my old computer for a new one, he just laughed. But it's the Internet that really spoils my day. Every morning I have to wade through piles of e-mails written by people who probably wouldn't have bothered if they had had to set pen to paper and find a postage stamp.

Once the novelty of surfing the Net wore off, I found that it's still much easier to read things in print than on a screen. The problem with the Internet is that it is time-consuming, cluttered with useless junk and it is impossibly difficult to access useful information on it.

I detect an impending rebellion against the effects of information overload, particularly from people with enough intelligence to realise that you can't fish and look at a computer screen at the same time.

18 July 1999

Hats off to the clever people who sell water to the vain and silly

The bottled mineral water business has to be one of the great scams of our time, ranking alongside the South Sea Bubble, Dutch tulip bulbs and kubus culture schemes as ingenious ways of parting the gullible from their money.

The clever thing with the water scam though (and this is where I have to admit to a grudging admiration for the perpetrators) is that nobody has ever been persuaded to buy water because the price was likely to rise. Nobody has yet lost money buying water, and its reputation as a commodity remains intact.

In more conventional rackets, such as the Dutch tulip bulb scandal for example, greed drove the price of bulbs higher and higher because 'investors' perceived a shortage of the right sort of tulip bulb. Eventually the bubble burst and the price of tulip bulbs came tumbling down, leading to the financial ruin of many.

Because of the abundance of water, all of it looking pretty much the same, nobody was going to chase the price up, so a more sophisticated system had to be found if people were to be persuaded to pay dearly for something they could get out of a kitchen tap for next to nothing.

As we saw with our own stock exchange last year, good old human greed can normally be relied upon to drive the price of shares way beyond what they are really worth. This is known as the greater fool liquidity theory. Eventually the market is unable to sustain the hype and when no more buyers can be found, the share price plummets to more realistic levels.

This is why so many information technology shares today are trading at substantially lower levels than just over a year ago. Many private investors hadn't a clue what these companies did for a living when they bought the shares. They just thought that anything to do with computers must make money. Today they are poorer but wiser.

While greed may be a major factor when you're looking to make a quick buck, there is an even more potent one – ostentation.

This is where the bottled water people have been remarkably clever. The advantage with pandering to people's vanity rather than their greed is that the scam has a longer life. So, by convincing people that they should buy bottled water because it is better for them than tap water, they create a consumer need that was never there in the first place. Suddenly it becomes trendy to walk around with bottles of expensive designer water and, before you know it, everyone is paying a fortune for something that is delivered to most people's homes for a few cents.

All that is happening is that the various members of the bottled water industry are having a colossal laugh at our expense. Just think about it. A vast amount of money is spent on designing, producing and advertising the bottles the water comes in. It's actually the bottle that costs all that money; the contents are virtually worthless. So by buying bottled water you are at least helping the ponytails in the advertising industry to win their Loeries.

The blurb on the labels must count as some of the most creative fiction writing around. There is always a secret spring, tucked away in an unpolluted mountain range where the cool, clear water runs over the stones and, once it has been purified to remove all the rabbit turds and dead amoeba, is bottled at source for your exclusive pleasure. If they told us it was collected in leather buckets by elves and pixies, we would probably believe them.

Then there is all that pseudo-scientific information which is intended to make us believe we are getting something more than just water. Most of the people I've seen walking around with bottled water couldn't even pronounce the names of the ingredients let alone tell you why it's a good idea to be swallowing them.

But like many other consumers, I too might have been unwittingly hoodwinked by the fancy packaging, the secret spring myths and even the list of ingredients had the producers not overstepped the bounds of credibility by putting a 'best before' date on their bottles. This is the ultimate proof that they think we are all a bunch of palookas. How can something that has been on the planet since the beginning of time suddenly need a best before date? On the other hand, how can you hope to keep selling water to vain, silly people if it doesn't either go bad or out of fashion?

25 July 1999

Just one hour of Mozart and you'll be able to set your video recorder

According to a reputable international magazine, scientists have discovered that people who listen to one hour of Mozart's music experience a 10% increase in intelligence.

It always amazes me that there is a branch of science entirely devoted to such studies, and I can't help wondering why they bother and what they do with such information.

Understandably, not all scientists wish to spend their lives in laboratories cutting up small furry animals or messing about with plasma.

Those of a squeamish disposition opt for these way-out studies, either because they have a phobia about working with rats or because they love to come up with astoundingly boring statistics before telling the rest of us how to lead longer, healthier and more fulfilled lives.

It wouldn't be so bad if they didn't keep changing their minds. One moment cholesterol is bad and people are advised to avoid fatty foods. Then, before you can say *filet mignon,* another team of scientists comes up with different research saying that a certain amount of cholesterol is actually good for you and it's all that healthy rabbit food you've been eating for years which is the real problem.

Is it any wonder the poor, bewildered public haven't the faintest idea what is safe to consume and what isn't?

The only sensible course is to ignore all scientific findings relating to food on the safe premise that future studies are bound to contradict them. Then you can eat whatever you fancy without worrying.

In any case, the collective stress caused by the publication of these reports is probably far more dangerous to your health than anything you can eat or drink.

While we do at least have a choice as to what to put into our mouths, we sometimes have very little say as to what goes into our ears. So if an hour of Mozart boosts intelligence levels by 10%, can you imagine what effect the sort of music they play in shopping malls and some restaurants might have on you?

Professor Richard Head, in his seminal work *The theory of Rap: a study in futility,* suggests that the pounding rhythms and repetitious, moronic lyrics of rap songs have a numbing effect on the central nervous system.

The patient's eyes glaze and stare blankly ahead and there is spasmodic and involuntary twitching of the limbs which can be mistaken for dancing if not correctly diagnosed. Nobody has bothered to measure whether intelligence levels alter after an hour of being exposed to rap music because it probably wouldn't matter anyway.

Whether Wolfgang Amadeus really is better for your intellectual growth than a good dose of *Tristan und Isolde* is open to question. However, assuming that the scientists are correct and an hour of Mozart really does make you 10% brighter, then the obvious question is whether a longer dose of Mozart is even more efficacious.

The theory of compound accrued intelligence would suggest that it is.

Let's assume you already have an IQ of at least 130 – which is a fair assumption if you are one of those readers who regularly make it through to page two of the *Business Times*.

After only an hour of listening to Mozart your IQ will leap to 143, which is already quite impressive compared with the majority of the population. You may even be able to understand the instruction manual that came with your video recorder.

Another hour and, thanks to the system of compound accrued intelligence, you hit the 157 level. Now you are clever enough to finally realise that all designer labels on clothes are little more than an elaborate confidence trick to part you from your money.

Finally, if you can cope with the whole of *The Magic Flute* or *Marriage of Figaro* at one sitting, your IQ would soar to around 190 – which means you're probably smart enough to realise that you should have been listening to Wagner in the first place.

The only problem with all this is that, like the sun, Mozart may be fine in small doses but excessive exposure can be harmful. Too much Mozart can eventually lead to what is known as 'acute recitative syndrome', which occurs when dreary domestic conversations are carried out in a high falsetto voice to the accompaniment of a harpsichord.

22 August 1999

Three cheers to all my unsuitable drinking companions

Hi, my name is David and I'm an alcoholic. This may well come as a surprise to you. It certainly came as a surprise to me because I only found out about it last weekend when I answered one of those reader questionnaires that newspapers love to run.

I was sitting in the garden watching masked weavers drop strips of grass into the swimming pool and nursing a pre-lunch gin and tonic when a headline caught my eye: Find out if you are an alcoholic.

So I put my glass down and answered the questions as truthfully as possible. Then I totted up the score. Six out of ten yesses. If you answer yes to two, the chances are that you are an alcoholic, it said. Three or more yesses and you are definitely an alcoholic. No ifs or buts about it.

Mind you, it wasn't difficult to get a high score considering the way the questions were worded.

'Have you ever felt remorse after drinking?' Well, not only have I felt remorse but I have lost count of the times I have woken with a blinding headache and sworn that I'll never touch another drop. Yes to that one.

'Have you been in financial difficulty because of drinking?' I suppose it depends how you define financial difficulty but with good malt whisky at about R260 a bottle one has to make simple lifestyle choices; does the dog get fed this month or do I buy the whisky? I did once mislay all my credit cards after a bender and that definitely counts as a financial difficulty in my book so that's two out of 10 already and I'm well on the way to the park bench.

'Do you turn to unsuitable companions and an inferior environment when drinking?' What a bloody stupid question. You wouldn't be drinking with people in the first place unless they were unsuitable would you? And what the hell's an inferior environment?

My favourite pub of all time is the Harbour Inn in Southwold. In fact, I'm rather hoping that the afterlife is a bit like the Harbour Inn, except that the drinks are free. When I was last there the paper was peeling off the walls and the bar was so dark that the pool balls were marked in Braille, but the pints of Adnams Bitter it served were as near perfect as one could hope for. I once watched a girl roll a cigarette with one hand there and have been in love with her ever since. Highly unsuitable companions, inferior environment but great beer. Score three on the dipsometer.

'Do you crave a drink at a definite time daily?' Are they kidding? How can you possibly appreciate an African sunset without a good stiff drink in your hand? The great news is that, as it takes eight minutes for the sun's rays to reach the Earth, you can quite legitimately have a drink eight minutes earlier than the official sunset. I have to admit that I also get a bit twitchy at midday and start reaching for the corkscrew and a decent bottle of sauvignon blanc. So that's four down.

'Do you drink alone?' What's that got to do with anything I'd like to know? You can be at a bar with five people all drinking mineral water so you're technically drinking alone if you're the only one with a proper drink in your hand. I frequently drink alone, partly because it saves on the washing up but mainly because I'm too damn mean to share a bottle of good burgundy with somebody who wants to float ice cubes in it. Five yesses and my vision's beginning to blur.

Finally, 'Have you ever had a complete loss of memory as a result of drinking?' I'm ashamed to say that I have, but it wasn't really a problem because the two girls I found in my bed the next morning remembered everything. So there you have it. Six honest answers and suddenly I'm Dean Martin.

Not that I'm particularly worried. Hemingway was hardly a teetotaller and Dylan Thomas packed the stuff away. It goes with the job. If you lock yourself up for hours on end trying to rearrange words into some semblance of order for a living, you'll either be driven to drink or start talking to yourself or both.

In the celebrity world in which I now move it's a great career enhancer to be into some sort of substance abuse. Coincidentally, I had been considering getting myself admitted to a trendy rehabilitation clinic to boost my public profile, so this news comes at a good time. The problem is there's such a long waiting list. The places are already crawling with movie stars trying to cure themselves of sex addiction, washed-up rock musicians and drug-crazed 'It' girls from London Sunday newspapers.

I think I'll just pour myself another drink while I wait for a vacancy.

12 September 1999

All that jazz and open air must really disturb the human brain

Judging by the disgraceful mess the following morning, the music at last Sunday's Zoo Lake jazz concert in Johannesburg must have been pretty awful.

Why else would so many 'fans' have devoted so much energy to trashing neighbouring suburbs if there had been anything worth listening to? I thought the point of music was to soothe the savage breast.

Although the posters advertising the free concert rather naively stated that alcohol and firearms were forbidden, there was no shortage of empty bottles strewn across the lawns adjoining the lake.

They were also scattered liberally throughout the neighbouring suburbs, along with discarded fast-food containers and all the other flotsam the so-called jazz enthusiasts brought with them to the event. Predictably, most of the litter bins remained unused.

Apart from leaving the neighbouring suburbs looking like a municipal rubbish tip, the rabble parked their cars in residents' driveways, ripped up paving stones to make ramps so that they could park their vehicles on the pavement, defecated in the streets and deliberately damaged private property.

I imagine that part of the thrill of visiting something like the Zoo Lake jazz concert is that it is held at a venue close to some rather upmarket Johannesburg suburbs. This gives the less fortunate a wonderful opportunity to vent their frustrations on the house-proud larneys of the north by messing up their suburbs and making them look a little more like squatter settlements.

The real sting in the tale though is that, as usual, it's the unfortunate rate-paying residents of the affected suburbs who will ultimately have to foot the bill for sorting the mess out. I doubt whether very many of the drunken hooligans at Zoo Lake on Sunday have ever bothered to pay a municipal bill in their lives.

One of the obvious problems with inviting 60 000 people to a free concert in a residential suburb is policing. Even with the help of reinforcements drafted in from other areas, it was unreasonable to expect the already overworked Parkview police to cope with a drunken crowd in an open area.

Surely it would be better to get them all into an enclosed stadium where you can turn water cannons on should the mood turn ugly.

Another problem with choosing Zoo Lake as a venue is traffic. There is simply not enough secure parking in the area to hold a major event.

Coincindentally, another open-air concert took place at the Johannesburg Country Club on Sunday. It was an evening of classical music sponsored by Rand Merchant Bank and the interesting thing is that, although alcohol was allowed in this case, there was little evidence of drunkenness, relatively little litter and no vandalism.

The only possible conclusion one can draw from this is that while classical music has a civilising influence, jazz is more likely to lead to public disorder and probably ought to be banned on those grounds alone.

The government should appoint a commission to investigate the psychological effects of being exposed to long drum solos and tedious meandering tenor saxophone breaks.

I think they would find that the average human brain becomes confused trying to make sense of the musical disorder and, in frustration, resorts to violent and irrational behavioural patterns.

Which is precisely why jazz is normally performed before small groups of people in dingy basement clubs. A group of 50 people saying 'Wow, man, cool' through a haze of stale cigarette smoke is a lot easier to control than a crowd of several thousand sitting in the open air without all the benefits of passive smoking. All you have to do to keep them happy is play an encore.

The harsh reality is that, as an art form, jazz is clearly not suited to open-air concerts. Neither is sobriety a good accompaniment to jazz.

If the organisers of last week's event had half a brain they would have known that attempting to ban liquor was an exercise in futility.

Instead, they should have handed a free bottle of Klipdrift to every visitor on arrival and by the time the music started they would have been as meek as lambs.

By the end of the concert, a combination of liquor, the noise and the sun would have had their heads throbbing so badly that all they would have wanted to do was go straight home and sleep it off.

Then it would simply have been a matter of burying the dead and hosing the whole area down at the end of the evening.

10 October 1999

Parliamentary pin-up calendar could reveal all about ministers

It is a sad indictment of our right to privacy when a cabinet minister cannot take all his clothes off in a public place without being snapped in the buff by the prying lens of a paparazzo.

A nude photograph of Minister of Environmental Affairs and Tourism Mohammed Valli Moosa appears in the October edition of the magazine, *Out There*, apparently without the minister's permission. For some reason, the phrase 'publicity stunt' keeps coming to mind but perhaps I am being too cynical.

The magazine's new editor judiciously blamed her predecessor for commissioning the story, adding that the photograph wasn't out of keeping with the story. I suspect this wasn't the first occasion in the proud history of journalism when a story might have been written to fit the picture rather than the other way round.

The minister's office said the photograph was taken without his knowledge and rather optimistically declared the matter to be closed. Fat chance. The press don't get thrown an opportunity like this very often. I'm surprised the ANC still don't seem to understand this and spend more time anticipating trouble.

If I had been working for the minister, I would simply have explained that he was auditioning for a part in the Kosi Bay Amateur Dramatic Society's forthcoming production of *The Full Monty*. Not only would this have been the only plausible explanation but it would also have impressed the cultural lobbyists, who feel the arts are being ignored by government.

The whole affair poses some interesting questions. For example, why is somebody so keen on taking candid photographs of naked cabinet ministers? Perhaps I will be approached, when I am next in Cape Town, by a man in a grubby mackintosh asking if I want to buy dirty postcards of politicians nudge, nudge, wink, wink, say no more.

Another possible explanation for the photograph could be that the new editor of *Out There* is looking to reposition the product, as we say in the media industry.

Despite sounding like a gay contact magazine, *Out There* is a macho, testosterone-enriched publication full of gritty outdoor types abseiling down rock faces, braving rapids in inflatable rafts and bungee-jumping over crocodile-infested rivers. The magazine's appeal to the armchair traveller is the vicarious adrenalin rush it offers readers without the need for them to move from the comfort of their secure homes or risk getting the paintwork on their new Toyota Land Cruisers scratched by all those nasty thorn trees.

Maybe the editor thinks it is time to change all that and feature a hunk of the month to boost the female readership. What could be better for our new open democracy than pictures of naked cabinet ministers, photographed in attractive settings that reflect their portfolios. It would demonstrate that they really do have nothing to hide.

For example, next month's *Out There* could feature Water Affairs and Forestry Minister Ronnie Kasrils discreetly draped over the branch of an indigenous tree, holding a watering can. Then, the month after, we could have a nice soft-focus picture of Finance Minister Trevor Manuel reclining seductively on a chaise with a strategically placed three-month Treasury Bill. Perhaps the ANC could even produce a calendar of parliamentary pin-ups to rival the famous Pirelli calendars. This could even be used as a fundraiser to swell party coffers before the next election.

*

One of the problems facing government at the moment is how to instil a respect for the rule of law among people who have been allowed to run amok for the past five years.

A case in point is the Braamfontein hawkers. The Greater Johannesburg Metropolitan Council has been trying to evict them because they have finally realised that the likelihood of attracting rate-paying businesses to office properties in the area is greatly diminished when informal traders who don't pay any rates or taxes are allowed to trade from the pavement.

If the government had enforced these rules from day one, instead of pretending that it was only white whingers who objected to the new dispensation, then they wouldn't be finding things so tough now.

The equal opportunity alternative is to raze Johannesburg to the ground and allow everyone to trade freely on the piles of rubble.

14 November 1999

Bringing home the desperate elegance of real-estate speak

I haven't been in the housing market as a buyer or seller for eight years now but I wouldn't miss the weekend's property pages for the world. There I have discovered a whole new literary form known as Desperate Real Estate Speak (DesRes for short).

It is a style of writing which skilfully ignores all the stifling rules of grammar, construction and spelling while, at the same time, conveying no useful information. If only we journalists were allowed to commit the same solecisms without the interference of fastidious sub-editors, then we too could soar to the dizzy heights of creativity and mixed metaphor which I am about to share with you.

Here's an *amuse gueule* from the Cape to whet your appetite. 'Are you a flower child – artie – somewhat eccentric? Enjoy walking barefoot, lazing in a hammock? Excellent!' Believe it or not it's an ad for a showhouse, not an invitation to a Sixties-style love-in. The only way you would know is because a picture of a house costing R785 000 appears above the text.

This is a perfect example of DesRes because absolutely no mention is made of the property which is obviously aimed at cash buyers because the chances of a barefoot, artie, eccentric hammock lazer getting a bond of this size are slim.

However, it is Gauteng that runs away with the 'Out to Lunch Sac de Vomitoire Award 1999' for two of the finest examples of DesRes it has been my privilege to read over the past eight years. Both properties are in upmarket Sandhurst and carry no price tag. In other words, if you need to ask you can't afford them.

The first is: 'A melody of enchantment – as though one has tiptoed into the celebration of a Hans Christian Andersen lullaby – a cradle of fantasy swaying softly between the timbre of colonial elegance and bewitching tribal rhythm.'

What is actually being described here is a thatched house but there is no mention of the property at all; there simply isn't enough space. Apart from the fact that Hans Christian Andersen wrote fairy stories and not lullabies, I wondered how one could possibly tiptoe into a celebration of one of his lullabies. Tiptoeing into the lullaby itself would be difficult enough. And if colonial elegance has a timbre I wonder what it sounds like.

The advert burbles on about fairies dancing at night and smiles laced with candy-stripes, strawberries and quaint tradition – a potent mix. Then under a bold headline 'Wonderland revisited' we are invited to 'amble through the looking glass into Pandora's Box because only through these small windows can you visit there'. You would think they could afford doors in Sandhurst.

The term Pandora's Box is normally used to describe an attractive gift that conceals an unpleasant surprise; an unusual way to describe a house you're trying to sell. Anyway, this is a minor problem because the property is apparently 'the ultimate incantation, that weaves a spell for those whose souls have learned to dream ...' So there!

There is an enigmatic PS which tells us that 'Alice doesn't live here any more.' That, at any rate, is a relief for the new owners who no longer have to endure boorish neighbours playing 'Living next door to Alice' at three in the morning. Apparently though, someone called Julia Twigg has left her magic footprints everywhere so book the carpet cleaners.

A final N.B. invites you to 'stake your claim before the pixies steal it'. That's all we need in Johannesburg's northern suburbs – a pixie crime wave.

The second property in Sandhurst's Midlands is modelled by the 'Pygmalion of Imagination' and 'born of the early Georgian period'. That means it was built around one hundred years before Johannesburg was established. Don't worry though. If you're looking for a home that is arrogant and self-assured in its elegance and reflects a cachet that whispers but never shouts then this one's for you.

It may be a good idea to save a fortune in costs by dispensing with the agent's services and sell one's property oneself but think what a blow it would be to the desecration of the English language.

*

I owe the hadedas an apology. It's the grey louries that eat the mulberries and leave large purple streaks on the side of the car. If I had paid attention during Monty Brett's bird identification course I would have remembered the ibis beak is for digging, not fruit eating.

5 December 1999

Thanks, Claudia, you've done the free press in SA a huge favour

When in Cape Town, I have to make do with inferior tools. For reference purposes, I have a copy of the *Penguin Dictionary of Quotations*, *Roget's Thesaurus* and an edition of *Shakespeare's Complete Works* (including, I am ashamed to say, an overtly racist play called *Othello*) on the veranda table where I work.

The two volumes of the *Shorter Oxford English Dictionary* would take up valuable space on the table which is more usually occupied by the whisky bottle, tumbler, ashtray, a bowl of olives and other such accoutrements of the jobbing writer, so they sit at my feet like a pair of obedient terriers.

The dictionaries were originally published in 1933 but my revised and corrected reprint is dated 1968. Interestingly, the word 'racism' doesn't appear in the main body of the dictionary. It does, however, appear in the addenda at the end of the second volume and is defined thus: 'the theory that fundamental characteristics of race are preserved by an unchanging tradition.'

This isn't much help to me when it comes to dealing with the Human Rights Commission's report into what they insist on calling 'racism' in the media. I suspect that what they actually mean is 'racialism' but I would be reluctant to charge them with malapropism just in case they accuse me of attempting to create a negative stereotype by subliminally suggesting that their grasp of the English language is less than perfect and their educational standards somewhat suspect.

It's well documented that the meanings of words alter over time, particularly when a word is constantly misused. Eventually the linguistic purists among us throw up our hands in surrender and give in to mob rule. So racism and racialism are now regarded as the same thing – which is rather a pity because there is now no word to describe the theory that fundamental characteristics of race are preserved by an unchanging tradition.

The interesting thing about all this is that concerns about racism are evidently a fairly new thing. More to the point though, racism has become a major growth industry and it's now possible to earn a good living looking for examples of it.

Someone who has managed to do this is the Human Rights Commission's Claudia Braude who has received R80 000 from the taxpayer to report on the media and racism.

My colleagues in the media have been rather unkind to Ms Braude on the basis that her so-called independent research is little more than a load of inaccurate, pretentious gobbledegook masquerading as a serious academic study. For a mere R80 000 what did you expect?

The report on racism in the media sprung into life after a complaint from the Black Lawyers Association and the Association of Black Accountants to the Human Rights Commission last year. I'm proud to say that the *Out to Lunch* column was singled out for particular criticism, which is why I have been following the process of investigation with more interest than I would usually have devoted to such fripperies. I still hold the view that a complaint about racism from two racially exclusive groups is probably a clue that this is all an elaborate millennium hoax on the part of Barney Pityana.

You may remember that, some years ago, an unfortunate young attorney was told by the government to hold an independent inquiry into Allan Boesak when he was accused of putting his fingers in the till. She did so and conveniently found no case to answer. The response was hoots of derisive laughter from the press, shock from the Scandinavian donors and a rather different legal view from the attorney general.

I submit that poor Claudia Braude was 'used' in much the same way. She was told to go and sniff out racism and like a good truffle hound she trotted off and did just that. She could hardly come back a few months later empty handed so, in desperation, she combed through the newspapers and resorted to inventing racist interpretations for pictures of marabou storks. The fact that she has made herself a national laughing stock as a result is a sad by-product of her unwillingness to go back and tell Dr Pityana the truth.

The members of the Human Rights Commission must surely have read Ms Braude's report before they released it and it's difficult to believe that they too didn't crease up with mirth every time they turned the pages.

Claudia Braude has done a huge favour to the free press in South Africa. Thanks to her report, nobody will ever attach any credibility to a study on media racism again.

23 January 2000

Call me a chimp or a gorilla, just not a human please

It seems as though government spin doctors have been hard at work rummaging through their dictionaries since the beginning of the year.

In what seems to be a case of simian semantics, it's claimed that incoming police commissioner Jackie Selebi called a black woman police officer a chimpanzee and not, as was repeatedly reported by the press, a gorilla. I imagine Sergeant Jeanette Mothiba is glowing with pride at having been promoted several rungs up the anthropoid ladder and can now be persuaded to drop her case of *crimen injuria* against her boss.

I suspect that Neville Melville, executive director of the Independent Complaints Directorate (ICD) who handled the investigation, had trouble keeping a straight face during the proceedings. I would have doubled up with mirth several times a day at such surreal goings on, but that's probably why they don't employ frivolous people like me to do such important, groundbreaking work.

What is odd, though, is how it now seems to be the media's inability to gather the correct facts of the case that resulted in the gorilla allegation in the first place. Even stranger is the fact that nobody involved has seen fit to correct the media's deficiencies in the past two-and-a-half weeks. It was not until the official hearing that we discovered Sgt Mothiba had been dubbed a mere chimpanzee and that, according to some witnesses, no gutter language (whether in colloquial Afrikaans or not) had been employed.

The fact remains that Sgt Mothiba clearly felt sufficiently offended to take action against her new supremo, and I doubt if she would have done so had she not enjoyed the support of many of her colleagues. She has also apparently indicated her willingness to withdraw the charge if a suitable alternative manner of resolving the issue can be found. This suggests to me that Sgt Mothiba, far from being a hothead willing to launch into litigation at the slightest provocation, is a reasonable, intelligent woman who simply wants justice.

The fact that some of her colleagues seem to have developed amnesia and can't actually remember Commissioner Selebi either calling her a gorilla or using offensive language can almost certainly be put down to self-preservation. It has been made very evident that this incident has embarrassed the government, the police and the new commissioner, so why would a mere foot soldier in the fight against crime wish to say anything that might limit his or her career prospects? The ICD has even succeeded in putting a positive spin on this one by claiming that a sergeant in the SAPS feeling free to lay a charge against her commanding officer shows how far along the rocky road to democracy we have travelled; even if the case *is* tossed out.

So all's well that ends well. The commissioner is cleared of using language more befitting a Quentin Tarantino movie and the term 'chimpanzee' is ruled not to be as offensive as 'gorilla', although I would caution readers against indiscriminate use of either in the company of police officers.

It's quite possible the whole affair has been blown out of all proportion by an irresponsible media and that Jackie Selebi's 'charm offensive' was merely his own idiosynchratic way of inspiring an already demotivated police force. However, he hasn't got off totally scot-free. It has been recommended by the ICD that he go for regular counselling sessions to Safety and Security Minister Steve Tshwete who will instruct him in the correct way to deal with subordinates. One solution would be to revoke all their constitutional rights and then he can call them whatever he wishes.

*

An ancillary issue and one that has caused me sleepless nights of late is the delicate issue of 'speciesism' created by the Selebi case. If I was a silverbacked forest gorilla watching humans slaughter one other in central Africa, I don't think I would be in any doubt as to which is the more intelligent animal.

So what gives the ICD the right to decree that being called a gorilla is insulting while being called a chimpanzee is acceptable?

Are your memories so short? Have you already forgotten Max the crime-fighting gorilla? You don't find chimpanzees hot-footing it after Gauteng's dangerous criminals. All they want is to hang around drinking tea and looking cute for the camera.

Unless gorillas receive an immediate official apology, I will complain to Claudia Braude.

27 February 2000

The rule of law is dead – we are living in a taxiocracy

I received an e-mail from a retired policeman earlier this year following my comments in this column about the mayhem on the roads over Christmas.

I posed the question that if I, a mere member of the driving public untutored in such skills, could spot a taxi that was obviously unroadworthy, why couldn't the traffic authorities? I suggested that it was the government's haphazard approach to law enforcement that was partly to blame for the high road death toll in this country.

My correspondent was a police officer when the taxi industry was born in this country. Here are his comments.

'The development of the taxi industry was marked by speeding and dangerous driving to make as many runs possible from residential areas to industry or city. The process was reversed at night. The next development was to hit out at anything that held the taxis up. Other vehicles going too slowly were shunted out of the way or even shot at. Unfortunately, the good cops got caught up while trying to do their job without fear or favour and were met by hails of AK-47 bullets or rammed by the taxis they were trying to control. The taxi drivers didn't have to kill many to get the message across.

'The madness then spiralled as the number of taxis proliferated and became uncontrollable as they united into armies of racing missiles ready to destroy anything in their path.

'I know what it's like not knowing as I go to work every day whether my wife and family will see me alive again. The magic word on the road is ungovernable. Do you really believe that a few convictions for drunken driving will put things right? Good luck, mate!'

There you have it from the horse's mouth. The police are terrified of the taxi drivers because they are outnumbered and outgunned.

While I have every sympathy for these views, it does seem to me that if we can't even control a bunch of rampaging taxi drivers we would be in serious trouble should anyone decide to invade us.

If the traffic cops really have lost the battle on the country's roads, as this reader suggests, then apart from their decorative value and an occasional spell at directing traffic, there really doesn't seem much point in having them.

Boy Scouts (who all receive basic training in helping people across the road) have similar uniforms and could be used just as effectively and much more cheaply at road blocks.

As far as traffic direction is concerned, the country is blessed with many skilled people who have been waving drivers into empty parking bays for years and would, no doubt, welcome some career advancement.

The great trek by members of the National Taxi Drivers' Association just over a week ago finally convinced me that the rule of law is dead and we are now living in a taxiocracy.

Their eloquent spokesman, Themba Mghabi, has made it quite clear that his members will brook no resistance from a democratically elected government and may well have to inconvenience road users again in the near future. It seems to me that, as well as being taxi drivers, they may also justifiably lay claim to being taxidermists – they have managed to well and truly stuff the government.

Few people can have missed the wonderful photograph on the front page of a daily newspaper showing drivers lining up along the N1 to Pretoria for a defiant collective pee. Do you remember the scandal of how the Nats spent a fortune of taxpayers' money putting hundreds of toilets in the bushveld in what was then the Northern Transvaal? Nice idea; pity about the location.

It was also perfectly obvious, apart from the illegality of blockading a major highway, that many of the taxi drivers became progressively drunk during the demonstration. Media reports also suggested that some were openly carrying weapons, that other motorists were harassed and that commuters coming into Johannesburg by taxi were forced out of vehicles. All in all, a most appalling display of anarchy – and not a single arrest to show for it.

I'm not sure if I understood things corrrectly when our new Minister of Safety and Security came to office but I vaguely remember something about 'zero tolerance'. I know we already have 'The Scorpions' but maybe the police should set up another unit called 'The Maltese Poodles' who can stand by and yap a bit whenever taxi drivers decide to go on a destructive orgy.

If the authorities really are too frightened to take on the taxi industry, we are in serious trouble.

26 March 2000

Winning a better class of flying duck above the fireplace

One of the by-products of something like a national lottery is the opportunity it affords the media to write sensational and moralistic stories about money not necessarily buying happiness.

When people who have never had much money suddenly win a fortune, their lives change. If they are real spoilsports, they shun any media exposure, pay off their bonds, buy a modest family car and carefully invest the rest of the money to pay for their children's education. Hardly riveting Sunday reading.

What we all want to read about is people who win a fortune and proceed to publicly destroy themselves for our amusement. The sort of folk who, on first hearing news of the win, immediately go out and buy several cases of champagne to bathe in. Even if somebody told them that bathing in champagne was rather a disgusting experience, they would do it anyway because they think that's what rich people do every day. Just in case you do win the lottery, it's worth remembering that rich people bathe in wooded chardonnay because it's cheaper and smells nicer.

Fortified by a bubbly bath, they then appear on the front pages of national newspapers dressed in bright green Crimplene leisure suits and reveal detailed plans for the disposal of the rest of the money.

A ludicrously expensive car always features high on the list as does a holiday on some exotic island for the whole family, including mother-in-law. A move to a bigger house in an upmarket suburb is a given.

Those winners who forgot to tick the 'no publicity' box like to pretend that the money won't change their lives. Absolute nonsense! What were they doing buying a lottery ticket in the first place if they didn't want to change their lives? At such long odds you could save your money and not change your life much more cheaply every week.

There's a strong case for confiscating the winnings from such people and redistributing it to those who can be relied on to squander the money properly.

The psychological benefit of watching others win a huge sum of money shouldn't be underestimated.

Firstly, it gives us an opportunity to gloat at the vulnerability of those who suddenly come into money and do things like moving into a smart neighbourhood, innocently believing that this will increase their social standing.

Their new neighbours, on the other hand, are bound to regard them as vulgar *arrivistes* and refuse to have anything to do with them. So, in an attempt to ingratiate themselves they buy a thoroughbred race horse and keep it in the back garden. When even this doesn't work, they revert to type and just put a better class of flying duck on the wall above the fireplace.

More importantly, though, it allows us to breathe a sigh of relief that we haven't yet had the burden of winning an enormous amount of money on the lottery.

It's inevitable that a large win attracts all sorts of scumbags and eventually leads to family squabbles.

Within a month or so of hitting the jackpot some reptile from the tabloid press will have dug around and found a distant relative of yours who is barely surviving.

Just as you think you've managed to fob off the long line of pan-handlers and old friends who suddenly make contact to 'just say hello and congratulations', a headline will appear in the *Sunday Times* ... 'Heartless lottery winner pours Chivas Regal on cornflakes as second cousin twice removed queues for stale bread'.

After that you have no option but to hand out money to all and sundry, and within months you're as broke as you were before the win.

My problem with the South African lottery is that the prize money has been so paltry that it's unlikely to alter anyone's life.

Admittedly, it's early days yet but you can't exactly go wild with half a million rand. It's barely enough to buy a decent luxury car. In fact, your time would probably be better spent sitting at home thinking up new dot com names to sell or fraudulently claiming the pension of a dead relative.

The only good thing about the lottery thus far is that people who have never paid a cent of tax in this country are willingly buying tickets at odds of 14-million to one and finally contributing to government coffers.

With any luck Trevor Manuel will be able to drop the marginal tax rate again in next year's budget. Socialism does indeed move in mysterious ways.

23 April 2000

How Seffrica's crigget boss got a call at three in the morning …

Where were you when Hansie confessed? If you can't remember, make something up and memorise it for future reference. You're going to need it one day.

So momentous was the occasion that we're all supposed to recall exactly where we were when we first heard the news of President Kennedy's assassination.

I'm always a bit embarrassed about this because I haven't the faintest idea where I was on that fateful November day in 1963. Probably out riding my blue and white Raleigh Lone Ranger bicycle or shooting crows with my catapult. I was ten years old, for heaven's sake, and not wildly fascinated by American politics.

Like Kennedy's assassination, Hansie Cronje's surprise *via dollarosa* confession that he hadn't been 'entirely honest' is one of those great historical events to which we will be able to fondly hark back for many years to come.

One person who will certainly remember where he was is 'Seffrican crigget' supremo Dr Ali Bacher. He was at a KwaZulu-Natal game reserve with Percy Sonn, entertaining Australian cricket officials.

Imagine the scene. They are sitting around the dying embers of the boma fire, picking the remains of a fine wildebeest supper from their teeth and wondering whether to pull the cork from another bottle of SA port-type wine. The evening has been dominated by an animated discussion of India's appalling smear campaign on the gentlemanly game of cricket.

At two-thirty they turn in knowing that they have to get up in just over three hours for an early-morning game drive.

As Dr Bacher drifts peacefully into the gentle embrace of Morpheus, his REM sleep is rudely interrupted by the shrill call of his cellphone playing *Waltzing Matilda*. One of the Australian officials has mischievously changed the ringing tone without his knowledge. He waves aside the mosquito netting and fumbles for the switch on the bedside lamp, looks at his wristwatch and realises that he's been asleep for only 20 minutes. A mild profanity escapes from his lips. It's probably another wrong number. Being listed in the telephone directory as a doctor has its drawbacks.

Pressing the answer button, he hears the gloomy tones of Hansie Cronje at the other end of the phone.

'I haven't been entirely honest,' burbles the hapless SA cricket captain.

'Thanks for sharing that, Hansie ... do you know what the bloody time is?'

'Yes, but I couldn't sleep so I thought I should ring and tell you.'

'Tell me what?'

'That I haven't been entirely honest.'

'Rather phone a priest, Hansie. I don't run a 24-hour confessional service and certainly not at three in the morning. Goodnight Hansie.'

Bacher turns off his cellphone but not before changing the ringing tone back to *Nessun Dorma*, plumps the pillow and tries to snatch a couple of hours of shuteye before his early-morning game drive call.

At six o'clock exactly he is awoken by the sound of a light knocking at the door. Half an hour later he is bouncing uncomfortably through the African bush with his antipodean guests in an open Land Rover, eagerly searching for signs of nocturnal savagery. Suddenly Bacher remembers the events of the previous night and turns to Percy Sonn.

'Would you believe it, Percy, Cronje phoned me at three in the morning to tell me he hadn't been entirely honest ... three in the morning, I ask you. Sometimes I wonder about that boy.'

'Are you sure it wasn't John Berks doing one of his hoax radio calls?' asks Sonn.

Suddenly their nostrils are assailed by the acrid smell of a decomposing carcass. 'Jeez, who's dropped their breakfast?' says one of the Australians, lapsing into the colourful argot of his native land. In the sky the vultures are already circling and a black-backed jackal is tearing at the flesh of a recently killed springbok.

'Hard to say what brought him down,' says the game ranger. 'He might have just run into a low thorn branch during the night and broken his neck. The interesting thing, though, is that within a few days there'll be nothing left of him. The vultures will have stripped his flesh, the hyenas will have crunched his bones and the ants will do the rest. The smell will have completely disappeared and you won't even know there's been a kill.'

On the branch of a nearby acacia tree, a pair of Indian mynahs cackle happily to themselves.

7 May 2000

It's unutterable. It's unintelligible. You guessed: it's SA's new motto

!KE E: /XARRA //KE ... No, this isn't the secret formula for something toxic that Dr Wouter Basson dreamed up in his apartheid laboratory. Neither is it a bad typographical error or even the work of a malevolent sub-editor.

That gallimaufry of seemingly random letters and jumbled punctuation marks is the country's new motto. The reason you probably don't recognise it is because it's written in an extinct language which means little to anybody, apart from a handful of academics. The people who originally used this language are, according to newspaper reports, long gone.

I think it's safe to assume that the country's new motto will go largely unappreciated by the majority of the population, most of whom speak one of our 11 official languages, which don't happen to include the language of the !Xam people, beautiful and lyrical though it may well be.

This is a great pity because I would have thought that the whole point of a country having a motto is that it should be pithy enough for all its citizens to remember and quote in times of exigency.

To go to the trouble of designing a new coat of arms only to add a motto that few people will understand strikes me as a piece of inspired perversity. What else can you expect from politicians? In fact, the new motto epitomises the attitude of most politicians, which is: the less we understand, the better.

We are told that the words of the new motto loosely translate as 'Diverse people unite' or 'People who are different join together' but, with respect, we only have the academic's word for this. The !Xam language is even deader than Latin, and for all we know the cunning linguists may have played a practical joke on us and we could be walking around with the !Xam equivalent of a blonde joke on our new escutcheon.

Surely it would have made more sense to have a motto in a language that most of the nation could at least recognise and pronounce. And that's another thing. It hardly trips off the tongue.

I'm prepared to bet that if you were to ask our politicians to read the country's motto aloud the majority wouldn't have a clue how to pronounce it.

So we have a motto that is both unintelligible and unpronounceable and the only thing I haven't managed to find out yet is how much this folly cost the taxpayer.

Not that the crest itself is much to get excited about. Two San figures apparently having an arm-wrestling match doesn't make much sense to me, and if the motto really means 'Diverse people unite', why do they look like identical twins?

And what the hell is that startled winged creature at the top, just under the spiked orange party hat? It looks like an eagle having a bad hair day, but I'm told it's a secretary bird with uplifted wings.

According to President Thabo Mbeki, this is a bird which 'slays serpents and thus protects us against those who would do us harm'. According to Roberts's *Birds of Southern Africa* (6th edition) however, serpents make up less than 1% of its diet. It feeds mostly on insects and is particularly partial to grasshoppers. If grasshoppers are not on the menu it will make do with rodents, lizards or baby birds. So what the president probably should have said is: 'It slays grasshoppers and thus protects us against those who would hop all over us.'

The good news is that the secretary bird is a high-flier, but only when it can be bothered. Most of the time it sits doing nothing or wanders around on the ground looking for something to stamp on and eat. Hardly an inspiring symbol for the country. Maybe we should swap it for a peregrine falcon, a bird of prey that combines good looks with the ability to kill its prey in flight while plummeting through the air at speeds of up to 380km/h, which is a good deal more impressive than stamping it to death on the ground.

Then there's that thing that looks like a multicoloured pyramid hanging around the secretary bird's neck. What can it mean? Don't let anyone tell you it's supposed to be a protea. An artichoke possibly, but certainly not a protea. Maybe those pyramids and inverted pyramids which make up the design are symbolic of the country's convoluted bureaucratic structures.

Before long, our new crest with its gobbledygook motto will appear on all official stationery. It will be painted on the President's brand new R300-million jet and on the sides of our fleet of VIP limousines. It won't appear on hospital linen or school textbooks, though, and for a very good reason.

Government doesn't have money for hospital bed linen or school books because it's too busy pampering its ego.

14 May 2000

Those jolly good days when the colonies knew their place

When I was at school most of the map of the world was coloured pink. The parts of the world not coloured pink were known to be inhabited by garlic-munching foreigners and heathens and, therefore, to be avoided at all costs unless you were either a missionary or a properly accredited explorer.

The non-pink areas also included those vast, inhospitable land masses occupied by bears, penguins and communists.

The US wasn't coloured pink simply because it was still a renegade, mongrel nation trying to establish its own identity in the world.

It was a time when five shillings (25p in the new money) could buy you a dollar. The expanse of water which separated England from the US was known disdainfully as the herring pond and anyone who seriously considered emigrating there was either assumed to be mad or suspected of being a fugitive from justice.

In those days the Americans wouldn't have dreamed of going to war without first asking the permission of the British prime minister.

Now the pink parts of a world atlas probably indicate gay-friendly tourist destinations, but in those days they represented the British Empire and thus, the civilised world.

The first lesson we ever learnt in geography was that the pink bits were 'ours'.

The reason that other parts of the world atlas weren't coloured pink was simple. British explorers had already visited those areas and decided that they simply weren't worth having. Either that or the Spanish had got there before us.

We were taught to be very proud of the Empire. One patriotic pupil even went to the trouble of cutting out all the countries coloured pink, redesigning his own perfect world by pasting them on the inside cover of his school atlas.

The basis of colonialism has been much maligned, but the whole point of the British Empire was to share the benefits of civilisation with those who hadn't had the good fortune to win first prize in life's lottery by being born English. Being invaded and made a member of the British Empire was a sort of a consolation prize.

No sooner had the Union Jack been run up the newly installed flagpole than the natives were busy learning exciting new skills from their benevolent masters. Things like how the teapot should be warmed *before* the tea is added and boiling water is poured on top. The art of shoelace tying was spread throughout the colonies by the British and the now ubiquitous umbrella was introduced to grateful subjects who, for centuries, had been using gigantic leaves to protect themselves during tropical downpours.

If there was any sign of insurrection in the colonies, the governor-general would ask the British government for a gunboat or two to be sent to sort the problem out. This proved difficult with some of the landlocked countries in the portfolio so, instead, malcontents would be locked up (for their own good) until they saw reason.

Much of the unhappiness sprung, no doubt, from minor outbreaks of ingratitude and the extraordinary delusion that home rule would be a nice idea.

However, once people were told how lucky they were to be part of the British Empire and to have a small share in a monarch who rode around in a solid gold coach back in London, they usually counted their blessings and made a nice pot of tea.

Sometimes the king or queen would come over and see how their subjects were doing in their far-flung colonies. The people would be issued with little Union Jacks and lined up in the hot sun for hours. They were carefully instructed to wave the flags only when they saw a black Rolls-Royce with no number plates coming towards them.

As there weren't many unlicensed black Rolls-Royces to be found in the African bush, this proved a fairly simple instruction to follow.

These days the map of the world looks more like a patchwork quilt.

The emotional and monetary cost of being kind to people who clearly didn't understand the *quid pro quo* of being part of the Empire (such as giving up the more fertile pieces of land and handing over the mineral rights) finally took its toll and the British very magnanimously allowed parts of their Empire to break away and rule themselves; initially under careful supervision to make sure they didn't cock things up.

The most hurtful thing, though, is that, having introduced the game of cricket to them, Britain's former colonies rarely allow them to win.

28 May 2000

No, I'm not just gazing at your breasts, I'm working out

I have never really been a fitness enthusiast. The whole business of falling out of bed early in the morning, driving to a health club and trying to find an empty parking lot before searching for a free cycling machine holds very little appeal and must surely rank as one of the more stressful ways to start one's day.

I'd much rather get up at a civilised hour (7.30 works for me), take a leisurely bath and enjoy a good high-cholesterol breakfast. Two fried eggs, plenty of grilled Thrupps' bacon and several cups of strong Columbian coffee followed by a small cigar while I listen to the news and contemplate how to fritter away the rest of the day. An occasional half bottle of champagne at breakfast is also good for the soul.

I realise that, according to common orthodoxy, this isn't considered a particularly healthy lifestyle, but it evidently works for me.

I have friends who religiously set off for a health club every morning, come rain or shine, to work up a sweat.

Others, who realised long ago that they don't have the necessary willpower to make it to a gym every day, employ their own personal trainers who arrive at their homes just as they are rubbing the sleep from their eyes to put them through all sorts of physical torture. I assume it's worth all the effort and expense.

With one or two exceptions, they look slim, healthy and fit and they clearly have lots of endorphins charging around inside their heads.

However, according to completely impartial observers, I also look slim, healthy and fit and I haven't been inside a gym for years. I realise that this must be extremely irksome for all those platinum-membership, lycra-clad clones who spend hours every week dancing to the thumping primeval beat of an aerobics class, but that's just the way it is. I originally thought that I was simply one of those fortunate people who possess a maintenance-free body but, thanks to exhaustive scientific research, I am delighted to learn that I have been working out for years without knowing it.

According to the *New England Journal of Medicine*, just 10 minutes spent staring at the charms of a well-endowed female is roughly equivalent to a 30-minute aerobics workout.

Gerontologist Dr Karen Weatherby (may the Lord bless her and keep her) and fellow researchers at three hospitals in Frankfurt, Germany, reached this wholesome conclusion after comparing the health of 200 male outpatients.

Half of them were instructed to look at busty females every day with the other half told to refrain from doing so. How they managed to resist temptation we are not told.

The study revealed that, after five years, the breast gazers had lower blood pressure, slower resting pulse rates and fewer instances of coronary artery disease.

'Sexual excitement gets the heart pumping and improves blood circulation,' explains Dr Weatherby.

'There's no doubt about it, gazing at breasts makes men healthier. Our study indicates that engaging in this activity a few minutes daily cuts the risk of stroke and heart attack in half. We believe by doing so consistently, the average man can extend his life by four to five years.'

So there you have it. Based on this research, I calculate that I have been working out for a minimum of 10 hours every day since puberty – which obviously explains the slim, healthy body not to mention the permanent beatific smile on my face.

While this research may come as great news for sedentary perverts, it hardly underpins the feminist cause, and it's all the more surprising that the head of the research team is a woman. The sisters won't be pleased.

'Have you any idea how disconcerting it is to have a man's gaze fixed on your breasts while he's talking to you?' asked one of my female colleagues as I began another strenuous 30-minute aerobic workout.

It's a dumb question. Unless you have breasts, you've obviously no idea what it's like having people stare at them.

Men evidently believe that women should feel flattered that we enjoy gazing at their breasts; particularly now that science has revealed that we're only doing it for health reasons, which also explains the heavy breathing during the workout and the occasional pulled muscle.

Men now have no business hogging the rowing machines and the cycle machines at the gym when all they need to do is hand the machines over to the women and watch their breasts while they exercise.

If Dr Weatherby is right, they can even finish their usual workout in a third of the time.

04 June 2000

Need advice? Statingthebloodyobvious.com will set you straight

I am no Faith Popcorn but I can't believe it can be that difficult for a moderately intelligent observer of the human condition such as myself to accurately identify future trends.

As a matter of fact, I've been doing so with spectacular success for years. Readers of this column will recall how I correctly predicted that socialist politicians purporting to represent the poor would still want to drive around in expensive luxury cars.

Admittedly, I didn't predict at the time that their wives would also expect the taxpayer to provide them with transport or that the rules of the game would allow anyone with more than one wife to have a free car for every wife. Surely this presents something of a dilemma. Do you simply marry a new wife whenever you want a new car, and which comes first, the initial flush of love or a new product launch? Maybe its time to re-work the lyrics to that old Nat King Cole song: 'When I fall in love, it will be for Rover.'

The only problem is that, unlike Faith, I never bothered to package my extraordinary insight and sell it to companies as in-depth research. To be absolutely honest, I didn't think anybody would be particularly interested in paying enormous sums of money for what was little more than expensively wrapped common sense, but this is clearly one trend I missed.

That's all about to change, though, and one prediction I can confidently make is that La Popcorn should start looking around for something else to occupy her time.

It's all about branding, of course, and once the *Out to Lunch* column becomes known as the mouthpiece for an infallible trend-spotting consultancy, I shall make my fortune and buy a wine farm in the Cape. My research already tells me that there is a potentially huge market for a dry style muscadel/pinotage blend among new wine drinkers.

I'm even thinking of starting a dotcom company called 'Statingthebloodyobvious.com' and listing it globally. By my calculation I should have about three weeks to milk all the shareholders' funds and divert them into my personal bank account in Sierra Leone before somebody starts questioning whether I will ever be profitable. This is known in the new economy as an exit strategy. You might have thought that investors would have learnt their lessons by now but my research tells me that, providing I tell analysts that I have no idea when I will break even, let alone become profitable, then there is a good chance my IPO will be a massive success. The less you tell the punters the more they want to buy your shares. That is until somebody spoils it all by selling their shares and taking profits.

The inherent strength of 'statingthebloodyobvious.com' over the competition is its courageous departure from conventional wisdom and its unique research facility. Instead of sending out lots of carefully worded questionnaires to a scientific sampling of style gurus, I prefer to take people to bars, buy them a drink and say something like: 'So what do you think of all this e.commerce crap then?' carefully avoiding any temptation to influence the results.

On the basis of exhaustive research I can now predict that the writing is already on the wall, not only for e.commerce but for technology as a whole. We (the corporate 'we' that is) have identified a strong build-up of public resistance to the idea of buying on the Internet. People are also fed up with spending money on things like cellphones or hand-held computers only to find that their unique features have a shelf life of about three months before a cheaper and even more sophisticated model hits the market.

Over the years consumers have been systematically robbed of quality experiences such as queuing only to find that the shop hasn't got what they want in stock.

Supermarkets have reduced the art of shopping to a mindless amble through pre-packed aisles. Not only are most supermarkets well stocked … they are overstocked, and the bewildering choice available is befuddling our simple brains.

E.commerce is even worse, with the added disadvantage that it removes all the sensory attractions of shopping such as taste, smell and feel.

Which is precisely why the trend will be away from convenience and towards specialist shops where you can taste the cheese, smell the coffee and tell the assistant precisely which Danish pastry you want.

And if they don't have what you want you can always order it over the Internet via your WAP cellphone.

11 June 2000

Exclusive: Satan says he was less than honoured by Hansie's slur

I was sitting quietly at home last Sunday, reading the instruction manual for my new do-it-yourself home colonic irrigation kit when the telephone rang.

'Is it possible to speak to Mr Bullard,' said a man's voice.

'Eez possible but who vant to spik vith him?' I asked the caller in what I hoped was a faultless Novokuznetskian accent.

'Ah, Mr Bullard,' said the caller, 'a commendable attempt to deceive me but a real Novokuznetskian always snorts at the end of a sentence. Anyway, now that I have your attention let me introduce myself. My name is Satan and I have a small favour to ask you.'

I was a little miffed, not only that the caller had so easily penetrated my vocal camouflage, but that he was now also on the verge of asking a favour from a complete stranger.

'Have we met?' I asked irritably.

'As a matter of fact we have,' said the lugubrious voice at the other end of the phone. 'It was at a party in Pimlico in 1979. I was the short red-faced guy with the corduroy jacket who persuaded the girl you had brought to the party to come home with me instead. You probably knew me as Lou Siffer back then.'

As it happened, I did remember Lou. His persuasive chat-up lines and smouldering looks had earned him an enviable reputation for getting off with other guys' girlfriends – a sort of Mick Jagger with dress sense.

However, he was also famous for throwing wild parties in his spacious Fulham flat. Lou was serving hot spicy food long before Thailand was officially discovered by the foodies. He made everything with extra chilli, including banana milkshakes.

His parties were always raucous. A neighbour complained about the noise once and the next day she spontaneously combusted outside Habitat in the Kings Road. Naturally, the IRA were blamed.

Miraculously, the booze never ran out at Lou's dinner parties. When stocks ran low he would dash into the kitchen, fill an empty wine bottle under a cold water tap and emerge triumphant with yet another fine claret. We never did find out how he did it. Whenever we asked him he would wink and say it was an old trick he had learned years ago, just before he got expelled from whichever educational establishment he had attended.

'Nice to hear from you again,' I said unconvincingly, 'what have you been up to lately?'

'Oh, a bit of this and and a bit of that,' Satan replied nonchalantly. 'I had extensive business interests in Eastern Europe a couple of years ago and my new company, *snatchedsouls.com*, has performed successfully in Africa. We've been doing very well in Sierra Leone and the Congo and have just expanded into Zimbabwe where business is, I have to say, looking terrific. I'm hoping to open a branch in Cape Town soon.'

'Great,' I responded unenthusiastically, 'so what's this favour that you want from me?'

'Well,' said Satan, 'apparently someone called Hansie Cronje has blamed me for the fact that he received unspecified amounts of money from Indian bookmakers. I've thought of suing for defamation but, believe it or not, I can't find a lawyer who will represent me. So I want you to put the record straight in the *Sunday Times*.

'Firstly, I've never met this Cronje guy in my life and certainly never told him to throw cricket matches. If stories like this get around it's only a matter of time before the English start blaming me as well and, as everybody knows, they're quite capable of losing without my help.

'Secondly, the suggestion that I am somehow to blame for Cronje's crookery is bad for business. I'm losing respect down here. The other devils say I have lost the plot and have already got their eyes on the top job. Here I am, trying to overthrow the powers of good, and I get dragged into some squalid little sporting scrap just because this Cronje guy can't wisely exercise the free choice he's been given. I've got bigger fish to fry and if people think I'm fooling about with small fry like Cronje then bang goes my credibility. I only deal in wholesale evil. I don't fanny about with retail clients like Cronje. His problems have got nothing to do with me and I want you to let your readers know that I am very upset at this slur on my professional reputation. I might even erupt a volcano under Fancourt.

'Do this one small thing for me, Mr Bullard, and I will make sure you are voted *Style* magazine's man of the year. Trust me, I've got fiends in high places.'

2 July 2000

Sharp marketing needed to make kugels want to chat about DNA

I fear that the importance of last week's announcement that scientists have deciphered nearly 90% of the three billion letters that make up the human genetic code might not have had the earth-shattering impact on the rest of humanity that the boffins had hoped for.

Give us a cellphone that can order 20 different varieties of pizza and we immediately see the benefits to mankind. Befuddle our under-utilised brains with big numbers and the complex notion that you can somehow map the individual DNA make-up of every human being and we don't get nearly as enthusiastic.

Scientists may have declared that they have 'read the book of mankind', but the rest of us are happy to wait for the movie.

It was probably ever thus. The invention of the wheel (with which this latest discovery has been compared as one of the great moments in man's long trudge to the twenty-first century) was also something of a damp squib among the riff-raff when it was announced by triumphant scientists.

Comments like: 'We've managed quite well without one so far' and 'I can't see any future for it and, besides, you have to balance something else on it first for it to really be any use' were heard emanating from the dank caves of doubting Luddite Neanderthals.

It wasn't until the marketing men got hold of the idea that people really sat up and took notice. It was only once the general public had it explained to them that round rocks roll downhill better than square rocks that they began to wonder how they'd ever managed without one. They started filling the wheel order books only to discover, to their chagrin, that nobody had yet invented the wagon.

Explaining the immediate benefits of The Human Genome Project may not be quite as straightforward.

If scientists could come down from their ivory towers for a moment and convey the significance of this discovery in language that most of us understand, they would have a much better chance of grabbing the public interest.

Get a decent advertising agency on the job and within days practically everyone would be fired with enthusiasm for all this stuff about secret information locked away in our 23 pairs of chromosomes. We'd soon be talking of little else.

Sandton kugels would linger over cappuccinos bragging about their guanine and cytosine and comparing the spiral staircases of their DNA.

If the boffins had told us that this discovery compared with the arrival of McDonalds in South Africa or the launch of a new BMW, we would have had a better grasp of how exciting it really is. But comparing it to man's landing on the moon is pointless because, as far as the majority of the world's population is concerned, man has always been able to land on the moon. The pre-lunar generation are now into their fifties. Space travel is no longer a big deal unless we happen to discover a planet with three-headed creatures on it. In which case somebody will immediately get the rights to merchandise the discovery and rush out three-headed creature dolls just in time for Christmas.

That, sadly, is probably the extent of our wonderment these days. To a generation weaned on dull repetitive music, junk food and fizzy drinks, things like pondering the size of the galaxy simply use up too much brain energy to be considered a worthwhile activity.

The only thing that makes me a little cynical about this whole genome business is how it was suddenly announced last Monday. It all looks rather stage-managed, which probably has something to do with the need for further funding. If they had mapped 100% of the human genome then that would have been something to crow about but, by their own admission, this is only a 'working draft'. It's a bit like claiming to have finished a jigsaw puzzle when there are still bits of sky missing.

According to my man in the lab with the bubbling test-tube, one of the problems with deciphering our DNA coding is that there is a lot of residual information among that sequence of three billion letters that we no longer need.

This 'junk DNA' is a bit like a dormant file on a computer and contains outdated information on things like how to walk upright and tactics for avoiding sabre-toothed tiger attacks.

So the scientists still have to wade through the rubbish and come up with an infallible DNA readout. Then it's A for Away.

Instead of lengthy hearings before something like the King Commission, we will be able to plug a machine into people like Hansie Cronje and discover that they were genetic scoundrels all along.

9 July 2000

Clear up the cockpit clutter and we can all become Biggles

Have you ever been down the sharp end of a Boeing 747 and taken a look around? Next time you're flying do yourself a favour. Pretend to be an unaccompanied minor and ask one of the cabin crew if you can visit the cockpit so you can sit with the captain. Apart from the clutter of throttle levers, pedals, steering columns and what have you, there are dials and screens all over the place – even more than in Jackie Selebi's new BMW 740i.

Admittedly, most of them are duplicates but this isn't just to impress the riff-raff. It's because the pilot and the co-pilot (they're the guys with the open textbooks on their laps) each need to know what's happening. So, if the pilot eats the poisoned bobotie during the flight and pegs it, the co-pilot can take over the controls (unless he's also eaten the poisoned bobotie), land the plane and no one will know the difference.

Heaven only knows what all those dials are for. After all, an aircraft can only go up, down and forward so you would think you would only need a dial for each of those; one for speed, another for height and maybe a rev counter. Oh yes, and an oil and petrol gauge, of course. That's eight dials maximum, which is quite enough for anyone to remember to keep an eye on.

With all this extra stuff to learn is it any wonder that aspirant aviators have to buy leaked exam papers to get their pilot's licences?

As if that isn't bad enough, there are switches and buttons everywhere, including on the ceiling. What they all do is anybody's guess. The question is, are they *really* necessary? There are suggestions that Boeing deliberately put in all these switches and buttons just to make the pilot's exams more difficult to pass.

For example, there is a panel of switches situated between the pilot and co-pilot which is considered essential equipment on any international flight. If you don't fully understand their function and when to operate them you can never become a qualified pilot.

On the extreme left is the 'instant simulated turbulence control'. This is one of the aircraft's multi-function switches and when activated it flashes on the 'fasten seatbelt' sign and plays a pre-recorded tape telling passengers to return to their seats before violently throwing the aircraft about. This, as any frequent flyer knows, happens as soon as all passengers have a full cup of hot coffee on their tray table. The cabin crew press a secret button in the galley when they've finished serving and the pilot does the rest.

Next to that is the 'acrid smell of microwaved vegetables switch'. This is turned on when the aircraft reaches its cruising height and just before the main meal is served. It connects to the aircraft's air-conditioning system and pumps the smell of cabbage down the aircraft. It's supposed to make you look forward to your meal but it generally has the opposite effect.

Unfortunately, once the 'acrid smell of microwaved vegetables' switch has been activated there is no way of getting rid of the stench during the rest of the flight apart from making an emergency landing, opening all the exits and letting fresh air blow through the aircraft for at least 24 hours.

The third switch is the one the flight crew use to interrupt the video and audio programmes just as the good bit is about to come on. A sequence of warning lights flash on the dashboard and the pilot and co-pilot can then pause the tapes at exactly the right moment to make a pointless announcement. 'Good evening ladies and gentlemen, this is the first officer speaking from the flight deck. For those of you who are interested, you can just see the lights of Maiduguri on the left of the aircraft.' Of course, nobody *is* interested but if he isn't allowed to sleep at three in the morning he doesn't see any reason why anyone else should.

After the pointless announcement the video programme sputters back into grainy life and the sound returns a minute later. The audio tapes skip the comedy sketch you've been trying to listen to since the flight began, which means you have to stay awake for another hour to hear it.

There's also a switch called the 'numb bum' control which makes all the seats go hard after five hours and another that blows a special gas onto your feet and makes them swell so that you can't get them back into your shoes when you land at Heathrow.

The good news is that the 'cash for pilot's licences' scandal is bound to finally expose how few of the instruments in a jumbo jet are essential. Make the cockpit simpler and we can all follow our boyhood dreams, pass the exams and become Biggles.

6 August 2000

In-between Hansie duty, Satan finds time to corrupt Harry Potter fans

I think it was the crudely drawn chalk pentagram in the playground of the local junior school that first confirmed my worst suspicions.

Later that week I was driving through the suburbs on neighbourhood watch with a friend.

The idea of neighbourhood watch is to make sure the criminal element knows there is a law-enforcement presence in the area. A flashing amber light on a bakkie with two overweight, middle-aged men in it apparently scares the hell out of them and they go and steal cars somewhere else.

If we see something suspicious, we're supposed to radio back to the police station. The theory is that a back-up squad car will roar up and arrest the miscreants. This is a nice idea but, unfortunately, not many of the radios work these days and there's no money to repair them. So we use cellphones instead, which is a lot easier because you don't have to say 'papa charlie to papa victor, do you read me, over' into a cellphone.

The situation is even worse with the police patrol cars because there aren't enough of them to go round. Even if there were, the police budget doesn't extend to filling them with petrol and they would probably run out of fuel before they arrive at the scene of a crime. So, if we see something suspicious while we're out on neighbourhood watch, we drive past very slowly and fix any dodgy characters with our 'I know what you're up to mate' look. I doubt if it has any effect, but we like to believe that we're doing the best we can in the circumstances.

Anyway, we were driving slowly through the leafy avenues of the northern suburbs of Johannesburg and had just turned a corner in Parkhurst to see about a dozen cats scuttle under a parked Landcruiser. At that point we had no idea that they could be witch's familiars.

However, later that same evening we heard the sound of sombre chanting coming from an area of open veld near the river. We turned off the car's headlights and drove slowly towards the diabolical noise. Suddenly the smell of sulphur and brimstone assailed our nostrils and we saw small hooded figures dancing around a gigantic bonfire.

There was a rumble of thunder and a massive cloven hoof thudded into the dry Highveld dust near the car. We looked up to see the gigantic figure of a goat with green blazing eyes wearing a grubby T-shirt with the words 'I Love Hansie' on it.

The horrible creature moved slowly towards the bonfire as a huge throne made up from what appeared to be the writhing, tortured bodies of damned souls materialised in front of him.

Satan (for it was he) sat on his monstrous throne and surveyed his loyal subjects for a few minutes, the stench of his demonic breath withering the branches of the surrounding trees.

Finally, he spoke. 'I'm glad to see you've been reading your Harry Potter books, children. Have you all finished the new one yet?'

There was some muttering from the dark lord's vassals and the hood fell from the head of one of the figures to reveal a neighbour's 11-year-old daughter. 'I had to help my mum do the shopping so I haven't managed to finish it yet, Mr Satan.'

'No excuse,' roared the evil one. 'You're not supposed to do things like help your mother with the shopping. Remember who it is you serve. Finish the book by next week because there'll be a test and you need 80% to pass. Anyone who gets less winds up as a virgin sacrifice at the next sabbat ... you are *all* still virgins, I hope? OK kids, any questions? If not, there's a table full of burgers, chips and diet coke over there and some Sony playstations to keep you amused until bedtime. If you'll excuse me, I've got to dash. No peace for the wicked. I've got another meeting with the South African Cricket Board at midnight.'

There was a roaring wind and the dry winter dust rose up like a red curtain and then settled again and the devil was gone.

The children had folded their satanic garb neatly away and were now dressed in designer takkies, t-shirts and baggy shorts.

'Hey, that was kif,' said a boy who had just cast a spell on all the garbage bags in the road which were now marching obediently to a central collection point. 'Certainly beats watching *The Carruthers Brothers* on a Wednesday night, doesn't it?'

'What amazes me, though,' said an attractive girl who had just bitten the head off a gekko, 'is that we would never even have known about the dark significance of JK Rowlings books if we hadn't read the letters page in the *Sunday Times* a few weeks ago. Just think of the fun we would have missed.'

13 August 2000

New evidence that talk is cheap in the President's office

I was paging through last Sunday's *Business Times* Appointments section desperately looking for a real job when an interesting advertisement caught my eye.

Just below our new national crest with its unintelligible motto and the proud words 'the Presidency: Republic of South Africa' was an invitation to apply for the position of Director: Media Liaison. Duties would include drafting and issuing media statements, and organising and conducting press conferences, media briefings and interviews. A bit like those smooth guys at The White House who stroll up to the lectern and answer questions on behalf of the American President. Clearly a powerful position and one that could easily lead to greater things, particularly for someone with a Machiavellian disposition.

After all, as spin doctor to *Le grande fromage* himself, here would be an ideal opportunity for a bit of public image enhancement. It would be difficult to resist the temptation to throw in the odd personal observation during press conferences or to drop some occasional juicy gossip to your favourite hacks in return for a long drunken lunch.

Before you know it you're leaking a secret policy document here, suggesting that the President is deeply unhappy with so-and-so there, and pretty soon you're the second-most powerful person in the country, getting invited to Dali Tambo's parties.

The power to disrupt journalists' lives by organising important media briefings at short notice would be too good an opportunity to pass up. Summon the buggers to Pretoria at six in the morning for an urgent statement on the president's proposals to deal with the illegal Inuit immigration problem, and then spend four hours explaining that exhaustive investigations have revealed there is no substance to rumours that Eskimos have been slipping into South Africa to harpoon our mating whales. Give them a cup of lukewarm tea and a couple of stale Marie biscuits and send them back to their dismal newsrooms to write their stories. What a fabulous opportunity to have some fun at the expense of the taxpayer.

Here was a job tailor-made for my considerable talents, I decided, and I was just about to send out for forms Z.83 and Z.27 (obtainable from any public service department) when I decided to take a look at the remuneration package. Whoaaa ... a commencing salary of R187 113 per annum!!

Admittedly, the package includes such mouth-watering benefits as a competitive motor finance scheme, home-owners' allowance, pension fund and medical aid, and I daresay BMW would give me a free 740i if I asked them nicely, but it's hardly a package designed to attract the best and brightest to the president's office. No mention of a platinum expense account card and use of the new Presidential jet for personal shopping trips to Dubai either, I notice.

Small wonder that our current crop of spin doctors are such a dismal bunch of no-hopers. As the saying goes: you pay peanuts, you get monkeys. After all, you can probably earn more than that as the features editor on Pig Breeder's Weekly and it's well known that top-notch journos these days are raking it in.

There can be only one reason why government is paying such a derisive salary for such an important position, and that is that the idea of anyone even half competent being paid what they're worth to handle the media is anathema to most politicians.

However, all is not lost. I hear that a lady called Carien Pieterse is approaching journalists and encouraging them to become spies.

Pussy Galore, Dr Holly Goodhead and Elektra King are admittedly names that would be more likely to lure me into the caliginous world of espionage, but beggars can't be choosers.

The prospect of drinking vodka martinis (shaken not stirred) all day, sleeping with mysterious women with Eastern European accents, and getting my hands on a government-issue Aston Martin are too good to miss.

I see that my colleague Hogarth was rather dismissive of this opportunity for journalists to multi-task last week, voting Agent Pieterse Mampara of the Week.

I can only assume that Hogarth's days of saving the world from evil geniuses who point laser beams at your family jewels are over. In which case, make way for the new generation.

I have even been putting in a bit of practice at Sun City's roulette tables. Unfortunately I lost the lot in record time which, admittedly, James Bond never does. I did manage to get the six-CD shuttle in the hire car to work, though, which bodes well for the standard-issue exploding fountain pen.

27 August 2000

What's the point of all this law when enforcing it is such a chore?

I've always had this strange ambition
to break with normal prose tradition,
and have a bash (surely no crime?)
to write this column all in rhyme.

The benefits are clear to see,
less words, same space and great for me
because I still get paid to fill
the bit above the ads that will
ensure safe passage to Tasmania
or offer business with Albania.

My only problem with this plan,
is finding words that rhyme and scan.
One can waste a lot of time
just searching for a bloody rhyme.

Shakespeare, Wordsworth, Keats and Spenser
took on a task no less immenser.
From seeking rhymes they wouldn't shy
but ee cummings didn't try.

He, lazy sod, just scribbled verse
that made no sense and (what is worse),
as he was from the Yankee nation,
completely left out punctuation.
Which made it difficult to tell
when to breathe in and to expel
the air from one's unwholesome torso.
A bit like yodelling, but more so.

But so much for the overture.
Space is scarce and I am sure
my readers want to learn about
our nation's follies, which I doubt
would be believed by half mankind.
So here's the best that I can find.

Two weeks ago (or maybe three)
Dullah Omar (for it was he)
gave out that it was very risky,
to drive a car while drinking whisky.
He added, in a serious tone,
that users of a mobile phone
would be in trouble if they thought
that they could talk and not get caught.

And so he ordered massive fines,
Offenders would be thrown down mines,
their cars impounded and their ears
cut off and fed to grizzly bears.
This was, he hoped, a warning shot
to demonstrate that he was not
a soft touch (as had been suggested).

For when Al Boesak was arrested
and came back home to face his trial,
Omar dashed off to the airport
to greet his hero with a smile.
Which many people thought quite sinister
behaviour for a Justice Minister.

But I digress, so let me please
speak of Omar's latest wheeze,
which is to make the roads more pleasant
by banning drunks and all those peasants
who talk on cellphones while they swerve
across the traffic, bloody nerve!
And those to whom red lights appal,
and so they hit the gas pedal,
instead of slowing to a stop
because there's not a traffic cop.

Laudable aims, we must agree,
and so it seems quite odd to me,
the cops have yet to take a stance.
So much for zero tolerance!

What is the point of all this law
when enforcing it is such a chore?
Tough talk is fine, but what is better
is sticking to the legal letter,
which seems beyond the ANC,
who look disorganised to me.

Why else would they waste their time,
banning statistics on crime?
If crime rates fall you can be sure
they'll let us know so fast and bore
us all to death with their success
at clearing up another mess.

Priorities seem a bit askew
when crooks walk free but me and you
don't dare to leave our homes for fear
of driving after drinking beer.

And so my space is running out,
my eyes are tired and I've got gout
from surfing on the Internet,
and drinking too much cabernet,
I think I'll end my piece just here,
go to the pub and have a beer.

10 September 2000

What drives the racism talkshop industry is the colour of money

I spent most of last weekend in front of the bathroom mirror practising my grimace. I also put in a strenuous couple of hours of brow-furrowing, did a bit of eye-narrowing and managed to almost perfect sucking air in through my teeth while shaking my head from side to side at the same time. Finally I decided to try a bit of hand-wringing just for good measure.

Sadly, all to no avail because no one has asked me my opinion on the recent four-day gabfest known as the National Conference on Racism. My carefully rehearsed gestures of deep concern will have to be reserved for more important issues, which is probably just as well because I would have struggled to put on a convincing act.

One thing that particularly struck me about the conference is that racism is probably one of the greatest growth industries in SA. I don't recall the ANC devoting nearly as much time and energy to conferences on commerce. Everywhere you look there are experts on racism eagerly beavering away at the government's behest to eradicate this evil from society.

The latest trendy job description I picked up from news reports on the conference is 'xenophobia consultant'. Their role is to prevent angry, unemployed South Africans from pushing sharp bits of metal into the stomachs of illegal immigrants who flood across our unguarded borders and steal their jobs.

Looking back at the conference, it would be hard to envisage a more vacuous gathering of economically useless individuals. As we have already seen from the Human Rights Commissions report on racism in the media, the burgeoning racism industry provides all manner of lucrative employment opportunities for work-shy folk who are either unable or unwilling to find real jobs.

What are real jobs? They're the ones that produce a product or service that we can sell into the world market to increase the wealth of this country; the sort of thing that countries like America do rather well. I don't see the army of ANC toadies and bleeding-heart liberals adding much to the country's GDP, but I notice they're always there with outstretched hands when there's money about.

It's surely no surprise that the conference ended with a suggestion from Penuell Maduna that affluent South Africans who benefited under apartheid should send voluntary cash donations so that the disadvantaged can be advantaged.

Pull the other one guv! Your government can't even distribute the money that it has legitimately raised in taxes or get its act together sufficiently to hand out the lottery takings. Which is precisely why you need to keep the racism pot on the boil because, like Uncle Bob up north, you might need to call on it when your constituents start asking what you've actually done for them before the 2004 election.

The rank and file watch the lot of you dressed up in smart suits and handmade shirts, swanning around in expensive German luxury cars and flitting around the world in private jets. Try telling them that you're only doing all these things to reinforce black aspirations and not because you rather enjoy the lifestyle of the very people you accuse of benefiting under apartheid … affluent whites.

And what exactly do you mean by 'benefiting under apartheid'? Apart from the howlingly obvious disadvantages of government job reservation, the disgraceful pass laws, the appalling black education system and so on, are you seriously suggesting that any white who contributed towards the national coffers under apartheid is guilty of vicarious racism and should be punished? You have only to track the performance of the rand against major currencies over the past 20 years to see that there was little benefit to be gained under apartheid for the average South African.

Most intriguing though is the way the ANC rushed to forgive the old order at both Codesa and subsequently at the Truth and Reconciliation Commissions hearings. So those who thought up and enforced the apartheid laws walk away unpunished while the blame is shifted from the generals to the foot-soldiers. The duplicity of politicians never fails to astound me.

Racism is no more an issue in this country than it is in America or Europe, for example. After all, the history of the world is a story of repeated subjugation. However, if the SA government really intends to foment racial hatred then it mustn't be too surprised if mob rule takes over and foreign investment dries up.

The last thing our pale foreign investors need is to have their SA assets seized as reparation for an unjust past.

1 October 2000

Cosatu's comic opera delivers superb display of utter brillance

I always enjoy Cosatu conference time and I often lament that Messrs Gilbert and Sullivan are no longer around to turn the antics of the workers into hilarious comic opera.

From the moment they all tumbled off their buses and launched into a spontaneous 'toyi-toyi' I knew they wouldn't let us down and that, with a bit of luck, we would be in for four days of inspired lunacy.

The extraordinary thing about the workers is that they honestly believe they are indispensable. Nobody seems to have alerted them to the fact that most of them could easily be replaced by machines which would do the job just as effectively. So they labour on under the impression that without them the entire economy would collapse. If that's the case, they reason, then all they would need to do is to withdraw their labour to bring the country to its knees.

Workers enjoy making this sort of impotent threat because it makes them feel powerful. In the egalitarian world in which they dwell, they rarely manage to turn their talents into a positive force.

If you are on the shop floor, it's regarded as very bad form to show too much initiative. Horrible things can happen. You might get promoted and earn more money than your former colleagues. You will then be accused of betaying your roots and turning your back on friends.

How much easier it is to bleat with the flock and blame the company's wicked capitalist management for deliberately keeping workers' pay low. The frequent use of emotive buzz phrases like 'accumulating wealth by trampling on the backs of the worker' has become a comforting anthem for those who have long given up hope of getting out of the rut they have dug for themselves.

Sadly, it is a harsh fact of life that not everybody is destined to lead. If this were not the case, armies would be all officers and no foot-soldiers and there would be no orchestras because everyone would fancy themselves as soloists.

Precisely the same rules apply to commerce.

Somebody has to head a company and he or she should expect to be rewarded for bringing special skills to the job. To suggest, for example, that a 'boss' shouldn't be paid more than 20 times the salary of the lowest paid worker is the sort of madness one frequently hears from the unions.

In the global market in which we now find ourselves, top executive talent is internationally transferable and goes to the highest bidder. Any attempt to 'rig' the market by putting a ceiling on the package will simply mean that we only attract those who can't make it elsewhere.

For precisely the same reasons, skilled management should be paid infinitely more than the workforce, simply because they are a rarer commodity.

Unfortunately most workers don't understand these things. Neither do they understand that it is not always management's fault if the company for which they work fails to compete in the global marketplace.

Members of the SA Clothing and Textile Workers' Union can toyi-toyi and ululate to their heart's content but that won't alter the fact that other countries produce cheaper clothing than we can. Arguing that they can achieve this only by employing child labour and paying slave wages certainly isn't going to shame customers into looking for more ethical suppliers.

The brutal world of capitalism is not noted for its altruism.

When I was in Hong Kong a few months ago I was shown the catering facilities at Cathay Pacific's corporate headquarters near the new airport.

In spotlessly clean kitchens covering 50 400 square metres, Cathay's catering services division prepares meals for about 35 airlines. A total of 1 600 employees work there to produce meals every 2.1 seconds.

In one kitchen I saw people cutting watermelons into the sort of bite-sized slices favoured by airlines. In another area a man was turning omelettes as he has done for the past 30 years.

It's mind-bogglingly dreary work. The shifts are 10 hours long and there is a half-hour lunch break. I asked the customer services manager who was showing me around whether they ever had any strikes or whether the workers took unusual amounts of sick leave. He pointed out that in Hong Kong a full-time job is something that people value. Those who are employed know that there are plenty of people eager to fill their position should they find a regular job too burdensome.

In a country with high unemployment like South Africa, one would have thought that the workers would be counting their blessings rather than constantly trying to bite the hand that feeds them.

15 October 2000

Introducing *Sloth*, the game show where everyone wins, every time

I suppose it had to happen. When M-Net's *Who wants to be a millionaire?* first hit the airwaves last year, the gauntlet was thrown down and rival television channels were challenged to come up with something better.

When you're faced with improving a quiz show in which contestants can win large amounts of money, you have only two options. One is to make the questions more complicated.

As most South Africans already seem to find questions like 'What was the first name of the lead singer of the 60s pop group Gerry and the Pacemakers?' way beyond their intellectual capabilities, that's not really an option.

So the only way to make the game more exciting is to put extra money on the table. This is partly to make it worthwhile for contestants to actually bother to turn up at the studio.

After all, the paltry R1-million available from Jeremy Maggs is barely worth the effort of phoning to get on the show in the first place.

The other reason for upping the prize money is that there is substantially more at stake. When a contestant gives a wrong answer, you want to feel the pain with them. As anyone who bought banking shares three years ago can tell you, there's nothing quite like watching a huge pile of money evaporate to give you that sick feeling in the pit of your stomach.

The attraction of high-stakes quiz games is easy to understand. Once you've stocked up on 702 T-shirts and won a weekend for two at the Ogies Holiday Inn, you naturally want to move on to greater things.

The prospect of making a fast buck for doing very little may be one of the baser human instincts, but we can't deny it exists. However, we can't all be politicians in Mpumalanga, so a more democratic way of distributing free money had to be devised – hence the popularity of the national lottery, the proliferation of casinos and the high-stake television quiz games.

Last Thursday SABC3 aired a programme called *Greed* which offers contestants the chance to win R2-million. All e.tv needs to do now is come up with a similar format, call it something like *Gravy Train* and offer a prize of R5-million.

At least with M-Net's programme there is some pretence to freedom of choice. *Who wants to be a millionaire?* it asks, giving us the opportunity to answer 'not me thanks' or 'I'm already a millionaire. Why don't you give me immortality instead?'

The SABC's *Greed*, on the other hand, assumes that we are all aspirant Gordon Gekkos. It's a raw and unsubtle appeal to our basest instinct and there is always a price to pay for that.

For example, you win half a million and within a few months you are diagnosed with some horrific disease and spend exactly half a million in medical bills to cure yourself. Those who the gods wish to destroy they first invite onto TV game shows.

Anyone who is familiar with the plot of Wagner's *Der Ring des Nibelungen* knows that the terrible curse on the stolen gold from the Rhine far outweighed any benefit it bestowed.

That doesn't alter the fact that most people will do anything, including betray friends and colleagues, just to increase the size of their pile. *Greed* will undoubtedly be a huge success with the sort of people who don't think it strange to spend a large portion of their lives watching other people make money.

What we need now is a companion programme called *Nemesis* which tracks the downfall of the lucky winners.

Why stop there, though? Invasive television programmes that expose human weaknesses and play on interpersonal conflicts are all the rage at the moment.

There's no shortage of people willing to have a prying television camera track their every move and publicly expose flaws in their personality if theres a large wad of cash for the winner. It saves them all the bother of becoming politicians. Look at the enormous success of programmes like *Survivor* and *Big Brother*.

The next move must surely be to make a junk TV series based on something other than money.

The seven deadly sins are an obvious inspiration and everyone could be a winner.

We could have a programme called *Lust* where attractive members of the opposite sex have to live together for three months. The one who has had the least sexual partners collects the cash more as a consolation prize than anything else.

Or maybe *Gluttony* would make good viewing. Tables could be piled high with gourmet food and the winner is the person who weighs the least at the end of two weeks.

The only foreseeable problem would be *Sloth*. There are simply too many contestants in the country.

22 October 2000

Keep your prize – I have naked women dying to honour me

Gutted. Sick as a parrot. We wuz robbed! Of course I should have known this would happen. As soon as I had RSVP'd, telling them I couldn't make the awards ceremony on October 6 at the Westcliff Hotel, I might have guessed that they would scratch me from the list of finalists. These glossy magazine people are much too precious to tolerate absentee winners at their glitzy functions, no matter how deserving.

I could easily have sent a pre-prepared acceptance video or they could even have linked up with me live via satellite, but these were clearly not options as far as they were concerned.

Anyway I had a perfectly good excuse. I was in Cape Town attempting to be stylish. I'd even gate-crashed a lunch with the editor at the very stylish Constantia Uitsig earlier in the week. I was positively oozing charm throughout the meal and naturally thought victory was in the bag.

So when Gwen Gill, the *Sunday Times*'s social scene guru, came up to me on the Monday following the awards ceremony and hailed me with something along the lines of: 'Ah, it's *Style* magazine's not-the-most-stylish man of the year,' it was as if a knife had been inserted between my ribs and twisted back and forth a few times.

'Surely a close second?' I asked, visibly paling. Gwen stirred her tea and said nothing.

'Mentioned in dispatches then?'

'Not even a mention,' said Gwen. 'Unless you count the MC's comment that you have to be young to be stylish.'

This is precisely the sort of fatuous remark one has come to expect from people who have only recently stopped using zit cream. All because I answered 'my bladder' to the tricky competition question asking: 'What motivates you to get out of bed in the morning?' No points for honesty there. I should have invented one of those poncy, phoney mission-statement replies and I would have romped home. 'I am motivated to get out of bed by the desire to expand my self-knowledge and thus empower people in my business to discover their inner strengths … oh, and the money comes in useful too.' Phoooey!

The kindest thing one can say about *Style* magazine's most stylish man and woman of the year competition is that the judges have obviously redefined the word 'style'. I hate to sound like a bad loser (which I am) but nobody I know has ever heard of the two winners. They don't even write a Sunday newspaper column, which I should have thought would have been a prerequisite for such an award.

Well, good luck to them, I say. A trip on the Orient Express is a high price to pay for being under the scrutiny of Gwen Gills' microscope. Wear the same pair of socks in public twice and you're swiftly relegated to social list D (where I hang out). Put too many coriander leaves in the green salad or serve soggy sushi and you will never hear the last of it.

It doesn't end there either. You will be expected to attend all sorts of ghastly social events and to mix with continuity announcers simply because you have been voted 'stylish' and are, therefore, assumed to be an asset to any party. Look at poor Callie and Monique Strydom, who are now firmly on the social A list when it comes to invitations.

Spend a couple of months as reluctant guests of some obscure, gun-toting group of terrorist socialists and as soon as you're released you achieve instant celebrity status and have to spend another couple of months as reluctant guests of some obscure, gin-toting group of terrifying socialites. As one who has, over the years, become accustomed to celebrity status, let me tell you it's no cake walk.

There are distinct disadvantages to the rabble wanting to touch the hem of your garments. There are advantages admittedly. Beautiful women throw themselves at you at wild parties and beg for your hotel room number. That sort of thing happens all the time and I'm constantly having to phone room service to ask them to come and remove semi-naked women from my hotel bathroom.

However, the downside is that the enormous stress of being an icon eventually takes its toll. For example, you start wearing sunglasses in restaurants in indoor shopping malls at night. You value your privacy so much that you get personalised number plates on your car and then realise that you can't even pick your nose when you're driving without someone recognising you. You always book economy class tickets knowing that you're famous enough to be upgraded to business.

Then comes the day when you're no longer famous enough to get an upgrade and you throw a tantrum at the check-in desk. And guess who's standing behind you in the queue? Gwen bloody Gill.

19 November 2000

SABC move to show dog video inspired more by money than ire

I did not watch the *Special Assignment* programme about the North East Rand Dog Unit's use of illegal immigrants as live bait. I saw some of the footage on news bulletins and I read most of the news reports and the many outraged comments that followed.

I hadn't intended to devote space to the topic because I thought it had already had enough airing, but last weekend a dog bit both my wife and I so I took this as a sign that I should write about the incident after all.

In my case, it was my own dog that bit us. We decided last Sunday that, instead of sitting in the garden and enjoying the sunshine like sensible people, we should take the dog to the vet to have a growth removed.

He is a large, normally placid Rottweiler, but a visit to the vet is not something any of us relish. So we doped him beforehand and put him in the back of the car. He was still frisky enough to get out of the car and chase cats at the vets' surgery so he had another injection in his back leg which was intended to calm him down.

Fifteen minutes later we were attempting to put him on a blanket to take him into surgery when he first struck. He grabbed my wife's right hand, chewed a few times and spat it out. The dog went into one surgery and my wife, quite pale by now, went into the other to wash the wound and assess the damage. While the dog was being operated on I took her down to the Linksfield Clinic for the usual cocktail of antibiotics, tetanus jab, anti-inflammatories and what have you. Then I drove her home and went off to collect the dog, sans growth.

He seemed very drowsy, but managed to stagger to the car. I was trying to help him in when he turned and bit my right hand. So, after taking the dog home to recuperate, I took myself off to the Rosebank Clinic (I was too embarrassed to return to the Linksfield), had the wound stitched and went back to the pharmacy to collect another dose of precisely the same drugs I had collected an hour earlier. The wounds are extremely painful but, in our cases, relatively minor and they were treated quickly.

Not so fortunate were the unhappy trio attacked by the police dogs solely, it seems, for the amusement of their sadistic handlers. They were repeatedly savaged and I doubt if their hosts took them off for medical attention when they had finished their training session.

The visual image is more powerful than anything a journalist, however talented, can put on paper. On the Wednesday morning following the programme my maid wasn't her usual cheerful self. It wasn't until I had read about the dog attacks that I put two and two together and guessed that she had watched the programme. When I got home that evening I asked her about it. She broke down and sobbed, asking me why these things are still happening in the new South Africa. I wish I had an answer for her.

The wisdom of the decision to make the footage public by showing it on national TV rather than handing the evidence to the authorities to deal with is open to debate. I would feel much more comfortable with the decision if I didn't suspect the motive had more to do with money than with exposing evil. It was inevitable that, once shown here, the video would be aired (sold?) internationally, not because anyone really gives a fig about how the SA police treat illegal immigrants, but because it is sufficiently sensational to boost viewership and get people talking, which it certainly did.

The first thing a colleague of mine knew about the incident was when a Sydney cab driver explained it to her in great detail. The content of the video is probably no more horrific than film footage of similar acts of brutality from around the world, but it does show white policemen setting their dogs on black people in the new South Africa and that alone makes it newsworthy.

Unfortunately, that negative image will eclipse many of the positive images the country has been sending out.

If news of the attack had simply appeared as yet another dismal newspaper story, most readers would probably have shrugged it off and turned to the sports pages. A visual image whips up all sorts of emotions, as we saw from the outcry. Where, I wonder, were all these people when the puppeteers of the apartheid system were busy negotiating safe passage from the current government?

The most nauseating aspect of this whole sordid business is that the video has been triumphantly presented as evidence that racism is alive and well in the new South Africa (as if we didn't know).

In which case, why is the vociferous SA Human Rights Commission spending so much time and energy concentrating on pictures of storks on rubbish tips when there are more important matters to attend to?

It seems hypocrisy is also alive and well in the new South Africa.

26 November 2000

The day they found giraffe skeletons on the ocean floor

A few hundred years from now divers will discover the perfectly preserved skeletons of two giraffes on the ocean bed just off the east coast of Africa, a few hundred nautical miles south of the Suez Canal. The astonishing find will make the front page of The All-African Sunday Times (a direct descendent of *The Sunday Times* you hold in your hand and one of the world's most influential newspapers by the year 2201) and the scientific world will be scratching its collective head to work out how they came to be there.

Did they make a wrong turn during the great migration, forget to stop running when they hit the beach and end up in the ocean before realising that they couldn't swim? Was the bit of the ocean bed where they were discovered originally a part of the African continent which slipped into the sea under the weight of European tourists? Or were these a hitherto undiscovered species of aquatic giraffe capable of holding their breath under water for 30 minutes before bobbing gracefully to the surface to graze on seaweed?

What the scientists will never know (unless *The All-African Sunday Times* has an excellent archive service) is that the two giraffes were tossed overboard during a 40-day cruise from Durban to Spain and back again. Along with another 22 giraffes and three white rhino they were unhappy voyagers on the animal equivalent of the cruise from hell.

The floating menagerie was originally destined for a Spanish zoo, but when the foot-and-mouth outbreak hit KwaZulu-Natal the Spaniards quickly changed their minds and sent them back home without so much as a brief shore excursion to stretch their legs. The fodder supplies ran low on board ship and the two hapless giraffes failed to adapt to a diet of horse feed supplied in Malta as an emergency measure.

It's rather like when an airline runs low on meals in economy class and you're left with no choice but fish. We humans know that the only sensible course is to wrestle the packet of airline biscuits open and watch the movie in the hope that they don't run out of breakfast before the trolley reaches us. Giraffes, however, are not seasoned travellers and don't know these things. A total of 22 giraffes survived, so the food can't have been that bad, but two of them gave up the ghost and, after complaints from fellow passengers about the smell, it was eventually decided to toss them overboard.

Those of you who have surreptitiously lobbed an eaten apple from a moving car will know that civilised people wait until there's no one around before winding the window down and hurling the nibbled, browning core into the verge and reaching for the wet wipes.

Can you imagine then what it must be like trying to dispose of two fully-grown dead giraffes? It's not just a matter of sidling along the starboard railing and furtively loosing the beasts into the swirling waves. You first have to scan the horizon for other vessels and wait until everything is clear. Only then can you heave the monstrous hulk onto the rail and, after a count of three, give it a hefty shove hoping it doesn't become entangled in the propeller or drop onto a surfacing nuclear submarine. A 'mayday' call that you've hit a giraffe is bound to be treated with some scepticism by coast-guards.

If any other ship's captain so much as suspects that you have been littering the ocean with bestial flotsam then you have the full wrath of maritime law to answer to. The Dumping of Dead African Animals at Sea Act (1963 as amended) quite clearly prohibits dropping anything larger than a banded mongoose into the water. The defence that the two giraffes went on a drinking spree and ran around shouting 'the highballs are on us' before throwing themselves into the water is unlikely to be believed.

In this instance though, it seems no one saw a thing and the two giraffes drifted slowly down to their watery graves.

The remaining animals arrived home in surprisingly good shape, we are told, although the rhinos could easily have suffered from the newly discovered 'economy class syndrome'. They spent the 40 days cooped up in narrow, purpose-built crates which didn't even give them room to turn round – accommodation more suited to travelling South African rugby supporters.

The surviving giraffes fared rather better. They were travelling business in the stretched upper deck and had a good view of their surroundings which, admittedly, was sea most of the time.

Inevitably one of the younger giraffes would have asked the question: 'Are we nearly there, mum?'

Can you imagine what must have gone through her mind when she saw they were back in Durban again?

Please help with widow!!!

10 December 2000

To shore up your status in Plett, increase your building noise

It is the duty of the rich to build fine houses, patronise the arts, create beautiful gardens and encourage disappearing skills by employing expensive craftsmen in order to leave something for posterity.

Great men are more often remembered for their aesthetic contribution to the period in which they lived than for the manner in which they made their fortunes, which is probably just as well.

In renaissance Italy it was not a matter of how much you had but what you did with it. In Florence, the Pitti family went bust trying to keep up with the extravagant Medicis. Ostentation was the order of the day and if your neighbour in San Gimignano built a tall tower, then you simply called your builder in and asked him to build you a taller one.

The great houses of England are replete with splendid examples of this one-upmanship.

Most of them were built by men who had either enjoyed royal patronage or who had prospered through commerce.

The grounds and considerable funds necessary to build Blenheim Palace in Oxfordshire were given by a grateful Queen Anne to John Churchill, the 1st Duke of Marlborough, as a thank-you gift for beating Louis XIV at the Battle of Blenheim.

The building took 20 years to complete, by which time the Duke had been dead for three years. The house is reckoned to be the greatest baroque residence in England, largely thanks to Vanbrugh's insistence on not using nylon carpet tiles in the entrance lobby.

In a different league, Cragside in Northumberland is a gallimaufry of gables, battlements, half-timbered walls and gargoyles set against the dramatic backdrop of a dense forest. Built by Richard Norman Shaw for Lord Armstrong between 1870 and 1884, it features a drawing room hacked from the rock and lit by large recessed bay windows set high above the room. Lord Armstrong was an inventor and industrial tycoon who made his fortune through engineering and supplying armaments.

The hiring of the top architects of the day, the import of expensive building materials, the laying out of ornate gardens, the commissioning of works of art and the collections of fine furniture may well have left something for future generations to gaze upon and enjoy, but their real purpose was to publicly advertise the wealth and good breeding of their owners.

Which is why we shouldn't be surprised to learn that the latest trend among the mega-rich in South Africa is to buy expensive houses and then demolish them to build something else.

This is particularly prevalent in Plettenberg Bay where apparently it's now *de rigueur* to spend several million rand on a property and then three times as much building a new home on the same site.

'Plett', as it is affectionately known, is not so much a place as a social melting pot. With a growing squatter settlement as neighbours and a stunning view of the ocean, it still manages to offer some of the most expensive real estate in the country. During the Christmas and Easter holidays it is so crowded one finds it almost impossible to move, but as the beautiful people fly back to their Jo'burg homes to mix with precisely the same people they've just seen at Plett, it becomes a ghost town again. Nobody in his or her right mind actually wants to live in Plett. All they want to do is build there, which is nothing more than the human equivalent of a male lion marking his territory by peeing on a tree.

It's all part of the power game. To buy a house for R5-million and then promptly demolish it tells the previous owner exactly what you think of his taste in architecture. After that, the trick is to build something high enough to obscure the sea view of the tycoon living directly behind you. There's nothing the rich enjoy more than pissing off other rich people.

Just to add to the misery of existing residents, its a great idea to build your new home while your neighbours are trying to enjoy some quiet coastal solitude, preferably during school holidays. So while they're lying on their sun decks, your workers can be sawing bits of steel and dynamiting parts of the property to make way for the underpool meditation room.

Normally builders knock off at about five in the afternoon, but when money is no object you can afford to pay them triple time to keep working through the night and annoy your neighbours even more.

Meanwhile you rent somewhere in a nice quiet place and leave your site manager to cope with the flack. When the house is completed, you fly down in your helicopter, take one look and order it to be demolished and rebuilt all over again.

And if that doesn't let them know who's king of the hill, then nothing will.

14 January 2001

My Annual Report shows a deficit in fixed social assets

The start of a new year is traditionally a time for introspection; a complete review of one's life in an attempt to make sense of the human condition.

Some people take this more seriously than others. I have a corporate accountant friend who, at the end of each year, mentally drafts a chairman's report to the shareholders.

He divides the various aspects of his life and parts of his body into separate profit centres and evaluates their contribution to the bottom line of wellbeing.

For example, the leisure department had a good year with an improved golf handicap, but overall career prospects suffered on the failed materialisation of a long-hoped-for promotion.

The food and beverage division's figures resulted in an expanded waistline, but head office reported a thinning of hair with conditions expected to worsen in 2001. The upgrade to a company BMW five series caused temporary sensory joy, but it has been another uneventful year in the genital department with no hope of an upturn in activity.

I'm nowhere near as organised as that but an article in the New Year's Eve edition of the *Sunday Times* prompted me to conduct a review of my life. It was a depressingly salutary exercise.

I was sitting by the pool at around 11.30 am, having just mixed a very fine dry martini (chilled glass, five parts Bombay gin, half part Noilly Prat, twist of lemon and washed olive) and thinking that I'd managed to hit life on the sweet spot when my eyes fell on Gwen Gill's article on the 10 hottest social events of 2000. To my horror I realised that I had attended only one of the 10, and that was purely because I was master of ceremonies for the evening.

Worse news was to come, though. Of Gill's list of the 10 worst social events of 2000, I was invited to only one (declined), which suggests that I can't even manage to crack an invite to bad parties.

I have already written in this column of my failure last year to make the finalists' list in *Style* magazine's Man of the Year competition. My ego had only just begun to cope with this injustice when I attended the *Sunday Times* Christmas party.

The newspaper runs a sort of Oscar awards ceremony where staff members are invited to nominate people in various categories for the coveted annual awards. Surely it is the ultimate accolade to be chosen as worthy of an award by your peers.

I realised I didn't have a hope in the most improved fashion writer category, but my hopes rose considerably when the best columnist award was announced and finalists were called to the plinth.

Well, not only did I fail to grab the trophy (Gill won by a length), but insult was added to injury when I was told that I hadn't even been nominated. It's one thing being an also-ran; quite another not even to be considered fit to run.

The *Sunday Times* office has a wall devoted to Winners, saluting those who have brought glory to the broadsheet. I have to walk past it every morning on the way to my desk.

It's a poignant reminder of my failings and I wonder, purely in the interests of political correctness, whether we shouldn't also have a board for Losers fixed to another wall.

Thus I found myself, in the words of the Old Testament, weighed in the balance and found wanting as I entered the new year.

I briefly considered enrolling for a Mike Lipkin course (free popcorn included), but decided to phone Lifeline instead. As it happens I was one digit out but didn't know that until my sad story had tumbled out to the patient listener at the other end of the phone. He admitted that he wasn't from Lifeline but said he could probably help me anyway.

He pointed out that all the top columnists in the UK have been in re-hab at some time or another. Without a chronic drug-sex-drink dependence and a few failed marriages, it's impossible to be taken seriously as a writer.

People like AA Gill, Will Self and Julie Burchill have notoriously screwed up lives and that has made them celebrities.

Surely their writing ability had something to do with it, I suggested. 'Yeah ... right,' he said after a pause.

Then there's the angst factor to be considered. It doesn't do to be too cheerful or to make writing look easy. For example, young Darrel Bristow-Bovey writes superbly but he has managed to affect an 'I suffer for my art' attitude, which means that he can indulge in mood swings. That's why he gets invited to all the good parties.

What my image urgently needs is a makeover. Perhaps a well-placed story about how I went on a drunken rampage and horrified onlookers by throwing a television out of a hotel window.

That way I might be in with a slim chance next year.

4 February 2001

If a low rand is SA's share price, it's an attractive investment

I received a telephone call from a distressed reader last week seeking my views on South Africa's prospects for the future.

My caller had clearly been exposed to far too many depressing economic forecasts and was wondering whether to finally jump ship and pack for Perth. What particularly bothered him was the ever-diminishing value of the rand, and so he sought my expert opinion on where I thought the currency was heading.

I was brutally honest and told him that I wouldn't hold out high hopes for dollar/rand parity in our lifetimes or, indeed, our grandchildren's. As I have mentioned before, this has nothing to do with Afro-pessimism but everything to do with Afro-realism. What is more likely to happen is that the rand will be heavily sold from time to time by all those dreadful, unpatriotic emerging market hedge funds and then improve a little and stabilise before getting smacked again.

This is the way of the financial world and we shouldn't feel especially singled out for rough treatment. As we can do little about it there's no point in letting it upset us.

You will probably have noticed that there is a two-week period of mourning whenever the rand plummets. During that period various financial publications attempt to analyse what is going on and apportion blame, the personal finance editors commission articles on what this will mean to the average person and talking heads appear on television to tell us that it's good news for exporters. The politicians remind us that the problem is not really the weakness of the rand but the strength of the dollar. However, once the two-week period of national angst is over we all get used to the rand trading at the new distress levels and forget all about it.

Financial market reporters start to talk about the rand having a good day on the markets (admittedly from the new low levels). Their excited voices inform us that the currency strengthened against both the dollar and sterling and we all feel marginally happier once again, even if we know that the ups will never make up for the downs.

Like many people, my distressed caller probably feels that a sinking rand is a sign of a greater malaise in South Africa. That may well be true, of course, but I prefer to think of the exchange rate as nothing more than the share price of the country. When people sell the rand the price falls, when they buy it the price rises. As any canny investor knows, there is nothing wrong with a share price that is apparently too low, providing it still has the potential to rise.

For example, South Africans become gloomy because of the rand's purchasing power abroad. That hasn't stopped us travelling, though. The only difference is that we are reluctant to waste money on a London hotel room when we can get better value elsewhere. That probably has more to do with the rip-off prices of London than the weakness of the rand. There are still plenty of affordable holidays to be had elsewhere in the world on our rather generous annual foreign exchange allowance, so we are hardly currency hostages.

The flip side of this is that the weakness of the rand makes South Africa an absolute bargain for visitors. As far as tourism goes it gives us a huge cost advantage over our main rival, Australia. If we can't double the number of our foreign visitors in the next three years then we might as well give up.

Ah, but what about all the crime that's putting off foreign visitors? I suspect most tourists have an incident-free visit to this country and return home singing its praises.

Spain's greatest problem is terrorism (acknowledged by the Spanish government) and yet the country still manages to attract more than 60-million visitors a year. In other words, what the country has to offer is regarded as reasonable reward for the remote risk of being blown to pieces by Basque separatists.

Visitors to South Africa clearly feel the same way, which is why so many of them come again.

Worrying about the decline of the rand is something that only currency traders, central bankers and importers should indulge in. If you're earning rands and spending rands then you have little to worry about, particularly if interest rates can still come down despite a weak currency.

However, if you're still unconvinced try this. Whenever you go out to dinner, pretend you're a Brit and convert the bill into sterling. At least it will give you a vicarious thrill and remind you why it's cheaper to live in South Africa and not England.

11 February 2001

Knowing what voters want hardly a turn-on for SA politicians

Judging by many of our local magazine covers, there seems to be a special offer on the actress Helen Hunt this month. Like Chicken Man, she's everywhere.

Her publicists have blitzed the world's media with 'Huntabilia' which is why it's almost impossible to find a magazine on the rack that doesn't feature the lovely Helen Hunt smiling out at us from the cover, together with an article explaining in tedious detail what she's been doing with her life since *Mad About You*. Actually that's not entirely true.

Magazines with titles like Mining Monthly and Water Effluent and Sewage Weekly have, thus far, bravely held out and printed nothing about Ms Hunt's career.

I'm told that, despite some animated discussion at the last editorial meeting, the honchos at one leading mining glossy firmly rejected proposals to put pictures of beautiful women on the cover of their magazine just to boost circulation. Good for them, I say. Is there anything more sensuous than a picture of a large piece of yellow machinery driving down a muddy slope? Unless it's a picture of a large piece of red machinery with improbably huge tyres (phwoar!) driving *up* a muddy slope.

Clearly a lot of thought goes into the covers of these magazines and it ill behoves us mainstream journos to mock them. If the likes of Catherine Zeta-Jones or Helen Hunt were judged more visually appealing than a Euclid R280 hauler then they would no doubt make it onto the cover. As the saying goes, it's horses for courses. Just because there are people out there who breathe heavily whenever they look at the cover of a mining magazine, there is no reason for the rest of us to snigger. We must learn to be tolerant.

However, back to Helen Hunt who is on the cover of so many magazines because she is promoting a spate of new movies (surprise). One of these is a film she has made with Mel Gibson called *What Women Want*. According to the blurb, Gibson plays a chauvinist advertising executive who finds he can suddenly hear what women are thinking, with predictably hilarious results.

This is bound to find huge appeal among South African men, most of whom *think* they know what women are thinking but merely lack the vocal confirmation available to Gibson's character.

The central idea is so clever that I am told a South African adaptation is in the planning stages. It is to be called *What Voters Want* and it is the story of a small group of politicians who find that they can suddenly hear what the electorate is thinking, but only after a period of prolonged deafness.

This gives them a huge advantage over the rest of the politicians who believe the voters are too stupid to know what they want, which is precisely why they elect politicians to do the thinking for them in the first place.

In the script there's a wonderful scene where the Minister of Fruit is explaining the complex details of a R43-billion watermelon procurement deal to the voters. He is telling them how terribly difficult it is to buy so many watermelons at one go without the help of qualified watermelon brokers who act only in the most altruistic way at all times.

Someone rudely suggests that some of the politicians or their relatives might also be watermelon brokers in their spare time and the minister attempts to explain how this would be impossible.

Still, the people are unconvinced, so the minister offers to set up a full and impartial investigation provided it's conducted by people who are politically acceptable and have good paper-shredding skills.

At this point the Minister of Fruit hears the voice of the voters in his head telling him they don't believe a word he is saying and that any impartial investigation is likely to be a sham.

At first he doesn't believe he is hearing such things and accuses the voters of being unpatriotic South Africans who are trying to bring about the downfall of the government and scare off foreign investors. He tries to ignore the voices in his head but they get louder and eventually he has no choice but to respect the wishes of the voters. When he realises that he really can hear what voters are thinking he never again tries to deceive the very people who put him into power.

The only problem with *What Voters Want* is finance. The script has been rejected as 'totally unbelievable even within the realms of fantasy' by one potential backer. Pity, because we need more good fairy stories.

25 February 2001

I can't stomach the gutless trash dished up in local TV shows

I shocked fellow guests at a dinner party recently by confessing that the Bullard household does not possess a satellite dish.

There was an embarrassed silence from those at the table. I went on to admit we didn't even have an M-Net decoder and, furthermore, had no intention of linking up to either service because we couldn't afford it. Further pitying looks followed as we were silently categorised 'poor whites'. We expect food parcels to be delivered shortly.

When I said I couldn't afford it I was talking about time rather than money. I already have to choose between the three SABC stations and e.tv and that's bad enough. Add the satellite channels and M-Net and I would be utterly confused.

Quite simply, there would be too much choice and that's never a good thing because it increases the chances of making the wrong one.

The point is, I hardly ever watch television at all these days because the programmes have become so awful – particularly our local offerings. Some are so dreadful that I have now taken to hiding the TV's remote control whenever we have overseas visitors just in case they chance upon the retarded *Toasty Show* or the abysmally banal *Cassie Live*.

Locally produced TV programmes are probably doing more damage to South Africas reputation overseas than all those unpatriotic emigrants who allegedly bad-mouth the country in London pubs.

Why is it that South Africans seem incapable of producing anything worth watching? Are we really a nation of morons or are the broadcasters committed to dumbing down the airwaves ahead of the next general election? Thankfully the dreadful *Carruthers Brothers* is no longer with us but we now have *Madam and Eve* which is almost as bad.

Compare the scripting and the acting of local shows with the much slicker American and British sitcoms on our screens and you realise we have a long way to go. We have cultivated a culture of the 'lowest common denominator' which allows sub-standard work to flourish, providing it meets politically correct criteria.

If I were the minister of arts, I would send the writers, actors and producers of these abominations to Robben Island and allow them off only once they had produced something that didn't embarrass the entire nation.

*

It's flag-burning season again in Iraq – this time in protest against unprovoked American and British air strikes on targets around Baghdad.

Thousands of Iraqis, many of them potential contestants in a Saddam Hussein 'lookalike' competition, took to the streets calling for revenge against Britain and the US, waving guns in the air and performing traditional Bedouin dances. This may seem an impotent retaliation against the combined military might of the two trigger-happy Western powers but it is a symbolic gesture, as is the flag burning.

One thing puzzles me, though. Are Iraqi householders required by law to keep a stock of American and British flags, or do they simply rush down to their local corner store and buy a fresh one whenever they feel the need to flambé a flag?

For example, should I suddenly wish to publicly set fire to a Zimbabwean flag as a protest against Mad Bob Mugabe's human rights abuses, I wouldn't have the faintest idea of where to get hold of one, apart from pinching it off the flagpole at the Zim consulate.

And yet the Iraqis, who have lived under the burden of international sanctions since the Gulf War, can seemingly lay their hands on inexhaustible supplies of Stars and Stripes and Union Jack flags in all sizes.

One possible explanation is that these are rejects that have been dumped on Iraq by unscrupulous sanctions-busters who couldn't sell them to anyone else in the world. Closer examination would reveal there were too many stripes and too few stars or that the white cross of St Andrew had been placed over the red cross of St George.

So the Iraqis could be burning non-existent national colours which rather negates all that strong symbolism.

This seems a little far-fetched though and it is far more likely that there is a lively cottage industry in Iraq dedicated to manufacturing the flags of potentially hostile superpowers just so that Iraqis have something to burn whenever they are bombed.

In fact, I wouldn't be at all surprised if some bright spark didn't start something akin to a 'Flags t' Burn' franchise throughout the Middle East to supply customers with convenient ready-to-burn, petrol-impregnated pennants.

I can't help thinking that demand should outstrip supply for some time to come.

1 April 2001

Racially intolerant Martians impress President Mbeki with their insight

At their last congress the ANC discussed the possibility of starting their own newspaper. At the time I helpfully suggested the title *The Daily Struggle* but, as usual, I didn't receive the courtesy of a reply from anyone in the ANC.

For the past seven years I have been offering the government useful tips in this column on how to run a country properly, and not once have I even received so much as a 'Thanks for the idea, the president is considering it' postcard.

A less patriotic columnist would probably have given up trying long ago. I however, like the boy who stood on the burning deck when all but he had fled, have no intention of deserting my post and will continue to supply the ANC with good ideas. If they choose to ignore them, that is their affair.

Predictably, plans for the daily newspaper came to nothing. That was probably because somebody pointed out that to produce a newspaper you need access to a printing press and a regular supply of paper.

As the government sometimes can't even manage to provide toilet paper for parliamentarians, I doubt if they would be any more successful at ordering newsprint.

You also need advertisers if you want to run a successful newspaper, and it's hard to imagine why anybody would want to advertise in a publication aimed at people who have little money to spend.

So, realising that the dice was loaded against them, the press barons *manqué* of the ruling elite decided to go the cheaper Internet route and start something called *ANC Today*; an interesting policy decision considering how few of the ANC rank and file have access to personal computers.

I eagerly logged onto *ANC Today* last Monday to catch its spin on the Tony (Sweaty Hands) Yengeni luxury car story. The page made no reference to Tony's gleaming strugglemobile.

Aha, I thought. Clearly they are under strict instructions not to write anything that might embarrass their masters. Then somebody pointed out to me that, despite the title *ANC Today*, the government's online organ only gets updated once a week. My suggestion is that they rename it *ANC This Week* but, given my track record thus far, I doubt whether they will take much notice.

I have to say that if *ANC Today* is hoping to eventually emerge from the Internet chrysalis and become a newsprint butterfly they have a lot of work to do. Where is the leisure page? Where are the cartoons, the crossword puzzle and the bridge column? There is absolutely nothing to attract Internet surfers who already have thousands of other websites to choose from.

For example, if I were editor (another hint chaps) I would run an online reader competition. *Match the photos of these democratically elected leaders with their luxury strugglemobiles and win a weekend for two in beautiful Harare (meals not included, please bring your own petrol).*

However, the *ANC Today* page is not totally devoid of humour. This week's edition features an article by the president which is unlikely to do much to stifle speculation that the pres is a few chops short of a braaivleis.

In a rather long and rambling article (you *don't* sub-edit the president), Mbeki imagines a Martian visiting South Africa and immediately being able to appreciate the difference between Zimbabwe and South Africa.

In a nutshell, this is because the Martian is not racist which leads on to Mbeki's main thrust of the article which points out that, unlike Martians, white people are racists and that is why they think Mad Bob disease could spread south of the Limpopo. Expect to see the words 'SA Welcomes Martians' written large in the mealie fields of South Africa before long.

The curious thing about this tribute to Martian racial tolerance is that the comrade Martian also happens to be a 'she'; a case of political correctness run amok if ever there was one. Maybe the president could confirm that 'she' is also a one-legged, lesbian, whale-loving Martian, in which case I'm sure we would all feel much better.

22 April 2001

Gauteng school text evaluators, lend me your ass's ears

Poor old Hamlet. The Gauteng education department's setwork evaluators have suggested that Shakespeare's tragic hero is an unsuitable role model for South African youth and should be booted from the syllabus. The problem is that he is 'not optimistic or uplifting' and the characters in the play not appealing to modern learners as royalty is no longer fashionable. Try telling that to King Goodwill Zwelithini!

We all know that Hamlet is a miserable bugger who wanders gloomily around the family castle dressed in black, sees his dead father's ghost at the most inopportune moments, dumps his girlfriend who then goes mad and drowns herself and hops into open graves at the drop of a coxcomb to play around with dead jesters' skulls.

As if this isn't enough, he is also prone to acute mood swings, wondering whether or not to kill his uncle and, just to show that he is not afraid of a bit of aggro, stabs his girlfriend's dad (who is hiding behind a curtain) and then tells the cops he thought he was killing a rat in his mother's bedroom. Talk about dysfunctional!

This is hardly the sort of material to feed the impressionable young minds of scholars brought up on a wholesome diet of *Yizo Yizo*.

The poncy literary types in their tweed jackets claim that Hamlet is a universal work and represents everyman but that's a load of old cobblers, as the Gauteng educationists know. If somebody had given the boy a course of anti-depressants and a few hours with a good therapist he would be as right as rain. Before you could say 'to be or not to be' he would have been invited onto the *Oprah* show to talk publicly about the problems of spending every waking hour wondering whether to kill your uncle. The thing is that Hamlet is a classic 'victim' and needs to see his situation from a more positive viewpoint.

Rather than allow a troupe-load of strolling players into Elsinore to perform obscure plays which will expose his uncle's guilt, he should let bygones be bygones, light a joss stick and read some Deepak Chopra. Small wonder that the Gauteng education department thinks *Hamlet* is a bad influence. Heaven knows, life is enough of a struggle without kids having to read all that depressing iambic pentameter stuff.

Julius Caesar has also fallen foul of the educationists because it is sexist and 'elevates men'. You can't argue with that, can you? Where are the shopping scenes? Why the sexist emphasis on unnatural childbirth?

A solution might be to call it 'Julia Caesar' and rework the script into something more relevant to South African 'yoof':

Julia, a fiftysomething housewife from Kempton Park, goes shopping on 15 March in the Capitol Shoppertainment Centre and Casino, loses a fortune on the one-armed bandits and is accidentally stabbed by a security guard from Brutus Security Services, who mistakes her for a cash-in-transit heister. Her son Mark Anthony, a promising young lawyer with a Sandton firm, sues the casino's owner for contributory negligence and Brutus Security gets sacked and goes out of business.

King Lear presents more of a challenge. Its been chucked onto the undesirable heap because it is 'full of violence and despair and the plot is rather ridiculous and unlikely'. It's essentially a play about land grabs, duplicity, the breakdown of family values and a lack of political integrity, none of which are remotely relevant to the new South Africa. Besides, the language is much too complicated and would necessitate the teachers actually reading and understanding the play before they attempt to teach pupils about it. Since that is an unrealistic expectation, it's much easier to declare the play 'undesirable'.

Paradoxically, *Macbeth* makes it past the finishing post, which is strange because it's probably one of the bard's darkest works and could hardly be described as either 'uplifting' or 'optimistic'.

Appropriately enough, though, *A Midsummer Night's Dream* is on the list of approved works. That's the one with the character with the ass's ears. I think the Gauteng educationists probably recognised a kindred spirit.

6 May 2001

Come now, Nedcor – do you really think we're *that* gullible?

How on earth can we expect politicians to keep their fingers out of the cookie jar when corporate South Africa sets such an appalling example?

In what must rank as one of the most extraordinary 'social irresponsibility' programmes ever, 16 (the number could increase) Nedcor executives have apparently been given the all-clear to carve off a substantial chunk of the bank's profits and share it among themselves.

In this particular case the profits are the result of Nedcor's shareholdings in IT companies but who's to say that, if this act of piracy succeeds, they might not also get their greedy little snouts into other troughs?

Many people will view this as just another example of unbridled corporate avarice. For doing absolutely nothing except being members of an exclusive group of mutual backscratchers, the 16 stand to pocket an amount of money that most South Africans couldn't hope to earn in 50 lifetimes.

Bearing in mind the high unemployment rate in SA, the widening gap between rich and poor and the delicately balanced relationship between management and workers, one has to question how appropriate such blatant self-enrichment schemes are.

Last week, *Business Times* ran a response from Nedcor chairman Chris Liebenberg which had all the hallmarks of a hastily cobbled damage limitation exercise. If that is what was intended, then it failed dismally.

We probably wouldn't have learnt about the 'incentive' scheme had it not been for Ann Crotty, a highly experienced business journalist of great integrity who shoots from the hip without fear or favour. She waded through the lengthy Nedcor annual report and found, buried on page 92, a nebulous reference to the deal.

Surely, if it is as good for the future of Nedcor as Liebenberg would have us believe, it would have been given more prominence. Bankers are certainly not known for their modesty, and if Nedcor was genuinely proud of this innovative scheme to keep great talent, then you can be certain that it would have appeared in large print on the first few pages of the annual report.

The fact that it is hidden away tells us everything.

Nedcor's claim that it is forced to offer such incentives to attract and keep good people is pure casuistry. Incentive schemes are intended to encourage competition within an organisation and reward the most successful. The basic premise is that you forego a sizeable chunk of your monthly salary in order to share in any profits that you may generate. There is a clear downside, which is that you will earn very little if you don't perform. However, that's the risk you take by electing to share in profits rather than receive a standard salary.

Nedcor's scheme does it rather differently. It pays its executives a massive salary and, on top of that, allows them to share in the fortunes of companies over which they have no control. Apart from the movement in the share prices of the underlying investments, there appears to be no downside. How can this possibly be viewed as an incentive scheme?

It's nothing more than a sweetener in exactly the same way as Tony (Sweaty Hands) Yengeni's growing stable of unexplained Mercedes-Benzes might also turn out to be a sweetener. Perhaps we should be arguing that the cars are an 'incentive' for Tony to choose the right weapons when he is spending R43-billion of taxpayers' money?

If the object of the incentive scheme really is to attract and keep IT talent that might be wooed away by a better offer, then why does it affect 16 executives? Apart from the fact that IT personnel are more offered than bid in the world market at the moment, are we really to believe Nedcor employs 16 young Einsteins it cannot afford to lose at any price?

If Nedcor is as keen on corporate governance as it claims, why is it so reluctant to name the lucky winners in this game of greed?

Could it be that most of them have absolutely nothing to do with the banking group's IT fortunes, past, present or future?

13 May 2001

They paid R160 000 to undermine the right to free speech

Hot on the heels of the story that three senior ANC figures are plotting to oust the President comes yet another wild conspiracy theory.

According to an advertisement placed privately in the *Sunday Times* last weekend by prominent black business people, there is 'a coalition of right-wing forces' who are attempting to portray the country and its leaders in 'the most negative manner possible'.

While I would normally argue that those prepared to pay R160 000 to see their opinions in print should have their integrity respected, I can't help wondering whether the money wouldn't have been better spent seeking the services of a reliable therapist. I'm sure special discounts can be arranged for group sessions.

The signatories to 'the Media vs President TM Mbeki' suggest that by questioning the leadership of the President only two years into his five-year term, the media are guilty of an unwarranted and irresponsible attack on the country as a whole.

As Samuel Johnson remarked, 'patriotism is the last refuge of a scoundrel'.

The signatories accuse the media of being hostile to democracy and damaging the image of the country with their constant negativity.

As the signatories inelegantly put it: 'to the rest of the world and investors it portrays our country as a place not to do business with.'

Surely by placing an advertisement claiming that there is a right-wing coalition undermining the president you run a far greater risk of damaging the country's international standing than you do by demonstrating vigorous debate in a free press?

To criticise a president and government at any time is the constitutional right of any member of society, irrespective of the majority the ANC enjoys. Are the signatories seriously suggesting that anybody who doesn't support the ANC should be silenced? If the criticism or comment is libellous then there is recourse through the civil courts.

The signatories waffle on about preserving and defending democracy but it appears that this right to free speech doesn't include whites or the media. Or is it simply a case, for them, of inappropriate subject matter? You can criticise something only if it has been sanctioned for criticism by the ANC politburo ...

There is no doubt in my mind that the ANC government has achieved much more for all the people of South Africa than previous administrations. Its delivery has been impressive and it is sad that the government itself doesn't make more of its successes. As I have commented before, the government urgently needs some good communications consultants. I still believe (perhaps naively) that the majority of senior ANC politicians are honourable people who have the good of the country at heart and I fervently believe that we now live in one of the most tolerant countries in the world.

As a SA resident I would obviously prefer the country to succeed and prosper. But to suggest that to criticise the president only two years into his five-year term is to subvert the will of the majority is dangerous lunacy.

George (Dubya) Bush recently celebrated his first 100 days in office, an occasion traditionally marked by in-depth public scrutiny of the president's report card. British Prime Minister Tony Blair is under constant media criticism for his handling of the foot-and-mouth crisis and practically every major politician in the free world is fair game for the media. It goes with the territory.

The tone of the document is offensively racist and suggests that the media are against the black-run government. A few black commentators apparently 'unwittingly' contribute to this campaign. Clearly the signatories don't hold a high opinion of their fellow black professionals.

Most nauseating of all, though, is the appalling sycophancy of the document, with its smarmy personal note of encouragement to Mbeki.

It will be interesting to see if any of the signatories are beneficiaries of future government contracts, won't it?

27 May 2001

That's the way, Chris, blame the media – it works for politicians

When I first heard that Nedcor had scrapped its controversial incentive scheme my pen was poised to write a warm, congratulatory article on the triumph of decency over what looked suspiciously like dodginess, even though the banking group had taken a painfully long time to react to criticism.

It was only when I read an interview with Nedcor chairman Chris Liebenberg on the Moneyweb Internet page that I decided any gushing on my part would be rather premature.

In what comes across as a somewhat grudging interview, a peevish Liebenberg is quoted as saying of the decision to drop the scheme: 'For every argument that was raised two others came up and it became impossible for us to make any sense out of the allegations raised.' What on earth is the man on about?

His complaint seems to be that someone actually had the audacity to challenge the divine right of boards of directors to award themselves large amounts of other people's money.

Eventually, it seems, the board threw their hands up in despair and capitulated because it became so difficult for them to understand the allegations.

What's there to understand? A small group of executives were about to enrich themselves on the back of a successful investment that Nedcor had made in information technology companies. They were taking no personal financial risks and the scheme had no downside for them. Neither was it linked in any way to the performance of those executives. It was corporate piracy, pure and simple. As an aside, it would be interesting to know how many black and female employees were included in the deal.

As even journalists managed to understand the issue, it's strange that the chairman of a public company found it so difficult to comprehend. Liebenberg still protests that the bank's motives were honourable.

Later in the Moneyweb interview the following appears: 'Liebenberg lays much of the blame for the row at the door of the media. He says many of the journalists who have written about the scheme in recent weeks have done so without interviewing the group and that has led to various issues being blown out of proportion.'

Now where have we heard these weasel words before, I wonder? I was just thinking that this was precisely the sort of response one would expect from a politician and not a businessman when I remembered that Liebenberg spent some time as the country's Minister of Finance although he wasn't, in the true sense, a politician. Unfortunately though, he seems to have picked up one of the politician's less-attractive habits of blaming the media for unearthing the less-salubrious side of life and asking tricky questions.

Liebenberg's complaint that many journalists who have written about the scheme have done so without interviewing the group is quite valid, providing he appreciates the difference between a journalist and a columnist.

It is common courtesy for a journalist to speak to all parties involved in a story before going into print. Apart from good manners, it is highly unlikely that a news editor worth his or her salt will allow a sensitive story to be published without adequate evidence that the journalist has checked sources and presented an unbiased report. This is partly to protect the credibility of the newspaper and partly to avoid costly legal action.

The role of the columnist, on the other hand, is to comment on the passing parade. Obviously we prefer to get our facts right but, as far as I am concerned, there is no requirement for a columnist to interview anyone if he is putting his personal opinions into print.

Over the past few weeks Nedcor has provided a textbook example of how *not* to handle a crisis.

Since Nedcor obviously has so much money to splash about, may I suggest that it consider employing someone at a senior level to advise board members on how to avoid making fatuous and potentially damaging public pronouncements? It would be money well spent.

24 June 2001

Stupidity is no excuse for the SAA debacle – off with their heads!

The more I read about the antics of the corporate world, the more I'm convinced that many South African companies are run by complete buffoons who couldn't be trusted to put a slice of bread in a pop-up toaster without cocking it up. Take the Coleman Andrews debacle for example.

Andrews apparently earned around R232-million for three years' work, which is pretty good going even by international standards of greed. Now that this news is in the public domain, all I see are Transnet directors running around protecting their backs.

When the story first broke the impression was created that Andrews's whopping salary was something of a surprise to the Transnet directors. How can this be so? Surely somebody would have had to approve the package and the severance pay would have had to be agreed on (we hope) by a remuneration committee. How can the board plead ignorance? If they really didn't know what was going on and didn't bother to find out then they should be sued for negligence.

Judging by the ducking and diving, the only explanation I can think of is that there must be a lot more dirt at Transnet than just Coleman Andrews's salary package. At the time of writing this, many members of the board had declined to comment to the media and Transnet's chairwoman, the preening Louise Tager, was said to be 'evasive' on whether the board planned to meet. The strategy seems to be to say nothing and hope the problems will blow over. Clearly, management's attitude to transparency hasn't changed much since Transnet was one of the great bastions of the apartheid system.

This is simply not good enough. While it is abundantly clear that most of the board members of Transnet have been hideously over-promoted, they should still be compelled to answer questions, however probing. Stupidity should not be a mitigating factor when it comes to finding out what really went on at SAA.

The reason for my call for scalps is that we are all shareholders in Transnet because it is still a state-owned asset. The government's aim since it came to power has been to 'privatise' state assets, which would raise money for government coffers and ease the burden on the poor taxpayer.

The privatisation programme has been painfully slow, as any one of the foreign banks which have been hoping for a bite of the cherry will tell you. The reason the process has been so slow is threefold.

First, the nature of the business means there are lots of hangers-on who have to be 'rewarded' for their input in the privatisation process. This slows the process down because reports and feasibility studies have to be produced which give the various consultants and political appointees an excuse to hold lots of meetings. Very little is achieved apart from increasing the fee-earning potential for the 'advisers'.

Second, the process of privatisation has been placed in the hands of government ministers who know little about the wily ways of capitalism. This is hardly their fault. They were struggle politicians who suddenly found themselves in positions of power and influence.

Perhaps they naively believed that everyone was pulling together with one glorious aim in mind. In which case it was easy to pull the wool over their eyes.

Poor Jeff Radebe, the Minister of Public Enterprises, is a member of the SA Communist Party, for heaven's sake. That's like throwing Christians to the lions.

Finally, the unpredictable financial status and abysmal management of some of the parastatals has been a major problem. If you hope to sell investors' shares in a company, I should have thought a reliable profit record and a capable board would be prerequisites.

Flogging your assets (as SAA did) and then leasing them back and showing the sale proceeds as a one-off profit in the income statement is hardly subtle accounting.

As far as the management of Transnet and SAA are concerned, their lack of business acumen is well documented. The question is, will they still have their jobs this time next year and, if so, why?

1 July 2001

ANC curiously silent on despotic abuses by Swaziland king

If this column had appeared in a Swaziland newspaper I would, without any doubt, be on my way to a Swazi jail. As it is, I had to weigh the pros and cons of writing about the despotic King Mswati III, who last week declared a state of emergency that allows him to ban newspapers, jail those who ridicule him and overturn court rulings which don't happen to suit him.

If I upset the absolute monarch (sounds like a brand name for a vodka) then I run the risk of not being allowed into Mbabane, the thriving capital of this African economic powerhouse.

Or worse, I might be allowed in but I probably wouldn't be allowed out again.

The royal goons would be instructed to get out the jump leads and send a few thousand volts through the more delicate extremities of my body – a popular method of dealing with journalists who persist in misreporting government propaganda.

I decided that, on balance, I could probably cope with the enormous sacrifice of never visiting Swaziland ever again. I have been there a couple of times and the country is remarkably beautiful but who wants to lend economic support to a disgraced regime in these enlightened times? Piggs Peak will just have to survive without me.

Given the enthusiasm for human rights in South Africa, it's surprising that our government hasn't been more vociferous about our tiny eastern neighbour. I wonder if this is because it is mainly blacks who are inconvenienced by Mswati's scant regard for democracy.

In Zimbabwe, a country run by a similarly power-crazed lunatic, we have witnessed the spectacle of whites being driven violently off their farms. Naturally this has much more televisual appeal than black-on-black problems in some remote African backwater. I doubt if CNN or the BBC keep a film unit on standby just in case little Swaziland erupts into anarchy.

This sort of hypocrisy is quite understandable in Europe where most people frankly couldn't give a damn what the darkies do to each other in Africa just as long as it isn't bad for business.

Here in South Africa it is inexcusable. The situation in Swaziland has been deteriorating for some time but last week's royal proclamation sends clear signals that absolutely no opposition to the king will be tolerated.

Political parties have been banned since 1973 in Swaziland so most of the country's citizens have little idea what democracy is all about. This might have been fine in the days when the image of the country was of a fairy-tale kingdom ruled by a benevolent monarch but clearly the Disney image doesn't hold good today. The Swaziland Federation of Trade Unions has frequently lobbied for political reform and has called for strikes and a blockade of South Africa's borders in an attempt to force the king to hold democratic elections. But, so far, to no avail.

A black colleague has explained to me that nobody takes Swaziland seriously. Apart from the annual reed dance where the king selects a new wife from the bare-breasted maidens dancing before him, nobody knows (or cares) very much about the country.

An article in *New African* in April 1998 suggested that the king had managed to resist pressure for change because of the high regard in which he is held by the majority of Swazis and because of his personal charm (Mswati received a private education in England). Three years later it seems that his reserves of personal charm have run a little low and he is having to resort to less subtle methods to hang on to power.

Hopefully the South African government won't remain mute on Swaziland's growing disregard for human rights but, as we know from experience, the ANC appears to suffer from selective morality syndrome.

The imposition of economic sanctions is not an option, but a strong signal of disapproval from our government wouldn't go amiss.

Meanwhile, Mswati has also forbidden anyone from impersonating him. It's just as well that Mad Bob Mugabe didn't think of that first or Mswati would have another problem on his plate.

22 July 2001

What 'Special Price' Yengeni had to say about his Mercedes

I rather like this new trend of putting full-page adverts in national newspapers for political purposes. A few weeks ago there was that squirmingly sycophantic open letter to President Mbeki in which some 'leading' black business personalities chirped on about how beastly the media were being to our poor president. Now Tony (Sweaty Hands) Yengeni has also contributed to newspaper profits by taking a full-page advert to explain his version of how he came by his luxury Mercedes-Benz and, just for good measure, slagging off those who dared to question his integrity.

Sadly, Yengeni's advertisement was not placed in the *Sunday Times* where it would have reached an audience of well over two million readers. I assume this was an oversight and not simply a spiteful retaliation for our breaking the story in the first place.

So, as you were deprived of Mr Yengeni's published explanation last week, I thought that, in the interests of democracy, I should give you a rough rundown of his main points, together with some annotation of my own. This will save Mr Yengeni the expense of having to run an advert in the country's top-selling Sunday paper. The media has calculated the cost of last week's adverts at around R250 000, which is a hell of a lot of after-tax money for a poorly paid politician to have to shell out just to protest his innocence. Knowing Mr Yengeni's penchant for negotiating discounts, I think we can assume that he got a 'special' rate. Even so, it would still have been well beyond the means of even the 'Chief Whip of Majority Party', as Tony signs himself at the end of the letter. Did he forget the name of his party, I wonder, or is he just trying to let us know how powerful he is?

It's still strange that Yengeni has taken nearly four months to come up with a simple explanation as to how and why he came to be driving a luxury Mercedes 4x4. But of course he is a busy man and probably hadn't the time to answer a lot of cheeky questions from opposition politicians and nosy journalists.

The financial explanations are rather dull but I was intrigued as to why

Yengeni chose this particular car as his 'strugglemobile'. Apparently it was suggested that it would be very good for Mercedes-Benz's marketing strategy to have a person of Yengeni's calibre driving such a car. After all, you need a good sturdy 4x4 to get into some of those squatter settlements before you order the destruction of people's shacks in the middle of winter. And the poor would hate to see their struggle heroes slumming it in a clapped-out old Nissan. So, being the unselfish fellow that he is, Yengeni decided to help Mercedes's public image by driving one of their cars.

However, it is the rather verbose conclusion to Mr Yengeni's unconvincing protestation of innocence that tells the real story.

Yengeni complains of an 'unprecedented concoction of distortion, rumour and gossip-mongering, outright lies and half truths' (so why didn't you say something earlier, Tony?) and goes on to tell us that the biggest casualty in this affair is not Yengeni or the ANC but South Africa and its people. 'Patriotism is the last refuge of a scoundrel,' as Samuel Johnson famously remarked.

Yengeni whines that the issue of racism has reared its ugly head once again and goes on to catalogue the vast corruption of the previous administration, saying that this is seen as 'being normal and acceptable'. He complains that the 'new warriors against corruption' maintain a deafening silence on this topic and that there has been no attempt to bring previous miscreants to justice. The big question is why?

Well, Mr Yengeni, it was your party that cut the deals with the old order, guaranteeing them immunity from prosecution when you came to power. Most of us would have been delighted if the ANC had exposed and prosecuted the corruption of the previous government, instead of helping to cover it up.

To suggest that the media had a go at you simply because you happen to have a black skin and to further claim that they are racially selective when it comes to reporting corruption, damages what little credibility you had left.

12 August 2001
Nothing like a bodice ripper to give a bad dog a good name

It may not be the new Harry Potter but, according to an article in last week's Sunday Times, the Iraqi literati are raving about Saddam Hussein's new book, *Zabibah and the King*.

Apparently the allegorical novel has been greeted by rave reviews and critics say it reveals a softer, gentler side to a man that most people associate with ruthless brutality and a fanatical hatred of the Western world.

Not that you would expect anything else. I would have been very surprised if anyone in Baghdad had been prepared to say in public that Saddam's literary masterpiece is, in fact, a load of old horse manure.

So we must give the great man the benefit of the doubt, even if the CIA claims that the sex scenes were ghost-written by Danielle Steele.

The book may not be widely available on the shelves of the Iraqi equivalent of Exclusive Books but I am sure that it's only a matter of time before Mills and Boon rushes out an English translation and negotiates the movie rights.

All of this is great news for civilisation because nobody likes to believe that someone is all bad. The negative image we have of Saddam testing chemical devices on his countrymen and building up a personal arsenal of nuclear weapons is bound to improve now we know that, after a hard day's persecution of his political enemies, he sits down at his laptop and knocks off a couple of thousand words of shimmering prose before bedtime.

He is clearly a right-brain man and, believe me, I know how difficult it can be to fill a page. I don't even have the excuse of having to fit my writing into a busy schedule of hiding weapons of mass destruction from visiting UN nosy parkers.

I wouldn't be at all surprised if this doesn't trigger a cultural coming-out amongst other despots looking for a kinder press.

Now that Saddam is out of the closet as a literary lion, maybe Colonel Gaddafi will finally reveal his little-known artistic talents. A gifted impersonator,

Gaddafi frequently keeps foreign dignitaries in stitches in his Tripoli tent by reciting entire Goon Show scripts word perfect.

His favourite voice is Bluebottle, I am told, although his Eccles impersonation is almost as good as Spike Milligan himself. Gaddafi's favourite party trick, though, and one that he frequently gives on the last night of OAU meetings, is a side-splitting rendition of the dead parrot sketch from Monty Python.

Nor is it known or appreciated that Robert Mugabe is a great blues singer and guitarist with a particular fondness for the sound of the steel guitar.

His cover version of *This Land is Our Land* did remarkably well last year in Zimbabwe, although critics accuse him of having a rather limited repertoire. A keen fan of Dire Straits and particularly the soaring solo artistry of Mark Knopfler on the *Brothers in Arms* album, Mugabe is planning a comeback concert next year together with an accompanying CD: *Zimbabwe Unplugged: Blind Bob Mugabe Live at the Bulawayo Spar.*

Slobodan Milosevic, although a rotter of note, apparently used to croon along to old Frank Sinatra records and was seriously considering a career as a night-club cabaret artist until he got into ethnic cleansing, which gave him little time to rehearse.

Before he was shot by ungrateful citizens in 1989, Romania's Nicolae Ceaucescu had a part-time job as a ventriloquist's dummy.

Most of Central Africa has been ruled by stand-up comics at some stage of its history. Some of them even doubled as illusionists, making enormous amounts of money suddenly disappear and then reappear in places like Switzerland. The audience still don't know how they managed to do it, but they do know that the trick is irreversible.

I even hear that Swaziland's eccentric King Mswati III has written a cookbook called *The Naked Chief*, based on recipes he picked up during his time at a public school in England.

Particularly popular, I'm told, is his spotted dick, which serves between eight and ten.

26 August 2001

At last, a use for all those balls and coathangers: traffic-light croquet

Now that spring is approaching, exciting things are happening at traffic intersections in Johannesburg. The man with the eclectic product range of white coathangers, tennis balls and a bag of black dustbin bags is still desperately trying to interest me in his merchandise every morning.

I have tired of trying to explain to him that he needs to diversify and sell people something they might actually need. I get the impression that he may have signed a distribution contract and has no choice but to carry on flogging white coathangers, tennis balls and black dustbin bags until the contract expires.

Obviously somebody must be buying the stuff. I find it rather hard to believe that there are still people in the northern suburbs of Johannesburg who don't have enough white plastic hangers or tennis balls already, but maybe there are people out there who are obsessive collectors of these things.

Just as some people collect carriage clocks or old Dinky cars, there are quite possibly those who have a meticulously labelled collection of white plastic coathangers cluttering their spare bedrooms.

Whether or not Sotheby's ever plans to hold an auction of previously enjoyed white hangers is hard to say, but stranger things have happened. I recall that John Lennon's socks were auctioned a while ago so maybe 'Lot 36 – A white plastic coathanger, believed to have been used to hang one of Nelson Mandela's famous shirts', is not so far-fetched.

What is needed here, though, is a little lateral thinking to help boost sales. For example, if a game could be devised involving 10 white coathangers, 50 black bin bags and three tennis balls, the hawker would then have a good reason to sell all three products together.

I was thinking of a sort of traffic-intersection croquet, perhaps where the players have to coax their tennis ball through the hoops of the 10 white coathangers with a rolled-up bin bag.

The coathangers are wedged, curly bit down, in drain covers at busy intersections and the players (two to a team) alternately approach the playing field from the four directions of the intersection when the light is green.

When the lights go red their tennis ball is 'out of play' and the opposing team swings into action. The object of the game is to get your tennis ball through all the coathanger hoops on the field of play in the shortest possible time without getting flattened by a taxi or having your cellphone stolen.

The winning team is given a windscreen sticker that guarantees that no hawker will try to sell them tennis balls, coathangers or dustbin liners ever again.

The most exciting news from my local intersection, though, is that the purveyors of inflatable hammers have now been replaced by condom salesmen: a subtle variation on the inflatable hammer theme, if you think about it.

There are huge piles of blue and white boxes by the roadside containing 100 condoms a box and they are being handed out by cheerful, smiling hawkers without even a hint of coyness.

I thought they might be part of a primary healthcare initiative on the part of the government when a box was first thrust through my window. But any illusion of government-sponsored sex was shattered when the hawker asked for money in return for the box.

So I handed it back. It was something of a relief to do so. Ownership of 100 free condoms carries with it a responsibility to use them. I asked one hawker what on earth I was going to do with 100 condoms and he told me to wear two at a time and be doubly sure.

A female journalist of my acquaintance thought she was being handed a box of tissues and only discovered the mistake when she tried to blow her nose on one.

The question is, why are we whiteys suddenly being offered bulk consignments of no-name-brand condoms? My guess is that it's all part of the preparation for greater things to come.

Now that prostitution is no longer an offence, the intersections will shortly be crowded with scantily clad young women offering sexual services. Like good Boy Scouts, we need to be prepared.

2 September 2001

Dishonesty in public life ought to be punished as treason

I'm not familiar with Frene Ginwala's reading habits. For all I know she may like to curl up on a winter's night with a cup of warm cocoa and a leather-bound copy of Hansard. Or perhaps she prefers something a little more racy. One thing seems certain though; she is definitely not a reader of the *Out to Lunch* column.

Her comments more than a week ago that Parliament must act urgently to preserve its credibility come a mere seven years after the very same sentiment was first expressed in this column. Despairing that the message wasn't getting through I have repeated it over the years, but with little effect.

I suppose we should find some solace in the fact that the Speaker of the National Assembly has finally realised that the public image of politicians is, as the Australians so elegantly put it, 'lower than the shadow of shark shit'.

This is not a problem unique to South Africa. Politicians are seen as self-serving opportunists everywhere in the world and that's generally because that is exactly what they are. As Lord Acton remarked: 'Power tends to corrupt, and absolute power corrupts absolutely.'

South African politicians like to believe that attacks on them must be motivated by racism but, in truth, criticism of politicians has very little to do with skin colour.

Scumbags come in all colours and when the people see their leaders burying their snouts in the trough, ducking and diving whenever they are asked reasonable questions and appointing their friends and family to influential positions, they become disillusioned with the democratic process.

Unfortunately, the dishonest and arrogant behaviour of the few gives the rest a bad name.

There will always be those to whom public office appears as an opportunity for personal enrichment rather than a chance to make a real difference to the development and growth of South Africa.

The worrying thing is not just that their behaviour is tolerated but that the ruling party is prepared to close ranks to protect them, which does absolutely nothing for Parliament's credibility or the country's reputation. How often has the public exposure of some malfeasance resulted in a lame internal inquiry and the convenient removal of the embarrassing incident from the pages of our newspapers?

It has become abundantly clear over the past seven years that the intellectual demands of Parliament are beyond many of its members. South Africa Inc needs to be run on business lines and the empty benches of the National Assembly suggest that it is not. A cull is long overdue.

However, it's not only the rank and file that need to be thinned. There are also some senior MPs who are a disgrace and it is in South Africa's long-term interest that such people are removed from office immediately.

I think it's time to reconsider the crime of treason, defined as 'the violation or betrayal of the allegiance that a person owes his country'. Let us take the case of the ANC Chief Whip, Tony Yengeni, as an example.

The *Sunday Times* revealed details of Yengeni's luxury 4x4 several months ago. Yengeni still hasn't adequately explained the unusual procurement and financing details of the vehicle. It may be that there is a reasonable explanation but we have yet to hear it. Until we do, the ANC has a huge question mark hanging over its claims to espouse 'transparency'.

Meanwhile the Yengeni case, among others, is well known to foreign observers and helps to reinforce the country's image of a basket case in waiting. It is impossible to put a price to the damage done to South Africa's standing by the controversy surrounding the arms deal, the frequent 'cover-ups' of political incompetence and the many incidents of dishonesty and lack of accountability.

All these are acts of treason in some form and should be punished as such.

28 October 2001

Don't despair: you can still go pretty far on a shrivelled rand

As we watch the rand shrink daily against most other currencies it's important to keep a level head. We know (because we have frequently been told so) that the 'real' value of the rand is actually much higher than the one we hear quoted on the evening news.

The only problem is the dreaded speculators who have pushed the rand to artificially low levels for their own nefarious reasons, many of them related to trading-desk profitability.

This has led to a situation whereby the rand has mysteriously become 'undervalued', which means that the current market value actually bears no relevance to the real value of the currency.

The only problem with this argument is that no one seems keen to trade the rand at the so-called 'real' value, which suggests to my whisky-addled brain that the rand isn't undervalued at all.

It may even be that it is overvalued, in which case we can all continue to wallow in gloom and give up hope of ever travelling overseas again. That might turn out to be a blessing in disguise because it will save us from the inconvenience of arriving at an airport eight hours before an international flight to face a battery of security checks, anthrax tests, penknife confiscations and the probing latex-clad finger of the internal body search. Faced with such customer care, who would opt for air travel?

Since September 11 it is probably not the fear of flying that has caused a substantial reduction in airline passengers but the attendant inconvenience of travelling by air.

Personally, I have never thought it a particularly good idea to get into a long metal cylinder packed with highly flammable liquid, but statistics suggest that you only really have problems if the cylinder hits something and the fuel catches fire, in which case you know very little about it anyway.

So airline travel is still a relatively safe way to go, probably more so now than it has ever been. It is also much cheaper in real terms than it was 20 years ago when the rand was trading at about R1.80 to the pound.

South Africans may not be aware that they enjoy some of the cheapest international airfares in the world. The problem is the perception of how little the rand will buy when you arrive at your destination, which leads to widespread national depression when the rand carries on plummeting.

If you still insist on staying in five-star hotels in major capital cities, your overseas holiday will certainly cost much more than it did a year ago.

If, on the other hand, you are prepared to shop around for alternatives, then there are plenty of destinations that South Africans can still afford.

Cathay Pacific tell me that they have seen an increase in bookings as adventure destinations such as Vietnam and China become more popular.

Australia is also proving to be a smart choice and it's interesting to note that a night in one of its upmarket bed-and-breakfast establishments will often cost you less than the South African equivalent, even though the rand is trading at around R4.75 to the Australian dollar.

Even a visit to Europe is affordable if you are prepared to travel out of the big cities and into the less crowded areas. A shared villa in Tuscany is still good value and there are some astounding package holidays in countries such as Spain.

The best news of all though is that you can bargain now as never before as the lemmings all cancel their holidays.

Those hoping for a dramatic recovery in the rand are likely to be disappointed. Any improvement is likely to be testudinal in pace and probably temporary. So the sooner we all adjust to the fact that the rand is unlikely to become one of the world's major trading currencies, the better.

The bad news is that the strong pound has made South Africa an affordable destination for loudmouthed, low-class Brits, who can now afford to eat at restaurants like Constantia Uitsig and 96 Winery Road.

For that reason alone, Tito Mboweni should be supporting the rand like crazy.

4 November 2001

My new mission: to put the fun back into fundamentalism

I've decided to become a fundamentalist. It's all the rage these days and, besides, everything else looks quite middle of the road by comparison.

If you can't be extreme, why bother at all?

The only problem is the small matter of choice.

I've had a good look around at the various fundamentalist movements on offer and, while I don't doubt their sincerity, I also can't really see what's in it for me if I sign on the dotted line.

For example, members of most extremist religious organisations seem to take the gloomy view that their particular choice of deity would have a serious sense of humour failure if they even looked as though they were enjoying life.

This is not particularly sound thinking because there is hardly any point in creating beauty and then forbidding people to enjoy it. On the other hand, if you just sit around and say: 'How lovely,' you can hardly call yourself a fundamentalist, can you?

So, in order to set yourself apart from the easily appeased, run-of-the-mill acolytes, you have to come up with a new set of rules based loosely on the first set of rules.

The idea is that the new set of rules is much more difficult to observe, which gives them their fundamentalist edge. Having had a look at various brands of fundamentalism and found them wanting, I've decided that it's high time someone put the 'fun' back into fundamentalism and came up with something more in tune with modern needs.

So I have just formed an extremist group of 'fanatical hedonist fundamentalists' to appeal to all those people who don't think that life's too bad but that it could probably be even better with a bit of effort.

Unlike militant fundamentalist organisations, we're not planning to blow up any cars, take hostages, burn flags, murder and maim anyone who disagrees with us or demand our own homeland. What we are going to do is devote our lives to strict adherence to hedonistic principles in the sure knowledge that a benevolent deity is smiling kindly down at our efforts. Which is not to say that we are one of those limp-wristed, pushover fundamentalist organisations.

Just because we don't let loose a furious volley of automatic rifle fire into the air if the froth on our cappuccino isn't creamy enough doesn't mean we won't rise up as one and seek justice and froth in the future. You don't mess with extremists if you know what's good for you.

Take dry martinis, for example. A slop of cheap gin, a slop of Martini all served with too much ice in a long glass may be acceptable to unbelievers, but to a member of the hedonist fundamentalist movement it would be anathema. We fundamentalists insist that the correct glass should be pre-chilled in the freezer for at least half an hour. A bottle of chilled Tanqueray's gin should be on hand and the recommended mix of 95% gin to 5% French dry vermouth (only Noilly Prat will do) should be shaken with a few ice cubes and poured lovingly into the chilled glass. Finally, a washed olive and a twist of fresh lemon peel should be added to the glass. Anything less is not a fundamentalist martini and should be sent back to the kitchen or poured over the waiter.

You would also be unlikely to find a hedonist fundamentalist watching *Big Brother* or buying a lottery ticket. This is not because of strict ethical standards. In the case of *Big Brother* it's simply a matter of always having something more interesting to watch and, as far as the lottery is concerned, most hedonist fundamentalists would regard the prize money as derisory.

It's interesting to note that the strict hedonist fundamentalist male dress code of Savile Row suits, handmade shirts and silk ties has been enthusiastically adopted by many ANC politicians who are keen to align themselves with the organisation.

The undisputed high priestess of the movement (which treats its womenfolk rather better than most fundamentalist groups) even manages to spend R72 000 a month despite only earning R17 000. Now that's real extremism for you.

2 December 2001

Bring on the Havanas and pass the port: There's work to be done!

A couple of years ago I cracked an invite to lunch at the head office of one of the country's larger mining conglomerates.

Guests were ushered into an elegant bar area next to the dining room and offered a pre-lunch drink by one of the stewards.

To my horror, my fellow guests ordered mineral water and soft drinks and, when it came to my turn, I really tried to say: 'sparkling mineral water please,' but it came out as: 'large Scotch and soda please.' There was a good deal of embarrassed coughing and shuffling from the assembled suits and I felt rather like one of those socially inept characters in a Bateman cartoon ... *'the man who ordered alcohol at a corporate lunch.'*

I suspect it was the presence of the company chairman that put the others on their best behaviour. Even during the meal the wine bottle was a rare visitor to the table and I noticed at least half a bottle of goodish red still sitting on the sideboard when we were ejected at exactly 2.15 pm.

I grew up in a business environment where lunch was not regarded as a luxury but a necessity. I'm not talking about taking 40 minutes off at 1 pm for a wholewheat roll and energy drink, either. The City of London in the 1970s was one large luncheon club. At about 11.30 am, the business of trading in stocks, shares and government bonds would gradually wind down as jobbers, brokers and fund managers made their way to one of the many city watering holes for a pre-lunch pink gin or whatever. Then, after a cursory glance at the state of the markets, we would all push off to a proper sit-down lunch.

First prize, though, was an invitation to one of the better city dining rooms. Not only was the quality of the food excellent but it meant that nobody at the table had to take part in an unseemly fight for the bill.

In those days, banks and stockbrokers vied with one another to provide the most extravagant lunch. The whole idea was to bolster business and political relationships and you can't do that over a mineral water and salad.

If anyone had ordered a soft drink before lunch we would naturally have assumed they were suffering from hepatitis. Most decent lunch rooms served a proper four-course meal with a wine for each course.

The quality of the company cellar was of the utmost importance and it was fairly common to be served well-cellared vintages.

One or two cheapskate firms introduced buffet lunches but they were regarded as highly suspect and to be avoided at all costs.

After the cheese board had been cleared away, the stewards would then offer a choice of Havana cigars and the port and brandy would be served. This usually happened at around 3 pm and meant that lunch would finally end at about 3.45 pm, which gave us just enough time to get back to our own offices, pack up our things and catch a train home.

Was this good for business efficiency, I hear you ask? Well, there was never any proof that it wasn't, but I can't say that the present minimalist lunch trends have done much to enhance shareholder value. I gather there are even some companies that ban the consumption of alcohol during working hours. If that had happened back in the 1970s, you would never have persuaded anybody to embark on a career in the financial markets.

These days, you are no longer supposed to enjoy your working day and key employees are expected to commit themselves to absurdly long working hours, including weekends.

Meetings drag on for ages and it seems that you are judged by the length of your working day rather than your creative output. This is muddled thinking. In the days when we still had long lunches we knew we had only a limited period in which to produce profits. Consequently, we were much more motivated.

Apart from providing a focal point in the working day, a good lunch offers the opportunity for people to laugh, share ideas, get to know one another better and support the local wine industry. The mineral water and limp salad brigade belong in a cave in Afghanistan.

20 January 2002

Outing culprits will do little to solve the rand murder mystery

Was it Colonel Mustard in the library with the lead piping or the Rev. Green in the kitchen with the dagger?

There has been some skulduggery up at the manor house and the rand has been found lying in a pool of blood, bludgeoned violently about the head and shoulders by persons unknown. Not actually dead but twitching spasmodically.

The zealous young Inspector Kevin Wakeford was on the case and has now handed over his bulging dossier of evidence to Superintendent John Myburgh for further investigation.

I don't see Wakeford as the moody Inspector Morse type, listening to hours of Wagner while he toys with a tumbler of malt whisky and goes over the details of the case in his mind until the missing piece of the jigsaw falls into place.

Neither do I see him as Hercule Poirot, whose tactic is to make everybody a suspect and to eliminate them one by one using 'ze little grey cells'. Did Wakeford perhaps intend to call all those who have dealt in the rand over the past couple of months into the dining room at precisely midday to announce the real villain? I think not.

No, unfortunately I see him more in the role of the bumbling Inspector Clousseau on this one.

It's well known that the SA Chamber of Commerce, and Wakeford, its CEO, in particular, have just emerged from a dismal year, with the organisation's reputation in tatters. Sacob claims to represent 40 000 businesses, which may very well be true if one is merely counting subscriptions. However, I question whether Sacob can really claim to speak on behalf of big business. So perhaps all the media noise and front-page coverage is little more than a publicity stunt to boost Sacob's flagging public image. After all, what could be more public spirited at this particular time than to 'out' the wicked folk who have been selling our poor rand?

The question is, are there any hard facts?

Wakeford has, as the saying goes, been acting on information received, according to media reports. 'Reliable sources have apparently indicated that certain individuals and institutions have colluded under false pretences to enrich themselves, utilising dubious financial methods and instruments.' Those are serious allegations and the obvious question is how Inspector Wakeford can know about this while the financial authorities still seem to be in the dark as to reasons for the recent weakness of the rand.

The reality of financial markets is that they can be dangerous and unpredictable places. By electing to open up our economy we put ourselves at the mercy of all sorts of speculators and short-term profit seekers.

Back in the pre-democracy days I worked in the bond market. Every so often, to demonstrate our opposition to the apartheid regime, we would go short of government stock if we thought interest rates were about to rise. In other words, we would sell what we didn't own in the hopes of buying it back cheaper. In order to deliver the stock we had sold we would borrow the same stock, at a price, from another market player and run the short position for maximum profit. Unfortunately it didn't always go as planned and we sometimes lost money.

The notion that a handful of unscrupulous layabouts have got together to manipulate the rand is pure fantasy. When you try to manipulate the currency markets you are taking a calculated risk. Even Mr George Soros has been hung out to dry by the markets.

So the idea that the fall in the rand is solely attributable to people acting illegally seems unlikely. Should that turn out to be the case then there are laws which can be enforced, although I wouldn't hold my breath for an insider-trading prosecution.

We urgently need to grow up in this country and to stop looking around for people to blame whenever anything unpleasant happens. The recipe for a strong currency is simple: decisive leadership, global competitiveness, a stable political system and the maturity not to be cry-babies every time that something goes wrong.

10 February 2002

Someone didn't get the joke but, frankly speaking, the laugh's on them

Official commissions of inquiry are strange beasts. Their principal purpose seems to be to deflect blame from politicians in matters over which they exercise no direct control.

Because they are run by lawyers, the findings of a commission will extend to 800 closely typed pages when they could just as easily have conveyed the same message in five.

Since most people can't be bothered to read 800 pages of lawyer-speak, the findings and the recommendations of a commission are usually ignored.

However, at least the creaking machinery of democracy is seen to be working and a few lucky folk get to earn a fat chunk of taxpayer's money by sitting around and waffling on about something they don't really understand while drinking lukewarm tea.

The official inquiry into the fall of the rand, already regarded as something of a joke by most thinking adults, recently blew any remaining hope of credibility by appointing Christine Qunta as a member.

Christine is a weekly columnist for *Business Day*, but moonlights as a lawyer. Her column, *Frankly Speaking*, is entertaining (even if she admits to being dumb to the subtle delights of opera) and her stock in trade is to annoy readers enough to make them want to write letters to the editor.

That sort of thing is good for business because it makes people talk about *Business Day*.

It also has a secondary advantage: the columnist achieves a status of minor celebrity, particularly if their photograph appears next to the byline. Poor Christine probably can't pop into Woollies for a bag of lemons without being recognised by her adoring public.

But that is the price of fame and, to a relative newcomer like Christine, being recognised in public must come as a thrilling alternative to being shut up in a room with all those stuffy old law books.

In her wildest dreams, I doubt she ever imagined that someone might take what she wrote seriously and appoint her to the commission on the rand's demise.

As an old hand at the business of writing a weekly column, allow me to let you in on a couple of trade secrets. In order to keep the editor smiling, give radio talk show hosts something to chat about and to remain in the public eye it is necessary, from time to time, to put forward contentious ideas in the interest of stimulating public debate. Newspapers are pure showbiz and the columnist's role is simply to comment on the passing parade rather than report on it.

There are weeks when, for sheer devilment, one writes an article devoid of all logic and common sense and simply intended to provoke hostile response; an article so surreal and over the top that only a complete idiot would take it seriously.

This is precisely what Christine did with her piece on who was responsible for the fall of the rand.

Talking about the biggest threat to the economy coming from a small and vocal group within the country she wrote: 'Motivated by greed and bitterness at the passing of the old order, they actively instigate and collude with those in the capitals of the western world who benefit from African, Asian and South American countries perpetually being emerging markets or developing nations.'

It's a spectacular piece of nonsense writing, worthy of Lewis Carroll or Edward Lear, but unfortunately somebody didn't understand the joke – and now poor Christine has been appointed a commissioner she has to pretend she was being serious.

Worse, she has to come up with evidence to prove that there is, in fact, some sinister plot on behalf of the world's most powerful nations to destroy the South African economy. It is a demanding task and will require all the imagination and creative energy she can muster. Hopefully her presence on the commission may encourage the others not to write in gobbledegook but in a form of English her readers have come to know and love.

And as she sits with her colleagues, meticulously examining the past year's foreign exchange dealing sheets of our major banks, my advice to her is to sit back, smile, and think of the money.

It's infinitely better than the rate for a freelance columnist.

17 February 2002

It's a bit rich of the WEF to debate poverty amid five-star luxury

On our first visit to New York, my wife and I stayed at the Waldorf-Astoria Hotel on Park Avenue. The Art-Deco splendour of the vast and busy foyer doesn't suggest that this is the sort of hotel to offer heavily discounted accommodation.

Our room was impressive, with a large onyx writing desk and a few couches scattered about in the entrance lobby, the vast bed a short bus ride away with a magnificent marble bathroom trailing off somewhere in the north-east corner.

A pair of louvred double doors opened to reveal a good-sized bar area that could be stocked at a moment's notice should we wish to entertain 30 close friends in our room.

Just for the hell of it, we ordered room-service breakfast. At 8 a.m. the next day, there was a sharp knock on the door, and two trolleys were wheeled in by immaculately dressed staff. On the trolleys' starched white-linen cloths stood jugs of fresh orange juice, silver pots of steaming coffee, toast racks and all the paraphernalia that goes with a room-service breakfast in a top hotel.

It was ludicrously expensive, but it's no bad thing to behave like a movie star every once in a while. We ate breakfast dressed in our complimentary white-towelling dressing gowns while we zapped through the 45 or so TV channels that you find in New York hotel rooms. Having blown a substantial part of our budget, we opted for a $4 breakfast (unlimited coffee) at a diner in Lexington Avenue for the rest of our stay.

In the early evening we visited the Waldorf's cocktail terrace for a couple of pre-prandial Manhattans while someone played Cole Porter's grand piano. There we discussed the relative merits of being rich rather than poor and, over the clinking ice cubes, came to the conclusion that it's much more agreeable to have money than not, particularly when you happen to be staying at the Waldorf-Astoria.

The World Economic Forum (WEF) has just vacated the same hotel, and I am still confused as to what this year's glitzy event was all about.

Normally held in Davos, Switzerland, the WEF moved to New York for the first time in 31 years to 'show support' for the city. That's very kind of them, I'm sure, but by holding the WEF in New York rather than some remote, icy location in the Swiss Alps, the general effect has been to highlight the benefits of having lots of money while apparently taking the mickey out of the poor.

Not that I am suggesting that the WEF delegates should be put up in the local Salvation Army hostel. It's just that sitting in the sumptuous opulence of the Waldorf-Astoria and agonising over the plight of the *wealth-deprived* while anti-globalisation and anti-capitalism demonstrators are being held at bay outside by heavily armed riot police strikes me as rather surreal.

The WEF is strictly an invitation-only do, unless you're prepared to pay up, in which case you're most welcome to attend. Someone mentioned a figure of $25 000 for a corporate ticket. The whole point of this is to keep the great unwashed out. The sort of people who might turn up in grubby anoraks and beanies and drone on about how the world's resources should be more equitably shared. It wouldn't do to have poor people discussing their own plight, would it?

So Klaus Schwab, the WEF supremo, prefers to decide who will and who will not be permitted to penetrate the tight security cordon thrown around the event. Leftie beardie weirdies and muesli munchers are certainly not high on his invitation list.

I turned on the telly one evening to try to make sense of it all, and there was a discussion forum in progress with our own Archbishop Desmond Tutu participating. Next to him was a nameplate that read 'Bono' and a man with wraparound sunglasses sitting in a chair holding hands with the Arch. Edward de, I wondered? But I was being literal rather than lateral, and it turned out to be a very rich rock musician who is extremely concerned about people who don't make quite as much as he does and is going to do something about it. That's nice, I thought to myself. Now I'll have to tune in to Davos next year to see if he really meant it.

24 February 2002

Why we need a sports minister – to keep the race issue in play

More than five years ago in this column, I asked how a country like South Africa could afford the luxury of a sports minister. At the time, the incumbent was Steve Tshwete.

He immediately launched an angry counterattack in the form of a letter which was printed, to huge critical acclaim, instead of my *Out to Lunch* column. Unfortunately, the *Sunday Times* couldn't persuade Tshwete to embark on a career as a columnist. He went on to become our Minister of Safety and Security with special responsibility for nipping coups and revolutions in the bud.

I phoned his office shortly after the publication of his letter and was put straight through to the minister who, instead of ranting and screaming, turned out to be very reasonable and pleasant. We even tried to arrange lunch but the minister's schedule made it difficult and, on the one day we did manage to find a mutually acceptable date and time, he was stuck in a traffic jam and his secretary phoned to cancel.

It's well known that men of the cloth recycle their sermons and that, if you are a regular churchgoer, you are bound eventually to hear a sermon repeated word for word. In the Church of England this isn't really a problem because most attendees are so old that they probably wouldn't remember having heard a repeated sermon before. So, if it's good enough for the C of E, it's good enough for me although, strictly speaking, this isn't a repetition but more a leitmotif.

Today's philosophy exam question: If Ngconde Balfour didn't exist, would it be necessary to invent him? No more than 500 words please, and write clearly on one side of the paper.

Five years on, I still question the need for a sports minister in a developing country with more urgent problems to be addressed. Surely it's a joke portfolio, designed more as a sop to a loyal ANC supporter who is not cut out for the weightier challenges of government.

You can imagine other ministers doodling on their pads or filling in their crossword puzzles when the president calls for a report from the sports minister during a cabinet meeting. Compared, for example, with Trevor Manuel or Alec Erwin, anything that Balfour has to say is relatively trivial. He hasn't had to negotiate the renaming of sports as Erwin has had to negotiate the renaming of port and ouzo, although I'm surprised we are still allowed to use the word 'rugby', named, as it is, after an English public school.

Unlike Manuel, nothing Balfour says is likely to affect the rand adversely or send interest rates shooting up and nothing he does can ever have a major impact on black upliftment.

Even if he appointed an all-black cricket team, that's only 11 previously disadvantaged people who would be affected. Unless Balfour invents a new sport with a team of a few hundred thousand, his policy of a demographically representative national squad at any cost is unlikely to touch the lives of many.

On the upside, he still gets good seats at all the major sporting events and he is a man who clearly enjoys a well-stocked buffet. Indeed, there are those who feel a leaner, more athletic-looking sports minister would be less likely to attract sniggers at international gatherings.

So what is the real function of the sports minister? Well, it appears his main purpose is to keep the race issue alive. While most South Africans have become colour blind, the issue of racism is important to a government that may need someone to blame if something goes wrong.

So it's Ngconde's job to keep reminding us how racial discrimination is preventing the talented Soweto girls' synchronised underwater orienteering team from reaching the Athens Olympics.

He may well be right, just as he may well be right about the paleness of the national rugby and cricket teams. The only way we will know for sure is if he is given sole responsibility for selecting the national sides as he sees fit.

If they go on to lose we can then demand the resignation of the politician responsible. As far as I can see, it's our only chance of getting rid of the sports minister.

17 March 2002

The price of fame and the strange, disconnected world of PR

I had a phone call from someone in 'peeeaaah' the other day. That's PR to you; as in public relations, the strange, disconnected world that is inhabited by disillusioned ex-journalists and young girls with big breasts and a perpetual sniff whose exposure to current affairs appears to begin and end with *You* magazine.

The 'peeeaah' was phoning on behalf of a drinks company and breathlessly asked me whether I was David Bullard, the writer. I cagily answered that, broadly speaking, I might fit the description of the man she was looking for.

'Oh thank heavens,' she said, 'because I phoned *The Star* and they said that you didn't work there any more and they didn't know how to get hold of you.'

I like to think that I have remained unaffected by the burden of celebrity status that comes with a weekly column in the *Sunday Times*. Not for me the Russell Crowe tantrums or the contractual stipulation that my star dressing room must be stocked with Chivas Regal 12-year old whenever I do a gig for the Rotarians.

I hardly ever ask for my hotel suite to be redecorated to my specific requirements before I deign to move in and have no intention of going into rehab to boost my flagging career. All is ask is that barmen address me by name and that restaurant owners will overlook the fact that I couldn't be bothered to book and will immediately find me a table in their crowded restaurant, despite the queue of patient customers who have been waiting an hour.

Anyway, reluctant celebrity that I am, I still couldn't help feeling slightly peeved that a peeeaaah who claimed to need my services as an MC so badly couldn't even be bothered to find out which newspaper I wrote for.

It was not so much vanity on my part as irritation and envy that there exists a lucrative industry founded on ignorance and stupidity and I'm not part of it.

Another peeeaaah heard that I wrote a column called 'Out to Lunch' but had never actually bothered to read it.

This resulted in a hilarious string of invitations to review restaurants for my 'food' column. I point out that my column, despite the misleading title, rarely had anything to do with food. 'so, what is it about?' she asked, no doubt hoping for another crack at free publicity for one of her clients. I found it impossible to answer her question.

Last week, a peeeaaah phoned and told me that a group of top businessmen were going to have a power breakfast and had specifically requested that I address them. This wasn't going to be second-tier stuff either. Only the most powerful in the land would be there to listen to my words of wisdom. I must admit to being slightly sceptical at the time because my experience of the top tier suggests that they are much too busy awarding themselves bonuses and unlocking shareholder value to toy with a couple of slices of overcooked bacon and a rubbery omelette while listening to the golden tones of Bullard.

I asked what they wanted me to talk about. 'Oh, the outlook for the economy, interest rates, where the rand is going ... things like that.'

Suddenly the penny dropped. The peeeaaah had been asked to find an economist but had misheard the instructions and was phoning a columnist ... an easy mistake, try saying both quickly to yourself.

A quick check of the other potential speakers on her list (poor seconds I hasten to add, should I be indisposed) revealed a role call of some of the best-known names in journalism. I helpfully suggested that we were all as capable as any economist of putting forward a view on the economy, and probably a good deal more entertainingly.

There was a frustrated sigh at the other end of the phone as the peeeaaah realised that she would now have to get hold of the names of some economists to phone. She'd already had to phone her friends to get the names of these damn columnists and hadn't even had time to find out what they wrote or who they worked for.

Then an idea struck. Did I, by any chance, know the names of any economists? 'Sure,' I said, 'there's Kenny Galbraith, Adam Smith, Jonny M Keynes and, if you don't think it'll put the audience off their breakfast, Tom Malthus.'

I'll bet you a pound to a press kit that at least one phone call last week began with the words ... 'Hi, is that Kenny Galbraith, the economist?'

24 March 2002

Take a tip from me: SA tourism is about to enter a bull market

Having just returned from three days as master of ceremonies at the Association of South African Travel Agents' annual congress, I admit to a new respect for those involved in the travel industry.

By normal business standards, their margins are appallingly low and constantly under threat. All sorts of unpredictable events such as September 11, surprise military coups on sun-kissed holiday islands, natural disasters and volatile currency swings spook the industry and – to add to their woes – travel fashions change all the time.

It's certainly not a business for the faint-hearted.

However, it seems that successful travel agents are made of sterner stuff. Judging by the ones I met at the congress, you need a mixture of unbounded enthusiasm for the product, a genuine desire to please your client and an amazingly thick skin to succeed.

I have rarely met people more devoted to their industry and, after a few days with them, the reason for their high pain threshold became clear. They know South African tourism has huge, untapped potential and are just waiting for the good times to roll. It is as if, a few metres below the dusty topsoil, a rich seam of gold lies waiting to be discovered. When that happens (and there are signs that it is already happening) this country will become one of the most popular holiday destinations in the world, with all the trickle-down benefits that brings.

The congress was held in Port Elizabeth this year – and I promise never to be rude about Port Elizabeth again. The weather was stunning with not a breath of wind until the day I left.

The beaches were clean and The Courtyard hotel where I stayed offered a level of service that I have only previously experienced in five-star hotels. All the hotel rooms face the sea and the rand price of my suite per night would just about pay for a round of drinks for four in a London hotel. Hardly surprising that foreign delegates were walking around in a daze at the comparative cheapness of everything.

It wasn't a difficult task, but I managed to tempt a few North American visitors to have a final after-dinner drink in a hotel bar on Thursday night. They grabbed the bill and, at less than $1.50 for a tot of whisky, it would have been rude not to.

Earlier in the week, I spent a day at the Shamwari Game Reserve and that, too, was an education. In my shameful ignorance I thought that Shamwari had simply introduced wild animals to the Eastern Cape to try to boost tourism and lure foreign visitors away from the Kruger Park. Not so. The animals were there long before we were and Adrian Gardiner and his team are busy restoring the area to its former glory. The reserve covers 18 000 ha of pristine bush with the added benefit that you don't need to worry about malaria. I spoke to some of my fellow guests about their impressions.

Most were first-time visitors to South Africa and had come here because friends had visited and returned home with positive feedback. They were, to a person, stunned by the beauty of the country, the service levels, the quality of accommodation and the bewildering choice of what to do and see. They will, they assured me, be back. They will, they promised, tell their friends all about it.

One of the major obstacles cited by the tourism industry has been a negative perception of this country abroad. Ex-pat South Africans bad-mouthed the country so nobody came ... or so the theory went.

I never subscribed to the view that an émigré with a gripe could destroy the prospects for South African tourism. What kept people away were negative political perceptions from our past. To an extent, this still exists.

But foreign tourists are not fools. They know that there is crime in every country and that every country has its social problems. The UK had one of its worst years for tourism last year.

As with most businesses, things tend to go in cycles and I have a gut feeling that SA tourism is about to experience an unprecedented bull market, both domestically and internationally.

I will certainly go back to the Eastern Cape. It is an unbelievably beautiful region and I'm only annoyed that I didn't discover it earlier. I think the locals have been trying to keep it for themselves.

31 March 2002

State's Aids stance means it wants a lean and mean workforce

I have, thus far, avoided the touchy topic of HIV/Aids in this column and for a very good reason. I am not HIV-positive and I know very few people who are HIV- positive and so it is, rather conveniently, not my problem.

At this point, I imagine, those of you who are HIV-positive or like to think of yourselves as concerned citizens are thinking of writing an indignant letter to the editor of the *Sunday Times* complaining (in the strongest possible terms) about my insensitivity and lack of compassion and demanding that he sack me. Before you go to all the trouble of finding a pen that works and a piece of notepaper worthy of a letter to this august newspaper, allow me to explain myself. I have just paid you the compliment of being refreshingly honest and I suspect that my lack of concern is rather more commonplace than you may care to think.

The vociferous and well-organised HIV/Aids lobby would have us believe that this is an issue which affects us all; it is not. Many people couldn't give a toss because it is not a problem that directly touches their lives. Besides, why should people who are HIV-positive be more deserving of public sympathy and government funding than tuberculosis sufferers, cancer cases or manic depressives?

For some bizarre reason, HIV has become the *maladie du jour*, the illness to be fashionably concerned about. Perhaps this is because we know so little about it but my natural cynicism tells me that anything fashionable today will, as like as not, be out of fashion tomorrow.

People wander around with those trendy red-ribbon brooches to show they care, which is all very well but what, apart from publicly demonstrating a cringing deference to political correctness, does a red Aids ribbon brooch actually mean? Are we to believe that the wearers are tirelessly working behind the Aids frontline, taking chicken soup to the sick and needy or changing the soiled bed linen of people too ill to move? I rather doubt it.

For the rest of us, it's all very well to get hot under the collar about President Mbeki's apparently weird views on HIV but are the rest of us any better informed? The endless debate on how to combat the problem of HIV/Aids has become so dreary and tedious that it ranks with the Middle East peace process as one of the longest-running and most repetitively boring news stories of all time. The relative merits of giving something called Nevirapine to the HIV-positive mothers of babies has been used as a political football for so long now that someone should think of blowing the final whistle. It's a game no one can win because nobody has yet been honest enough to address the real issue.

If the government is going to commit itself to providing drugs to those with HIV it would have to do so at the taxpayer's expense. Given that the majority of those infected are not the most economically productive members of society, this would amount to preserving the lives of those who are unlikely to make any significant economic contribution to South Africa at the expense of the economically active.

To put it in business parlance, it's a lose-lose situation. It's a negative return on investment because it is highly unlikely that the children of poor HIV-infected parents will lead bountiful lives, walk into well-paying jobs and become valuable members of the SA economic machine. Not impossible I grant you, but highly unlikely.

So the government has to make a difficult decision. Does it hand out taxpayer-sponsored, life-preserving drugs to the poor, knowing that, by so doing, the drain on the exchequer can only grow, or does it take the view that a smaller, healthier and more economically viable population is in South Africa's long-term interest? I believe it has decided on the latter but, because HIV/Aids is such an emotional matter, it has to fudge the whole issue by pretending it is not convinced that Nevirapine is the right drug to hand out.

Unless we are living in an Orwellian topsy-turvy land, we must assume that the Minister of Health, a qualified doctor, is there to promote the good health of all South African citizens. Since there is not a shred of evidence to suggest this is the case, I can only assume that her best intentions (not to mention the Hippocratic oath) have been over-ruled in the interests of a socio-economic master plan for a lean and mean, economically sound future South Africa. John Stuart Mill would have been proud of her.

5 May 2002

Should Mark have spent so much to send himself up?

Should Mark Shuttleworth, or 'M Wattnbopt' as the Russians prefer to call him, have spent so much money sending himself up?

This question was asked recently on *Cape Talk* and I tuned in just in time to hear fellow columnist Max du Preez's views on the subject.

Max prefaced his comments by admitting that he had an aversion to rich people, thus leaving the audience free to dismiss his contribution as the ramblings of an embittered, underpaid hack who probably doesn't even know how many noughts there are in a billion.

One of the more unfortunate side effects of a career in journalism is that it instils in many of its practitioners an irrational loathing of those who make bucket loads of money.

The fact that they sometimes make it legally is immaterial.

While discussing the current malaise of the print media at a luncheon last week, I explained to my hosts that the salary for the position of deputy editor of a well-known magazine was all of R9 000 a month. I don't think they believed me. Is it any wonder that many of the best and brightest leave journalism and move on to greener pastures?

Those who remain certainly don't do it to become rich. Fortunately a career in journalism has many other compensations, not the least of which is working with other slightly offbeat people who enjoy an occasional drink.

From a free press perspective, it's probably better to employ the sort of people who are naturally suspicious of anyone with more than R500 in their current account.

A wealthy journalist soon becomes part of the establishment and the natural inclination to strip away the veneer of respectability and expose the canker beneath is tempered by the fear of offending those with influence. British newspaper editors are a fine example.

They love to be invited to 10 Downing Street for dinner with Tony and Cherie or, better still, to a weekend at Chequers (the Prime Minister's country house). Which is why so many of the British newspapers have dumbed down and now feature David Beckham's injured foot as front page news. It's left to fearless and irreverent publications like *Private Eye* to expose the likes of Peter Mandelson and Jeffrey Archer.

Max du Preez has been in the newspaper business long enough to build up a healthy reserve of bile and, rather predictably, he thought that the $20-million or so that Comrade Wattnbopt was spending on his jaunt into space could have been spent more usefully. As this amount probably represents a few months' interest to Shuttleworth, it's essential we get things in perspective. If I offer to buy Max a glass of fine malt whisky, will he rather go for a cheap blend and insist I donate the difference to a charity? I hope not. So what right has he to say how Mark Shuttleworth should spend his enormous fortune?

The fact that Shuttleworth made so much money at such a young age is to be celebrated as a vindication of the free market system. If he decides to blow the whole lot on extravagant mansions, fine champagne and fast cars, that is his prerogative. After blasting off into space I doubt whether even the acceleration of a Porsche GT 2 would give him an adrenalin rush.

Although he has made some crass comments in the past, Mark Shuttleworth is today the toast of South Africa and that is how it should be. Unlike the freeloaders who have been discussing (they claim) peace in the Congo at Sun City for the past two months, Shuttleworth's upliftment has cost us nothing. The positive spin-offs for South Africa are likely to be many and if it drums into the thick skulls of the average American that South Africa is a country and not just the bit of Africa below the equator, it will have been worthwhile.

My only misgiving is this 'hip to be square' (read: Hip2B^2) ad campaign accompanying Shuttleworth's space mission.

It's one thing to encourage 'learners' (dread word) to pay attention during maths and science classes. It's quite another to produce a generation of pustular youths with pebble lens glasses, bad personal hygiene and a row of retractable ball-points in their breast pockets. Nerds lead miserable, lonely existences, often resorting to cybersex as a substitute for the real thing.

Which is why maths and science should rather be promoted as sexy, not square ... even if it is a lie.